"What are you doing here?"

Casey motioned Nathan to keep up, and continued talking. "I tried the house and your cell phone, but when you didn't answer I figured you were at the office."

"That's where I should be, but something's come up and we need to discuss it face-to-face."

Casey stopped abruptly. "What?"

"Nothing that can't wait until you're out of those muddy clothes."

She made a face, but didn't argue. "I'll be back in a jiff." She started for the barn, but came back. "I don't suppose you brought clothes? I can't put these on again."

"I did pack a bag. Just in case..." He let the words trail off. He'd come with no real purpose other than breaking the news that Gwyneth was in town and that his company was on the opposite side of her father's legal battle. But Nathan had also hoped they might spend some quality time together. Now that idea seemed not only advantageous but imperative.

He'd been at Willow Creek less than fifteen minutes and he felt like a defendant arriving in court without the slightest hope of clearing his name. Hell, he didn't even know for certain what the charges against him were. Only that he was probably guilty.

Dear Reader,

They say you can't go home again. I think "they" are wrong. Sometimes the only way to reclaim your dreams is by going back to your roots. This might mean rebuilding a few bridges with the people you left behind, but for some, the effort can lead to amazing insights.

You probably know people like Casey and Nathan. They fell in love, got married, then got so caught up in the business of life they lost track of each other. The love is still there, but there's so much junk in the way—turkeys, a best friend's imminent delivery, a barracuda in stilettos, fairy shrimp and endangered salamanders—that they feel like strangers living in the same house.

For Casey, moving back to California means dealing with her father—the first man to break her heart. But time and distance have blurred the edges of her hurt, and for the first time in her life, her father needs her. For Nathan, the fresh start on the West Coast means his goals are within reach—if he's willing to put business over family.

Researching a book is sometimes a tough job—unless it includes touring San Francisco Bay on a "three-hour" cruise with good friends, good food and good wine. My heartiest thanks to Eric and Roz Johnson of the Point San Pablo Harbor and Marina for the up-close and personal look at the underside of the Golden Gate. You'll also see mention of the East Brother Light Station B and B in this book. Talk about "escape"—you can reach this gorgeous Victorian only by boat. My thanks to Fred and Colleen Slagter for introducing us to this amazingly romantic retreat. To see photos from these adventures, drop by my Web site at www.debrasalonen.com and check out my blog.

Happy reading,

Debra (who is happy to be home again—with Superromance)

A BABY
ON THE WAY
Debra Salonen

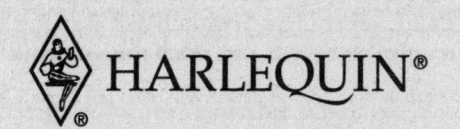

HARLEQUIN®

TORONTO • NEW YORK • LONDON
AMSTERDAM • PARIS • SYDNEY • HAMBURG
STOCKHOLM • ATHENS • TOKYO • MILAN • MADRID
PRAGUE • WARSAW • BUDAPEST • AUCKLAND

ISBN-13: 978-0-373-71386-8
ISBN-10:   0-373-71386-X

A BABY ON THE WAY

Copyright © 2006 by Debra K. Salonen.

This edition published by arrangement with Harlequin Books S.A.

® and TM are trademarks of the publisher. Trademarks indicated with
® are registered in the United States Patent and Trademark Office, the
Canadian Trade Marks Office and in other countries.

www.eHarlequin.com

Printed in U.S.A.

ABOUT THE AUTHOR

As a child, Debra wanted to be an artist. She saved her allowance to send away for a "Learn To Draw" kit, but when her mother mistook Deb's artful rendition of a horse for a cow, Deb turned to her second love—writing. She credits her success as an author to her parents for giving her the chance to realize those dreams. She and her high school sweetheart, who have been married for over thirty years, live in California surrounded by a great deal of family, quite a few dogs and views that appeal to the artist still trapped in her soul.

Books by Debra Salonen

HARLEQUIN SUPERROMANCE

910—THAT COWBOY'S KIDS
934—HIS DADDY'S EYES
986—BACK IN KANSAS
1003—SOMETHING ABOUT EVE
1061—WONDERS NEVER CEASE
1098—MY HUSBAND, MY BABIES
1104—WITHOUT A PAST
1110—THE COMEBACK GIRL
1196—A COWBOY SUMMER
1238—CALEB'S
CHRISTMAS WISH
1279—HIS REAL FATHER

SIGNATURE SELECT SAGA

BETTING ON GRACE

HARLEQUIN AMERICAN ROMANCE

1114—ONE DADDY TOO MANY
1126—BRINGING BABY HOME
1139—THE QUIET CHILD

For Fred & Colleen—the coolest friends by far

CHAPTER ONE

"I NEED YOU, Casey T."

Casey Kent knew of only one person in the world who called her by that nickname. Her father. A man who'd always gone out of his way to make it abundantly clear he didn't *need* anyone. Especially not a daughter, who should have been a son. A son worthy of taking over the Willow Creek ranch.

Casey took a calming breath and maneuvered her chair closer to her desk. She nudged aside the brief she'd been studying and rested her elbow on the smooth surface. A neat desk was part of her trademark as an organizational wizard. "Hello, Red, what's up?"

"We're under attack," he answered. His voice was the same gruff bass she'd heard her whole life. But something was different.

Was that a twang of fear? No, couldn't be. Roderick James Buchanan or, Red as he was called, wasn't afraid of anything or anybody. Her Aunt Meg used to say the only person her father feared was Casey's mother, but since Abigail had died when Casey was six, she had no real memory of her parents' relationship. She only knew her father. A man she'd worshipped and adored until he'd washed his hands of her.

"What kind of attack?" she asked to be polite. Her father's troubles really didn't concern her. He'd sent her away when she was fifteen. Banished her from the world she knew and loved and shipped her off to Boston to live with her maternal aunt.

Margaret Dawson-Merryweather had been quick to admit that she wasn't the motherly type. Smart, savvy and socially ambitious, Meg's life had revolved around her politician husband, their A-list friends and her charitable foundations. But when Senator Merryweather, who was nearly twenty years Meg's senior, had passed away after a brief illness, Red had been all too happy to send his daughter back east to fill the empty spot in Meg's life.

After a few months of thinking she might die of homesickness, Casey had accepted her fate and grudgingly allowed Meg, who had never been around teenagers in her life, to turn her tomboy niece into a refined woman of the world.

Did Casey still miss the fifteen-hundred-acre ranch in the Central Valley of California where she'd spent her formative years? On occasion. Like whenever she heard her father's voice.

"You're still running cattle, right?" she asked before he could reply. "It's not Mad Cow, is it?" As an environmental lawyer working with one of the largest nonprofit land protection consortiums in the country, anything that affected the herd population in California would have repercussions.

"No, nothing like that," Red said impatiently. "It's those goldang turkeys. We're gonna be overrun with 'em, if you don't git your behind out here and do something about it."

Turkeys? Casey frowned. Was it possible her father's mind was slipping? This was only April—half a year away from Thanksgiving.

"You've lost me. What about turkeys?"

He made a huffing sound that seemed to imply she was the slowest thinker on the planet. A surge of acid in her belly made her reach for the roll of antacids tucked unobtrusively in her paper-clip tray. Rocking back in her chair, she peeled away the wrapper and worked one free. *Good for my calcium,* she told herself. Another voice worried about the possibility of an ulcer. That practical Boston twang sounded a lot like Meg, who had been gone almost three years now. Casey still missed her.

"Some big turkey outfit bought the Booth Ranch. Word has it they're going to build the biggest turkey holding pen in the state right across the road from me. Can you picture the smell?"

How does one *picture* smell?

She shook her head to focus on what he meant. Lately, she'd developed a bad habit of making light of serious subjects—or so her husband claimed. "Is everything a joke with you, Casey?" Nathan had griped last night. "This is our life we're trying to plan."

Ours? Or yours? she'd been tempted to ask. Nathan Kent was on a professional roll. His latest win in court, which had made national news and posted Nathan's young-Richard-Gere-in-glasses photo all over the place, was well deserved. She could firmly attest to the number of hours he'd logged on his client's behalf. And the payoff, it appeared, was a golden ticket west.

Despite the fact Casey had made it abundantly clear from the day they'd started dating that she didn't want to return to California to live, Nathan had accepted his law firm's offer to run their San Francisco branch. "It's the only way I'll make partner, Casey. We'll be closer to Oregon and Washington. Didn't you say you were interested in looking there to live if we left the east coast? And the salary increase means you'll be able to stay home and nest for as long as you want," he'd argued. Nathan was a masterful debater.

Returning to the conversation at hand, she asked, "How do you know this?"

"How does anybody know anything around here? Someone blabbed. But in this case, it's not just a rumor. I saw the paperwork myself. They have an application in with the county. Somebody showed me a picture of one of their operations down south. The hatcheries are big enough to be seen from space. They process something like half a million birds per cycle."

He said the last as if they were talking nuclear weapon production. "That does sound like a lot of turkeys, but turkeys are a legitimate agricultural product. People have a right to build on land that's zoned agricultural. Sometimes, that stinks."

"That's the best you can do, Miss Fancypants College Educated Lawyer?" her father shouted. "Ag stinks. Live with it? I don't think so. I was here first. I just planted a quarter section of nut trees. I'm not going to watch my investment get ruined by the smell created from half a million turkeys. I'll fight them with my dying breath."

His impassioned speech forced Casey to hold the receiver a good six inches away from her ear. When she thought it was safe, she tried again. "I can tell you're upset about this and I'm sorry, but I don't know what you expect me to do about it. I'm in the middle of a move. Life is chaotic around here."

"You're headed back to California, aren't you?"

An uneasy feeling crept through her bones. "San Francisco. Is that still considered part of the state?"

"Close enough. And last I heard your husband is going to be the breadwinner while you sit twiddling your thumbs."

"I've never twiddled in my life," Casey said indignantly.

She hadn't told her father about hers and Nathan's ongoing efforts to get pregnant. For several reasons. One, she and Red weren't close, and even if they were she would have held off sharing the news for as long as possible so he wouldn't worry.

But after a year and a half of working with a prominent group of fertility specialists, their efforts had been a bust—sperm and eggwise. "You're both operating under too much tension," one counselor had suggested.

Nathan was right. His promotion meant Casey didn't have to work. Unfortunately, the downside could well offset that small gain. Although closer to his quest of making partner, Nathan's job came with no guarantees.

He'd need to put in long hours—hours that might further impede his sluggish sperm's swimming abilities.

Plus, there was the whole question of family. His and hers.

Nathan's mother, a widow since shortly before Nathan had graduated from high school, lived in Granite Bay, an affluent suburb of Sacramento. His younger brother, Kirby, was a graduate student at UC-Davis and sister, Christine, was married and lived close by. All three relied on Nathan for free legal advice, monetary support and emotional comfort. Casey shuddered to think how much more dependent his family would become once Nathan was within driving distance.

Casey had felt rather smug that her father was self-sufficient enough never to ask for advice—legal or otherwise. But that was before the turkeys came to roost.

When Casey had argued that returning to California meant she and Nathan would be in their family's respective backyards, her husband had tried to point out the positives. "You and Mother have never been able to build a real relationship, and it's time you healed the rift between you and Red. They're going to be our baby's grandparents, you know."

Casey put a hand to her much-too-flat belly as her father complained about her unenthusiastic response to his call to arms. "I tried you first, since you're my daughter, and this is your heritage we're talking about. But if that's the best you can give me, I'll call your husband instead."

Casey sat up sharply. "Don't do that. Nathan is

swamped with last-minute details. His company is throwing him a going-away party tonight and the movers come in the morning. We're staying at a hotel this weekend then fly out Tuesday."

"The planning department hearing isn't until the twenty-fourth of May. That'll give you plenty of time to unpack and read up on it. Where should I send the paperwork?"

To your real *lawyer,* she almost said, but she knew the joke would be lost on him. Casey was a girl. She might have graduated at the top of her class and passed the bar the first time out, but girls didn't have the same *stuff* guys did. Her father was a misogynistic old fool, and she knew better than to let his bias get to her.

"I doubt if there's anything Nathan or I can do, but I'll look it over for you. Fax whatever you have to this number. Mark it to my attention."

"Okay. I gotta run. Mother's giving birth."

"Mother?" Casey squawked. "Mother the Pig?"

"Yup."

It took her a few seconds to realize this couldn't be the same sow she remembered from her youth. "I thought you gave up raising pigs years ago."

Red made a snuffling sound that told her she'd called him on a subject he didn't want to talk about. "Man's gotta have a hobby, right? I started a breeding program a few years back. Get 'em through the wean-to-feed stage then give 'em to local 4-H and FFA kids to show. I think we're up to Mother number ten. Jimmy would know for sure. She's a Yorkshire-Hampshire-Duroc cross. The Hamp makes her a good mother, but I got nine students hoping for a fair project this year, and you know how tricky birthin' is. I can't afford to lose a single little weaner."

You know how tricky birthing is. Just the kind of reminder a woman who was trying to get pregnant didn't need to hear. But since her father wasn't privy to hers and Nathan's baby-making efforts, she really couldn't hold the reference against him.

Her beloved mother had died in her seventh month of pregnancy. A blood clot in her leg had traveled to her lungs and wreaked havoc before Red could get her to a hospital. The family had been in the mountains checking on Red's small herd of cattle when Abigail had become stricken. A leisurely spring picnic that had turned awful. Both Abigail and the baby boy she'd been carrying died.

Casey glanced out the window at the buds that were just starting to unfurl on her tree. Mother's Day was coming up. This year Casey wouldn't have any excuse not to visit the grave where her mother and infant brother were buried.

Clearing her throat, she forced her mind back to the present. "Okay, then, I'll let you go. Fax that information when you can and I promise to take a look at it. I'll give you a call when we get into the new apartment. Good luck with the pigs."

She stared at the phone a minute after hanging up. Red was a good man, and he'd tried to be a good father after Casey's mother had died. He and Casey had been a team. They'd done everything together—the way a father and son would have. Over time, they'd healed from their staggering loss and had gotten on with life, but in the process, Casey had focused all her love on her dad. Which meant, when he sent her away, her heart had broken into too many pieces to ever put back together.

NATHAN KENT LOOKED at the stack of legal briefs on his desk and sighed wearily. Too much work and not enough time. The story of his life, lately.

The red hatch marks on his calendar stopped today— his last day in the office—but that didn't mean he wouldn't have to lug at least half of these files home with him tonight. After the party.

While the movers were filling boxes and carefully wrapping up Casey's antiques, the majority of which would be headed into storage, Nathan would be down the street at Starbucks e-mailing notes to his secretary and colleagues about what needed to be done next week.

He didn't know why he cared. After today, what happened in the Boston office of Silver, Reisbecht and Lane was not his concern. He would still be closely associated with the firm, of course, but he had to transfer his focus and energy to the satellite office that would soon become his private domain.

This was his chance to lead, to prove his worth in more than billable hours and PR opportunities. Reinvigorating the San Francisco branch was the key to making partner, and Nathan lay awake at night fantasizing about that. His friend and mentor Nolan Reisbecht, a senior partner in the firm, had been instrumental in giving Nathan this shot, but he'd been clear about what was expected in return.

"We need you to go in there with both guns blasting, Nate." Nolan was the only person allowed to use the nickname Nathan hated. "The place is a mess. Bunch of lazy-ass freethinkers who probably smoke dope on their lunch breaks."

Nolan was eighty. He didn't actually work in the office, but he could be counted on to know what was happening in all four branches of the firm. The San Francisco office, by far, had the worst performance rating, dollar-wise. Nathan's job would be to turn that around. Hopefully, without the use of firearms or explosive metaphors.

His cell phone rang, but since it was in the pocket of his coat, which was hanging over the back of a chair across the room, he let it ring. Whoever was calling would either try his office number or leave a message. Probably, the caller was his wife.

Casey wouldn't let him carry the phone on his person because she said the radio waves and low-frequency emissions might adversely affect his sperm production. And since she still wasn't pregnant after a year and a half of trying, he couldn't very well argue with her.

They'd seen a bevy of specialists. They'd both been tested, probed, X-rayed and generally humiliated. For all practical purposes, the blame appeared to be resting on his sperm. "We call them sluggish swimmers," one doctor had stated. "They eventually get to the egg but don't have the motivation to dig in and fertilize her."

Nathan Kent—top of his class, editor of the law review, darling of the media—had lazy, unmotivated sperm. Who knew?

Or cared. But he did care. He loved his wife and wanted her to be happy. He loved the life they'd created together—nothing like his parents' contentious relationship. The only time he remembered his mother and father getting along well was before the births of his siblings, Christine, who was five years Nathan's junior, and Kirby, who came along six and a half years after her.

Nathan and Casey didn't fight. They got along great, but beneath the calm outward appearance they showed the world, he had a sense that Casey was miserable. Her aunt had been the first to suggest a baby.

"Don't do what I did, Casey," Meg had chided shortly before her death. "Don't wait to love someone else's child. You might not be as lucky as I was. Have your own family while you and Nathan are young and healthy. What happened to your mother was a fluke. She wouldn't want you to make important decisions based on fear."

Nathan hadn't gotten to know Meg for long, but he'd admired and respected her as an outspoken woman who didn't mince words. Casey had been emotionally devastated by her aunt's death. He was pretty sure that loss had somehow prompted Casey's decision to get pregnant.

Nathan had greeted the suggestion with a certain amount of ambivalence. Casey's mother and unborn sibling had died from a pregnancy-related embolism. Not something that was hereditary, of course. But what if? He couldn't imagine a life without Casey, but eventually he'd acquiesced to her argument. "We're established professionals with good health insurance and a lot to offer a child," she'd pleaded. "Let's do it."

And they'd given it a good shot. They'd even involved medical specialists, but each month Casey's period had appeared she'd go quiet for a few days. No drama queen fit of depression for his wife, but he couldn't help thinking her outwardly positive demeanor was for his sake.

Then this job offer had come up after a sudden, very hush-hush scandal in the San Francisco office that had resulted in two lawyers being disbarred.

Secretly, Nathan couldn't help but feel relieved that he wasn't going to be moving a pregnant wife or wife and infant to a new city. Keeping up with the demands of his job were quite enough, thank you. "At this point, I don't have time for sex," he muttered. Which was not something he ever thought he'd hear himself say.

The sound of his office door opening broke into his thoughts. Jannelle Norris, his secretary of five years, poked her head in. "Excuse me, Nathan, Casey is on line one. I buzzed you, but you must not have seen the light."

Fifty-five. Dependable. Unflappable. Nathan was going to miss her. They made a good team. Unfortunately, she wasn't free to move with him. Jan's husband was nearing retirement but couldn't leave his Public Works job for another few years.

"I was wool-gathering, as my wife would say. Thanks."

"You're welcome. And don't get so busy thinking about the things you have to do that you forget about the party. The company went all out. Should be lovely."

"Not a problem. We'll be there." A second later, he hit the white flashing light. "Casey?"

"Hi. How's your day going?"

"Hectic. I have to bring three other associates up to speed on cases that have been ongoing for months."

Her "Hmm" sounded completely disinterested. Or was he projecting? They worked on mirror opposite projects. The people she tried to help were usually battling his clients who wanted to build a shopping mall on the wetlands she hoped to save. The one law in their marriage that seemed to work was: no shop talk at home. He hated to think how screwed up they'd be if they actually knew what the other person did during business hours.

"What's up? You're still coming tonight, aren't you?"

"Of course. I bought a new dress. Well, vintage, but new to me."

Nathan smiled indulgently. Together they made an obscene amount of money, but Casey refused to shop at conventional retail outlets. "I won't support sweatshops and brutal working conditions just so I can wear some designer label. That's what secondhand stores are for," she told anyone who'd listen.

"We'll meet at the restaurant, right? I don't think I'm going to have time to go home and change. You know how crowded the train is this time of night." Which was why he kept several changes of clothing in his office.

"Got it. I just called to give you a heads-up. Red is on the warpath. He's gunning for a turkey consortium that wants to move in across the road from him. He thinks that since we're going to be in the neighborhood and we happen to have credentials, we should get behind him."

"Oh, Lord," Nathan said, his head beginning to pound. Bad enough his mother and siblings would soon be in his pockets, but now it appeared his father-in-law was going to seek free legal advice, too.

"Don't worry. I should be able to keep him off your back for a few days. At least enough time to let you get settled."

Casey often referred to her father by his nickname. When they'd first started dating, Nathan had assumed the man was a deadbeat dad, instead of the person who forked over huge gobs of money to send his daughter to several of the best schools in the country.

"Great."

She laughed. "Sorry. That's what comes from having a Y chromosome. Red trusts you to do him proud. I'm just a girl with a law degree, but for once, I'm kinda glad. He needs a gladiator, and since Russell Crowe is busy, you're the man."

Nathan loved his wife's laugh. He'd once called the sound a sprinkling of fairy dust. But not when she tried to be flippant about anything associated with her father. Despite his financial backing, Red Buchanan had a lot to answer for in Casey's book.

"I'm going to be in meetings right up to the minute we break for the party, so if he tries today, he'll miss me."

"Don't sweat it. He's faxing the paperwork here. I'll bring it home with me and pray it doesn't get lost in the move. But, hey, if it does, it does. Turkeys can't fly, so how fast will this happen?"

Nathan almost smiled at that one. She covered her

pain well. Of course, she'd had a lot of practice where Red was concerned. Less when their marriage was at issue, but she masked that hurt, too. Most of the time. Tonight would prove a challenge to them both. He was leaving a place that felt like home and saying goodbye to the people he felt closest to, which, he knew was a hell of a thing to say when his wife was going with him.

RED BUCHANAN STOMPED into the barn that was his second home. Hell, for the most part he lived here. If it weren't for the kitchen, which is where he wisely kept his bottle of Maker's Mark, he'd probably never spend any time at the ranch house across the field. This barn, which was an original structure he'd upgraded over the years, was the heart and soul of Willow Creek. Two new buildings had been added in recent years. A metal-sided retail sales office that doubled as a packing warehouse for the product his seven-year-old pistachio trees were putting out and a cozy little two-bedroom house he'd built the year Casey had graduated from college—just in case his daughter decided to return home once she finished school.

Instead, she'd married another damn lawyer. As if the world didn't have more than enough as it was. Maybe one of these days, they'd spawn a few more little legal bastards. Although, technically, he didn't suppose they'd be bastards. They'd be his grandchildren. Abby would have loved grandchildren.

"Red," a voice called.

Jimmy Mills, Red's right-hand man, was standing beside a hog pen that had been erected inside the barn to accommodate Mother's delicate condition. Red's prize hog got first-class treatment when it was time to deliver a new crop of piglets.

"Hey, Jim, how's our girl doing?"

The dust-colored canvas of Jimmy's jacket lifted and fell with his shrug. March and April had been unusually cool this year, with winds that seemed to suggest an iceberg was parked right off San Francisco Bay. "It's hard to tell with pigs. She seems bored, if anything. I put in some fresh straw, and fixed the lights for the babies, but heck if I know. You're closer to her than me, you ask."

Red chuckled. Animals were his hobby. They sure as hell weren't making him money. He'd phased out of the cattle business when land in the valley had become so expensive he couldn't afford to take a loss every year on his beef herd. But he'd stubbornly retained the pasture between the house and the barn for his critters. Over the years, he'd tried a few novel varieties including llamas and emus, but cows and pigs were his sentimental favorites. Nut trees had made him rich, but they weren't nearly as interesting.

"Just got off the phone with Casey T.," Red said, angling sideways to squeeze past his new loader. The bucket was tipped down, but the arm was raised five feet off the ground. A dangerous height. He needed to remember to lower that arm before someone ran into it.

"You did, huh? She excited about the move?"

Red glanced at his helper. If there was any justice in this world, Jimmy would have been his son-in-law instead of the prissy suit Casey married. But, no, she'd saddled herself with Nathan Kent, who may be an okay fellow, but he wasn't no Jimmy. And, dammit, Red knew he had no one but himself to blame for the way things had turned out. He'd overreacted—by far his worst trait, although he had quite a few to pick from—the summer afternoon when he'd discovered his daughter half-naked in the arms of the young cowboy he'd only recently hired.

Jimmy had been seventeen. He'd had a Sundance Kid look to him, and Casey and her best friend, Sarah, had mooned over him like he was a movie star. But when doodling little hearts with the words Mrs. Casey Mills in it had changed to rolling around in the hay, Red had called his sister-in-law in a panic.

"Casey is experimenting with her sexuality," Meg had said. "She's a young girl without a mother, Red. She's got to find out this stuff some way."

Red had finally understood that Casey was not now and never would be the son she'd pretended to be. Her genes weren't made to play that role, no matter how much the two of them wanted to think otherwise. She was a suntanned beauty with no feminine wiles. Defenseless. That's what he'd made her, and Red had hated himself for letting his late wife down.

He'd immediately shipped Casey off to Boston to live with Meg—to learn "girl stuff," he'd told his daughter. Casey had wept, thrown a tantrum and even tried to run away, but in the end, Red had prevailed. And she'd never forgiven him. Ever. And that bitterness would not be assuaged when she discovered Jimmy was currently living in the house Red had built for

Casey. For reasons Jimmy chose not to share with his employer—even though he publicly claimed Red was like a father to him, Jimmy's wife, Sarah, Casey's former best friend—had kicked him out of their home in town two months earlier. Sarah, who was one of the sweetest women Red had ever known, was also pretty darn pregnant.

"I just had Becky fax those papers to her and that fellow she's married to. Maybe between the two of them, they can figure out what we gotta do to block this damn turkey business."

Jimmy let out a troubled sigh. "I stopped by the café this morning. Fred Reed was there shooting his mouth off about what a good thing this is going to be for the county's economy. He's just crowing because he made a healthy commission on the land."

Red reached through the metal wire to scratch Mother's ear. The five-year-old sow was showing her age. Her ears were tattered from the occasional skirmish. Pecking orders existed in pigpens, too. "Fred's an opportunist, but I never thought he'd turn on us like this. Hell, if he'd given me a chance, I'd have bought the land. I've been thinking I might like to plant Fuji apples. Or maybe I could talk Joe Marchini into showing me how to grow radicchio. He's the biggest grower in the country right now."

Jimmy stood back and stuffed his hands in the pockets of his jeans. He was still a good-looking fellow. Red had yet to figure out why Sarah had kicked him out, especially with a baby coming. But Red knew less about women than he did about growing radicchio. What he

did know was that his daughter was coming home soon,
and even if she couldn't stop the turkeys from going in
next door, he was one happy man.

CHAPTER TWO

CASEY STOOD at the second-floor window of her new home—a five-room apartment in the lower Height district of San Francisco—and gazed at the shiny silver vehicle parked on the street below. Her new car—a Lexus SUV. If she weren't a mature woman of thirty-three, she would have stuck out her tongue at the abominable vehicle. But that would have been childish. And she wasn't a child. She was an intelligent, informed consumer who'd intended to purchase a hybrid car as soon as she got settled. A car that would have reflected her strong beliefs about saving gas and not contributing to air pollution.

Unfortunately, yesterday, Nathan had returned home with a previously undisclosed perk. A company car. A pricy silver beast equipped with every amenity and techno-gadget known to man. The look of triumph in his eyes when he'd handed her the keys had robbed Casey of the ability to speak—which considering what she would have said was probably a good thing.

"John and Gordon surprised me with this today," Nathan had said, running his hand along the fender with the same admiration he once would have reserved for Casey's thigh. "I had no idea they intended to give me a car. But isn't it great? Now we don't have to spend any out-of-pocket cash."

Her consumer's voice had been strangled by the wife who'd wanted desperately to celebrate his triumph. They'd shared so few positive moments in the past year. She'd pretended to be impressed and hadn't asked what kind of miles per gallon she could expect to make.

"We should be able to get along with one car until I can get over to Granite Bay," he'd added.

His mother was storing the 1969 Ford Mustang that Nathan had bought in college, but hadn't trusted to make it east to where he'd been accepted into law school. Since he couldn't bear to part with the old rust bucket, he'd stored it on blocks in his mother's garage. As soon as he'd learned of their impending transfer, he'd arranged to have the convertible overhauled by a family friend who specialized in vintage cars.

Casey gave the shiny hood one last glance, then walked to the glass-topped table they'd used on their patio in Boston. Their antique dining room set wouldn't fit in the apartment. It was currently stacked—along with the great majority of her prized possessions—in a climate-controlled storage unit in San Jose.

Patience, she silently counseled. *Think of all the dusting you won't have to do.*

Except she missed her things. Most of the fine antiques had been left to her by her aunt, but when Nathan and Casey had first started dating, they'd spent several weekends a month hunting through estate sales from

Maine to Pennsylvania. Casey had loved to make up histories about the pieces they'd brought home with them.

She couldn't remember the last time they went shopping for anything together—even for groceries. She looked at the four unpacked boxes stacked beside the arched portal leading to the kitchen. Her husband was a gifted cook who knew all the best places to buy organic in Boston. Lately, they'd been eating every meal out or on the go.

No wonder I can't get pregnant. She rubbed a painfully tense muscle in her neck. *I'm malnourished.* The thought made her smile. *And I need a massage.*

She'd forgotten how much work moving could be. They'd gotten the keys to their new apartment last Thursday and had spent the better part of the weekend cleaning the place to make it ready for their furniture, which had finally showed up nine days after leaving Boston.

They'd unpacked quite a few boxes together, but not before Nathan accused her of harboring treasures that had mated in the dark confines of the moving van, producing clutter—her avowed enemy. What he didn't seem to grasp was the fact their brownstone had had ten times the space as this place—for considerably less rent per month.

Yeah, yeah, this joint is a rip-off. Get over it. Casey sat down on a sculpted metal chair, curling one knee under her on the sage-green pad. Money was a "nonissue," her husband liked to say. "With you being home, our overhead will be less. We'll spend less on clothes, transportation and dining out, so we should be fine," Nathan had reassured her.

But this was the first time since college that Casey had been unemployed. She had a trust fund left to her by Meg, but Casey had no intention of touching it. The money was earmarked for land and a home. Somewhere. She was certain there would come a day when she and Nathan would need to escape the rat race and reinvent themselves. If their marriage survived this move.

"If…" she murmured.

It was becoming increasingly obvious that Nathan wasn't happy. His new workplace was a disappointment, she knew, but he was great with people and would have it whipped into shape in no time. She used to tell people Nathan was a Little-League coach in the making. He could make both parents and players behave themselves. But, this time, he seemed awfully quick to throw in the towel. Last night, he'd told Casey he was considering requesting a few transfers from the home office.

Her first reaction had been one of dismay. Casey knew without being told the list would include Gwyneth Jacobi. A legal shark with lustrous black hair that matched the black spike heels Casey always saw her in. Heels Casey often felt were aimed at her back.

How did one register a protest without looking like an insecure wife? And how did it come about that she *was* an insecure wife?

Nathan was handsome, polished and refined. He was also honest, reliable, trustworthy and loving. Less so on the loving part lately, but that might be attributed to the circumstances surrounding their infertility. It seemed as if they never made love these days because it felt right. Now they performed according to her biological clock.

But that wasn't wholly her fault. The doctors said Nathan's tired sperm was partly to blame, as was a slight tilt to her cervix.

The diagnosis irked Casey. Here she'd wasted all those years taking the pill when she could have had a blast and never worried. "Yeah, right," she muttered under her breath. Like that would have happened. She was probably the most sexually repressed person she knew. Although that was only a guess, because she was too repressed to talk about her sexuality with any of her women friends—of which she had very few.

But she didn't need to see a shrink to know that having your father find you in the hayloft with your boyfriend's hand down your pants wasn't the best way to experience your first sexual encounter. Especially when your father punishes you by sending you to live with your aunt on the opposite side of the country. "It's a wonder I'm not frigid."

"What?" Nathan asked, entering the dining alcove at his usual efficient pace. He pushed aside the *San Francisco Chronicle* help-wanted ads that she'd been perusing earlier. Even though she'd agreed to take six months off before looking for a job, Casey wasn't convinced she could handle a life of leisure.

"If you get pregnant in that time, great," Nathan had said, taking it upon himself to summarize one of their many discussions of the subject. "If not, then we rethink the baby-making agenda. Maybe we weren't meant to be parents."

Meant to be. Fighting words, in Casey's opinion, although she rarely argued with Nathan. She loved him and was confident they shared the same basic values, even if they arrived at the same point by slightly different paths. But Casey refused to blindly accept that certain things in one's life were preordained. Casey's first introduction to Fate had been after her mother and baby brother had died. She'd been too young to understand the concept, but the word had haunted her. In her dreams, Fate was an ugly man who chased her, night after night.

Nathan tossed a folded map on top of the newsprint. "I thought you threw these out. Your cell phone has GPS technology. If you're lost, you can ask it for directions."

Casey knew that made sense to him—buying a two-hundred-dollar phone to replace a $1.95 map, so she didn't point out the fact that she was lucky if she remembered to turn the damn thing on. "Some of those maps are from places we've been. I plan to scrapbook them some day."

"Since when did *scrapbook* become a verb?" he asked, filling his metal travel mug with Peet's coffee from his French press.

"In the late nineteen-nineties, I think. It's a big business now. Homemakers throw parties for their friends and sell all sorts of specialty stuff. Like they once did with Mary Kay or Tupperware."

"Hmm," he said, obviously tuning out her answer.

Such was the status of their communication. Thank God for e-mail or they'd never know what was going in each other's lives. Assuming, of course, he read her missives.

"Are you still planning to leave this morning?" he

asked, helping himself to the financial section of the *Chronicle*. His gaze skimmed the want-ads header, but he didn't ask for an explanation. Another indicator that he wasn't completely in tune with Casey. There'd been a time when he would have spotted the page and known what was going on in her head.

"I guess so," she said, walking to the counter where she'd left an electric kettle on simmer. A small cloud of steam unfurled beneath the glossy white cabinets. The countertop was one-inch-square black-and-white tile that matched the pattern on the floor, although the squares underfoot were larger. Casey hated the decor— she'd have chosen one or the other, but not both. The combination made it feel like she was cooking in a funhouse. "Are you absolutely sure this is a good idea?"

"Yes," he said decisively.

Nathan's ability to make decisions without second-guessing himself was one of the things she admired most about him. It was an asset in the courtroom, as well as in life. Casey was much less confident, although she went to great lengths not to let people know it.

"I could go next week, instead…when we're more settled."

"Everything will still be here when you get back," he said, glancing over his shoulder. The hallway was half the width it should have been thanks to the stacked cubes of corrugated cardboard. "Believe me, I won't have time to look at a single box. This is neat compared to my office. Did I tell you I fired two people yesterday?"

She stopped pouring boiling water into her French

press, which was identical to Nathan's except it was filled with herbal tea since her fertility doctor had suggested she give up caffeine.

The brew wasn't nearly as rich and aromatic—or flavorful—as coffee, but it dulled her craving for a hot beverage in the morning. And since the blend was made especially for her by an herbalist in Boston, she drank it faithfully.

"No," she said. "I believe that must have slipped your mind. Being small and inconsequential and all."

He ignored her facetious tone. "One of them was our HR person. I swear, the woman hired all her college cronies and never had a bad thing to say about anyone."

"Maybe they were all perfect until you came along."

"Sure. Right. Even the guy who lost fifteen settlements—including five pro-bono cases that should have been shoo-ins?"

"How do you know they should have been shoo-ins? You couldn't possibly have read all fifteen transcripts since you got here."

He stood up and reached for his jacket. "I didn't. I couriered the files to Gwyneth. She reviewed them and e-mailed a breakdown."

Casey turned back to her tea so he wouldn't see the sneer that curled her lip.

"I'm thinking about getting a dog," Casey said without intending to.

"No."

She pivoted on the heel of her slipper. She'd overslept—again. She didn't know why jet lag affected her more than it did her husband, but her new sleep pattern seemed to consist of tossing and turning until three then awaking too bleary-eyed to get up when her husband did. "I beg your pardon," she said, facing him. "Our deal was kids and animals once we left the city."

Nathan gave her a look she called his "How could anyone as stupid as you still remember to breathe?" look. He seldom turned it on her, but Nathan wasn't a patient man and this move had sucked up what little tolerance he had. He walked to the bow window to pull back the sheer curtain that the former tenants had left behind. "Blocks and blocks of apartments. Thousands of cars spewing noxious exhaust fumes. Even more thousands of people—rapists, child molesters, carjackers living around every corner. This is still a city, Casey. Only the zip code has changed."

"That isn't fair and you know it. But I refuse to discuss this issue when I'm in my robe and you're in a suit."

"You opened the subject."

"Without expecting a verbal onslaught by a lawyer dressed for work. Go. I'm not prepared to do battle." She tried to keep her tone light. There had been too much heavy talk between them lately—or rather, too much skirting of heavy talk. "I won't be here when you return, you know."

"Coward," he said with a hint of the old humor and charm that had won her heart.

"Ha," she countered, waving the spoon she'd just picked up. "Anyone who is brave enough to face down my misogynistic father can't be labeled a coward."

"Quit casting aspersions on my father-in-law. Red is misguided. Misunderstood. The product of a generation that didn't know women were strong warriors who only pretended to give men power."

She stabbed the half a grapefruit Nathan had left in a bowl on the counter. Thoughtful or too lazy to put it away? How shrewish to even think that. "Well, as long as you agree with me, then we're okay."

"Call me when you get over the Altamont. Mom says the traffic through Pleasanton is truly hideous."

"During the commute," Casey qualified. "I'll be fine. If anything goes amiss, I'll ask the car to call you. I've seen the commercials. These cars do everything for you but steer."

"I'm sure it's not quite that simple, but you'll be fine. You just haven't been behind the wheel for a while, and Californians take their driving seriously. I don't want them to run you over."

He walked to her and gave her a quick kiss on the lips. Casey closed her eyes and leaned in for something longer, but he'd already moved on, collecting his briefcase.

He looked so damn handsome. And single, she thought for one impossible moment. *Oh, god, no. Let it be my overactive imagination.*

I won't worry if he says, "I love you." But he didn't. He didn't even pause to wish her a safe trip or give her a smile. He was already deep into work mode, switching the rest of his life to another channel.

Casey locked the door behind him. As Nathan said, this was still a city. Last night, she'd watched a man urinating on a light pole, like a dog—except he didn't lift his leg. Casey wasn't looking forward to seeing her father, but she was anxious for a little fresh air and countryside. She hadn't been home to Willow Creek in far too long.

And if a zillion turkeys were soon going to be her neighbors, she'd better get there and breathe the clean air fast, she thought with a naughty grin. Her father might not be amused, but somehow Casey couldn't help thinking that Red's battle with fowl was too ironic for words. She just hoped he'd resigned himself to the reality of the fact that, although she'd give him a few legal pointers, she wasn't going to lead his troops into battle. Casey had given up fighting with her father—even on the same team—years ago.

NATHAN KEPT HIS PACE brisk for the first six blocks, but then—in typical San Francisco style—the street started a vertical climb. His breath turned hot and his legs began to quiver.

He'd promised himself this new move would include daily exercise, which is why he was walking to the office. He'd always done his best to include a workout in his routine, but over the years the demands of his profession had eaten away at his resolve. Now, his knees creaked and his chest was heaving as if he'd run a marathon. He had run in marathons in college, so he knew the feeling that came from pushing his body beyond the point of giving up.

Nathan prided himself on never giving up. Which probably explained why he felt so conflicted about his marriage. He loved his wife, dammit. But this past year had been difficult. Adversarial. He and Casey seemed constantly on the opposite sides of the bargaining table.

Every issue—right down to where to eat at night—had become a power play. He'd started communicating with her by e-mail just because he couldn't muster the energy it took to argue. Or, worse, be supportive.

Ever since they'd found out their third IVF procedure had failed to take, Casey had seemed unnaturally needy. His ebullient, savvy wife had been humbled by the process. After each medical appointment, her pride and self-confidence dimmed like a hundred-watt bulb during one of California's infamous brownouts. And as much as Nathan wanted to be supportive and understanding, he wanted his old life back even more.

He knew that was selfish, unfeeling and downright callous, but his self-esteem had taken a bruising, too. What man likes to learn that his sperm was made up of sluggish swimmers? He'd vowed after the last go-around that he would never again let his spermatozoa be put on trial without adequate counsel.

Fortunately, Casey's doctor had agreed they needed to take a break. "Step back from the plate and regroup," he'd said. "I'm wondering if this imminent move hasn't played a part in some subconscious sabotage."

Nathan hated the man. No matter how carefully each member of the reproductive team couched the words or hinted at excuses, the failure of Casey to conceive still came down to one thing: Nathan couldn't get his wife pregnant. He couldn't perform one simple act of procreation. And his ego was smarting every bit as much as Casey's.

They'd licked their emotional wounds in silence and embraced a new plan. "I'm not crazy about moving to

San Francisco—it's way too close to you-know-where," Casey had said. "But maybe a change of venue will do us both good."

Unlike Nathan who'd always intended to return to his home state someday, which was why he'd taken both the California and Massachusetts State bar exams right out of college, Casey thought of herself as an east-coast girl. Even after learning of Nathan's transfer, she'd made no effort to get temporary privileges in California.

"I'll know when it's right to get back into the game," she'd said, waving away Nathan's suggestion that it didn't hurt to be prepared.

To Nathan, this complacence proved something he'd always known. Casey might have one of the sharpest legal minds he'd ever encountered, but her heart wasn't in the practice of law. Never had been. That was why she'd accepted a job with a low-paying national land conservancy instead of joining him at Silver, Reisbecht and Lane. Not that he was complaining. He and Casey were too competitive to work side-by-side.

Besides, he often bragged that while he played the corporate game, she was his civic conscience. Still, when his sperm had come under fire, he'd been tempted to point a finger and say, "You try working eighty billable hours a week while juggling three high-profile cases and see what happens to your reproductive system."

Fortunately, Nathan had learned a long time ago when to keep his mouth shut. He'd watched his parents spar with words far too often as a child and had done his best to keep his arguments confined to court, where the rules were clear and a judge would intercede before the barbs got too vicious.

Nathan stopped a block from his building. He tried not to look too obvious as he lifted his arms to let the brisk breeze air-dry some of his perspiration. This isn't going to work, he decided, glancing at his watch. He couldn't spend his day in close quarters with this disorganized, uninspired group when he wasn't at his best. Nor could the boss show up late when he expected his employees to be at the legal grindstone promptly at eight.

Maybe he'd join a gym. If Casey wound up helping her father with his legal matters, she would probably spend time in the Valley.

Nathan hadn't paid much attention to Red's battle—something about an abundance of turkey manure polluting the water table and befouling the air.

Taking a deep breath, Nathan righted his shoulders and set off again. He was knee-deep in shit of a different kind and he couldn't shovel it all alone. He needed to hire some new blood. Or get an infusion from a known source.

A tingle he would have preferred not to feel made its way through his abdomen. Yesterday, after a particularly frustrating meeting with his staff, he'd impulsively fired off an e-mail to Gwyneth Jacobi. "Have you ever thought of working in San Francisco?"

He tightened his grip on his briefcase. Gwyn was a friend, a comrade-in-arms. He liked her mind and respected her work ethic. Wasn't it natural that he'd want a team player like her working for him?

Nathan was saved from lying to himself when one

of the men who had been up for his job joined him in the elevator. The man whose name Nathan couldn't remember made eye contact with him and mumbled a gruff, "Good morning."

Nathan nodded in greeting, then pushed the button for the twenty-fifth floor. A trickle of sweat escaped from his sideburn, but Nathan snubbed it out with his thumb.

"You walked to work?" the man asked, obviously surprised.

"Yes. My wife needed the car. Her father lives in the Central Valley and she's headed over there to see him."

"Where in the Valley? I'm from Visalia originally," the man said.

Nathan, who was trying desperately to remember the fellow's name, mumbled, "A ranch near Chowchilla, which is—"

"I know where it is. In fact, I'm handling a potential complaint against one of our largest clients, GroWell Ag, Inc. They're planning on building a new operation on some land they bought, but now the locals are crying, NIMBY."

Eric. Eric Mathers. That was his name. Stanford grad. Underutilized.

"*NIMBY?*" Nathan repeated. He knew the term, of course, but a sudden sense of dread made his thought processes freeze.

"Not in my backyard," Eric clarified. "GroWell's land clearly has an ag-exclusive land-use designation, but the neighbors are claiming foul," he said with a wink. "Pun fully intended, of course."

Nathan's mouth went dry. "Come again?"

The elevator door opened. Eric, who was probably fifteen years older than Nathan and twenty pounds heavier, stepped out and waited for Nathan to exit. As they started toward the double doors with the elegant gold lettering, he explained, "The fowl in this case is turkeys. GroWell is one of the largest turkey farming operations on the west coast. They've had to battle for every single new setup, but they always win." He paused with one hand straight-armed on the wooden push bar. "I always win for them."

Eric's tone wasn't bragging, just firm.

"That's good to know," Nathan said. Only years of not-blinking in court kept him from swearing, but once he reached his corner office, he did just that.

"Damn," he muttered, tossing his briefcase atop the stacks of folders, files and briefs that still needed his attention. Of all the legal firms in all the cities of the west coast, why did GroWell have to pick his? Nathan didn't like the movie *Casablanca,* but he'd seen it twice to humor his wife, and suddenly he was feeling a lot of sympathy for Humphrey Bogart.

CHAPTER THREE

CASEY WANTED TO hate the car.

But she couldn't.

The Lexus drove like a dream. The leather seat cushions were sinfully comfortable, the controls exactly where they should be, her visibility kingly. And something about the vehicle reminded her of learning to drive behind the wheel of her father's truck, a cantankerous Ford F-100. Flat-out the most disreputable-looking heap of junk on the road, that truck had made her feel in control of her destiny.

A complete illusion, of course. Not three months after her driving lesson, she was on a plane for Boston to live with her aunt, who made her take driver's training from a company that specialized in teaching young girls. Casey's teacher had been an overweight, bald man who bathed in Calvin Klein cologne. She'd passed the test, procured her license then didn't get behind the wheel again until college.

No wonder I'm such a lousy driver, she thought, reaching down to turn up the stereo. *I never get any practice.*

She didn't think that was going to be a problem any

more. In California, everyone drove. As evidenced by the number of cars on State Highway 132, which linked I-5 to Highway 99, the main two arteries running the length of the state from north to south.

Whoever had installed the presets of the channel selector must have fixed them on Bay area stations. Once she passed the sprawling city of Tracy, all that came in was static. She hit the scan button and stopped it at the first clear station. Country-Western. She hadn't listened to the music in years, but still felt a soft spot for it in her heart. She and her best friend, Sarah Myerson, had grown up singing along to the sad, crazy, broken-heart tunes.

After the song was over, two voices picked up a dialogue that obviously had been going on before Casey started listening.

"We're taking calls from listeners on the topic of dating ethics. Miss Priss here maintains that women never date a friend's ex, while men show no such restraint whatsoever. Is this true? Give us a call. Enquiring minds want to know."

"No," Casey said vehemently. "Absolutely not true. Female friends are every bit as lascivious as male friends. I speak from experience."

"Here's Mike in Bakersfield. What's your take on this topic, Mike?"

"I married my best friend's ex-wife."

"His wife? Wow. How's that working out? Does he still talk to you?"

"Sure. We see each other socially. He's remarried, now. It's not a problem. They got married for the wrong reasons and once she was free, I made my move."

"There you go. All's well that ends well, I guess," the male commentator said with a chuckle.

His female counterpart spoke. "That's just the man's point of view. Notice the lack of women callers. We don't do that kind of thing. It's not kosher."

"Damn right," Casey muttered. "But that doesn't mean some women don't do it. Sarah sure as heck swooped in on Jimmy once I was out of the picture."

And now they've got a baby on the way.

Another song came on just as traffic from some road work picked up requiring her full attention. She tuned out the voices on the radio and in her head until the next caller—a woman—started to speak.

"You're wrong. It does happen. Not often, but there are women out there who don't have any integrity. They'll take any guy who shows them a little attention—even their best friend's ex. I know. It happened to me. I not only lost my boyfriend, but my best friend, too. That's what really makes it so hard to get past. The hurt lasts a long time. Way past the point where you could give a rat's behind about the guy."

Casey chuckled and nodded. "Isn't that the truth?"

She and Jimmy had broken up before Casey had left for Boston. She'd done the honorable thing, the right thing, and set him free. She'd known he wasn't the type to write letters, nor could she expect a gorgeous young cowboy like Jimmy to wait. She'd been reasonable, practical and grown-up. But her fifteen-year-old heart never completely forgot, nor quit dreaming about him— his kiss, his smile.

Casey was still a virgin when she arrived in Boston,

but she and Jimmy had shared something special and unique. First love. And Casey had expected her best friend—the person who knew "everything" about her relationship with Jimmy from first look to first kiss—to understand and respect that.

And Sarah had for a while. She and Casey wrote faithfully every week at first. Then every month. Eventually, they sent holiday greeting cards, usually with a photo or two. Then those stopped, too.

Casey found out about Sarah and Jimmy when she came home for Christmas her senior year. A mutual "friend" was quick to tell all. The two had been an item ever since the homecoming dance that fall. Sarah had created quite a stir by bringing a date who wasn't a student. A cowboy two years older than her.

Casey never talked to her friend again. She learned of the couple's engagement and subsequent marriage through Red, who seemed to have completely forgotten that Jimmy was the boy in the hayloft with his daughter. Jimmy continued to work for her father, earning the title of foreman. Red often spoke highly of Sarah, who seemed to fill the role Casey had planned for herself with impossible style and grace.

As always, Casey was the odd man out. And now, she was on her way home. To somehow save the day. Unfortunately, Casey had been so sure she'd never return to California to live she hadn't bothered to take the bar exam in her home state when she had the chance.

Now, she couldn't have argued on her father's behalf in court even if she wanted to, and she wasn't totally certain she did. As the call-in people on the radio could attest, old grievances were often the most enduring.

"OH, MY LORD," Casey whispered under her breath an hour later as she mentally tallied the number of cars and pickup trucks parked in Red's long, eucalyptus-lined driveway. "Everybody for thirty square miles must be here."

So much for the quiet reunion she'd envisioned. She wondered why Red hadn't warned her that there would be a crowd here. "Well, duh," she muttered. "Why do you think?" Because he knew she would have put off coming. For being an absentee father most of her life, Red still knew her well. Too well.

She eased the Lexus over the bridge that crossed an irrigation spillway Casey had always euphemistically called a creek. Every spring, she and Sarah had floated on air mattresses from the house through the pasture to the main road where Red's barn was located. On days like this, Casey noted, looking around.

Not much had changed from the last time she was here. The house could use a paint job, but Red was good about hiring help to maintain the general appearance of the place. Always had been. Probably because Casey's mother had insisted on it.

Abby Buchanan had grown up with money. The daughter of a prosperous Wyoming rancher, she'd gone against her parents' wishes and married an upstart cowboy who swept her off her feet and took her to California. Casey had loved hearing her father's stories about the early years when they'd struggled. He'd made it sound glamorous. But her aunt had set Casey straight when she moved to Boston.

"Your mother worked her bottom off just to keep them out of the poorhouse. It wasn't until your father swallowed his pride and borrowed enough money to buy a small ranch that they began to prosper. And that probably wouldn't have happened if not for you."

"Me?"

"As soon as your mother found out she was pregnant, Red called our father and mended enough fences to buy Willow Creek. Frankly, I never thought Red would settle down long enough to make a go of it, but Abby couldn't have been happier. Not that she ever complained about traipsing around the rodeo circuit. As far as your mother was concerned, Red Buchanan could do no wrong."

Not for the first time, Casey wondered how differently things would have turned out if her mother and baby brother had lived. But wishing had never gained her much in the past, so she put aside the "what-ifs" and got out of the car.

Her cream-colored, silk-blend slacks looked deceptively casual, yet elegant. She'd rolled back the sleeves of her navy blouse far enough to display a refurbished gold-and-diamond watch she'd purchased from her favorite "junk" dealer in Boston. Casey didn't think of herself as vain but she'd dressed with care for this meeting. Meg always said the right clothes were as good as armor.

She stepped away from the vehicle and studied the small black remote in her palm to make sure she pressed the right button. She sure as heck didn't want to set off the alarm. Her thumb depressed the button and she started to drop the key in her purse just as a sudden baying made the hair on the backs of her arms rise.

"Oh, God," she said with a groan. "The dogs."

Lifting her gaze, she watched as four beasts charged out from the wraparound deck. *Mud. Paw prints on silk. Nuts. Nuts. Nuts.*

Casey frantically withdrew the key again and dove for the door latch. The car gave a little jolt and a siren wailed a woo-woo-woo in harmony with the barking.

She spun around to face the animals. "No," she shouted, holding her arm out straight. Like that would do any good. Everyone knew that while Red might be a good rancher, as a dog trainer, he was worthless.

She closed her eyes and crouched against the car to minimize the damage. She had other clothes in her suitcase, but this was by far her best outfit and now she'd walk into the gathering looking like something the dogs hauled in from the field.

A sudden, crisp whistle pierced the air.

The barking stopped.

Casey straightened and looked over her shoulder. The four drooling beasts—a deerhound, a chocolate Labrador with a graying muzzle and two mixed breeds—all vaguely familiar to her, sat frozen, eyes turned toward a tall, lanky cowboy who descended the steps of the porch with casual grace.

"Jimmy?" she croaked, her voice a high-pitched squeak that made her face heat up. This wasn't the way she'd imagined meeting her old flame—nearly treed by her father's ill-mannered dogs.

"Hi, Case," Jimmy said, his tone huskier than she remembered. Of course, the last time she saw him he'd been a boy. Now, he was a man. A gorgeous hunk of a man.

Why couldn't he be balding and bowlegged as she'd hoped? Instead, his dark-blond hair was brushed away from his face, the sides and back short to accommodate a hat, no doubt. Her father wore his hair in the same style, although Red's waves were pure white.

"Your dad said to keep a lookout for you in case the dogs tried to ambush you. I had them locked in the mudroom, but they must have escaped."

Casey turned off the car alarm and started toward the house, detouring to avoid the quartet that squirmed and whined, obviously waiting for a word from the man. "I truly appreciate the rescue. I have a feeling mud and drool are the two things that would never come out of these pants."

"That would be a shame, since they look so good on you."

The compliment surprised her. This adult Jimmy possessed a polish and confidence his youthful counterpart would have killed for. The Jimmy she'd known had been tongue-tied around girls and excruciatingly shy—two traits she'd found utterly endearing.

In an attempt to avoid the things that needed to be said between them, she smiled her thanks then asked, "Who are these mutts?"

"Jonesy, Dufus, Cry Baby and Rose," he said, pointing to each one. The dogs gave him a look that could only be described as devotion.

"Are they your official fan club?" she asked when she reached the steps.

He shrugged casually. "Your father made me take them to obedience class after they treed the UPS guy. Now, we've bonded."

Jimmy moved to one side as she mounted the stairs, her hand gripping the worn railing. "I'm guessing Red has quite a crowd in there."

He nodded. "Half the membership of the farm association, I figure."

"I wish I'd known. I'd have chosen another time to come."

His wry grin confirmed what she suspected.

"Which is why Red failed to mention that he was holding a meeting here today."

"That would be my guess, but you know your dad. He plays his cards close to his chest."

Casey had heard that saying for years but she'd failed to understand how apropos it was—not just to her father, but to the man she married as well. Nathan kept things bottled up inside him and avoided her attempts to bring his feelings out in the open. She'd find herself stifling her emotions in return. She often likened it to living next to an active volcano—look out when it blows.

Red, on the other hand, let loose his pent-up emotions on a regular basis—yelling, stomping his feet, slamming doors, reducing his housekeeper to tears or driving his daughter into the open arms of the first handsome young man who professed to love her. Nathan was far too civilized to yell. He just kept everything inside, and, like Casey, ate far too many antacids.

"I suppose it's too late to turn around and run," she said, her hand on the levered door handle.

"I don't think the dogs would like that." His obvious humor kept the words from sounding like a threat.

Casey smiled despite her sudden attack of nerves. Good thing she'd skipped breakfast or her stomach might be giving her trouble. She righted her shoulders and took a deep breath. "Legs don't fail me now," she murmured.

Jimmy must have heard because his low chuckle followed her indoors. But he didn't. Before closing the door behind her, he said, "Good luck. I have to check on Mother and her new brood. If Red asks, I'll be back in an hour or so. And I'm taking the dogs with me in case you need anything from your car."

Casey found it odd that Jimmy would duck out in the middle of a meeting, but she kept her opinion to herself. She followed the sound of voices down the short hallway to what her parents had called the family room—a vast open space that included the kitchen and dining areas, plus a seven-foot hearth and cathedral ceiling with skylights.

As she scanned the room, picking out more familiar faces than she'd expected to find after so long an absence, her gaze fell on one person she hadn't expected to find. Sarah. Coffee carafe in hand, the very pregnant woman was refilling the cup of an older woman who looked vaguely familiar. Except for her rounded belly and faint smudges under her eyes, Sarah looked just the same—sweet, charming, easy to love. Her trademark Julia Roberts smile was firmly in place. Too firmly?

Casey brushed the thought aside. Sarah and Casey

had been best friends from the day the Myersons had rented a mobile home from Red on a nearby quarter of land, but even after Sarah's father was elected sheriff and the family moved into town, the girls remained close. Distance couldn't come between the two.

No, it took more than mere miles to end their friendship. It took a boy. Jimmy.

And now, something was wrong between Sarah and Jimmy. Casey didn't have any details because her father was a deplorable source of gossip, but when she'd asked who was living in the guest house, Red had muttered, "Jimmy. For now. And that's all I'm going to say about it."

Sarah straightened and put her free hand to her lower back. The cotton of her lilac-colored maternity top draped lovingly around her pregnant belly. A prickle of tears made Casey look away sharply.

"We can't burn 'em out 'cause nothing's built yet," a man in a sweat-stained Ducks Unlimited ball cap said.

His voice was vaguely familiar, but Casey couldn't place a name with the man's corpulent face.

"Now, let's not promote violence when there's a deputy present," Casey's father said. Then he slapped his knee and pointed. "Oh, wait, that was Deputy Franklin speaking."

Jerry Franklin? District all-team quarterback when I was a freshman? Casey suddenly felt old.

Everyone laughed, including Jerry.

Someone at Red's elbow whispered something to him and pointed in her direction. Her father's impressive shock of white hair turned her way, drawing a matching response from the majority of the people in the room.

"Casey T.," Red boomed. "You made it." He moved his arm like Moses parting the Red Sea and a path materialized. "Everybody. You remember my daughter, Casey, don't you? She's a lawyer now, and she's come to save us from the turkey menace."

Casey tried not to groan and roll her eyes. She was nobody's savior. That was Nathan's strong point—bailing companies out of trouble with the IRS, helping affluent young sons and daughters of wealthy families beat their raps, screwing the deserving public out of millions of tax dollars. Casey's clients were remote parcels of land that deserved to be recognized as valuable wetlands or pristine prairie or whatever made it special in the eyes of the environmental community.

"Hi, everyone," she said with a quick wave.

A muffled clapping sound made her cheeks turn hot, but she kept her chin up, knowing one set of eyes belonged to Sarah. She walked to her father and gave him a hug. Red Buchanan was a bear of a man—larger than life and full of energy. She'd never known him to back down from a fight and wasn't surprised that he could engender this kind of support for his cause.

"I'm just an observer," she said, addressing the crowd. "I'm not licensed to practice law in the state of California."

"Not yet," Red said. "But, don't worry, honey, I talked to Judge Miller and he said he'd put you in contact with somebody who could offer you some sort of umbrella to let you handle a couple of trials until you take the exam."

Casey's stomach turned over. She knew that professional courtesy was common practice, but she'd hoped her father didn't.

She put on a fake smile and said, "We need to talk."

Red looked at her a moment then told his guests, "I think we got the basics down. You all know what to do and if you have any questions give the two co-chairmen...I mean, co-chairpersons, a call. I'm gonna be politically correct one of these days, right?"

A few good-natured replies said otherwise.

Casey looked around, wondering who the two unlucky saps were.

A man in a faded flannel shirt and bright-yellow suspenders called out, "Where can we get their numbers?"

"Well, Sarah's in the book under Mills, and you can reach Casey right here."

Casey's mouth dropped open far enough to drive a truck in. *Oh, Red, what have you done to me this time?*

AFTER CHECKING the files for current clients, Nathan needed a few minutes alone in the executive restroom to clear his head. Casey's father's arch-nemesis was indeed one of his company's premier clients. Fortunately, Eric Mathers was on Nathan's "keepers" list, so the client would have experienced representation in the upcoming battle. But Eric's last two trials had ended in monetary awards far less than had been sought and Nathan wanted to place a strong litigator in the second chair.

Normally, he'd have overseen the case personally, but that wasn't possible given his wife's father's association with the opposition. Nathan would have to make damn certain there was no room for finger-pointing or accusation of collusion. In theory, the case looked open and shut, but Nathan had learned long ago that where people were concerned never to count on probability.

When he returned to his desk, he found a surprise. A big one.

"Hi. I hope you don't mind, but I asked your secretary to let me in."

Nathan stopped dead in his tracks. "Gwyneth, what are you doing here? Didn't we just talk yesterday?"

She was dressed as if she'd just stepped out of court—a severely cut black wool suit with knee-length skirt that showed off her superb calves and high heels. A glimpse of white silk at the V of her ample cleavage.

"We did, and I'm hoping I didn't read more into your tone than you'd intended, but I sensed that you needed my help. So, here I am. Please tell me I didn't overstep."

Nathan swallowed hard. He could almost hear his mother saying, "Be careful what you wish for lest you get it." "You're not wrong. I'm up to my eyeballs here and I do need help, but what about Boston? There will be hell to pay—"

She cut him off. "Actually, when I presented my case to the partners, they agreed that I was the logical choice since this is where I started right out of college. I only worked here a few months, but one quick call from Nolan Reisbecht and I had my privileges reinstated. Just so you know, I'm only on loan for a month until things even out."

"Where are you staying?"

"The company apartment. Didn't you use it when you came west to check things out?"

He had. He and Casey. They'd planned on using the five days as a minivacation, but she'd wound up contracting some kind of bug the first day and had spent most of the time in the bathroom.

Gwyneth's body language said a hug was expected, but he used the pile of folders his secretary had handed him on his way past her desk to keep it formal. Casey wasn't going to be thrilled about this development. Although they'd never talked about Gwyneth directly, he knew that his wife was sensitive to his colleague's dramatic flair and blatant sexuality.

"Well, that's fabulous," Nathan said, motioning her to sit down. "You're a welcome sight. I managed to dig myself an enormous hole in a very short time, so grab a shovel."

She moved with the haughty grace of a runway model. She stepped to the desk but didn't sit down. Instead, she leaned over and placed her hands flat on the scattered papers that he'd left in uncharacteristic disarray. "Can we be frank, Nathan?"

Nathan willed himself to keep his eyes on her face, not her cleavage. "I think so."

"I came here for one reason. And one reason only. You."

Damn.

"You may not realize it but you've been the person I've tried to emulate in my career. I'm not done learning from you, Nathan. But, ultimately, you should know that what I really want…is your job."

Nathan let out the breath he'd been holding and rocked back in his chair. "Why does that not surprise me?"

"I didn't think it would. You're smart and savvy. You know the score. You also know that I want your ass, but since this is the workplace and I'd never do anything to compromise my chances for advancement, we'll have to leave any extracurricular activities to outside the office."

She spoke so fast Nathan might have thought he'd imagined the reference to his posterior if not for the rakish look she shot him. "I'm going to need a day to unpack and get settled. If you have anything you want me to look at before tomorrow, bring it over after work. You know where to find me."

After she left, Nathan closed his eyes. *Casey, why aren't you waiting at home when I need you?*

He picked up his cell phone and hit the speed-dial number to connect to Casey. "Hi, there. Sorry I missed your call. Please leave a message."

His initial smile—he loved the sound of her voice— gave way to an annoyed frown. Where was she? Locking horns with her dad or getting reacquainted with her old boyfriend. Johnny or Dusty or something.

He tried to picture Casey in some cowpoke's arms but not a single image came to mind. But Gwyneth popped right up like the damning slice of temptation she was.

He reached for the phone on his desk and buzzed his secretary. "Do you know if there's a rental car agency close by?" He was driving to the valley this weekend. Gwyneth could use the time to play catch-up on the files. And Nathan could use the time to reconnect with his wife. Before something irreparable happened.

CHAPTER FOUR

SHE FOUND JIMMY right where she thought he'd be—working on the tractor. He was wearing a pair of filthy coveralls that might once have been brown but now were several shades of grease.

The meeting had broken up an hour earlier, and Casey had spent the time since then trying to convince her father that she wasn't up to co-chairing the committee with Sarah. Naturally, she could have saved her breath. Sarah had conveniently slipped away with a nod at Casey and a "Doctor's appointment. Gotta run," to Red.

Frustrated and out of sorts when she'd realized her father and his close circle of friends weren't planning to take a break from their talking and drinking any time soon, she'd changed into jeans and a T-shirt and walked across the field hoping to find a sympathetic shoulder to cry on—figuratively speaking.

"Hey," she said. "Buy an old friend a beer?"

Jimmy scooted away from the upraised arm of the tractor. "Hi, Case. I wondered how long you'd last with the rabble-rousers. Nothing like a mutual enemy to bring people together, right?"

She nodded. "Sure seems like it." She looked around, trying to get her bearings. Only the age and make of the equipment seemed to have changed. "Does Red still keep a fridge…?" She stopped, spotting the ancient brown refrigerator in the corner. "Can I get you something?"

"A Pepsi, I guess."

She tried to hide her surprise and as she walked to the far side of the barn, she reminded herself that she really didn't know Jimmy. She'd assumed that he would follow in her father's social drinking footsteps, but why she thought that, she couldn't say. Other than a few polite exchanges at holidays, they were strangers. And yet, they weren't.

She opened the door. Four brands of cola and a case of her father's favorite beer. Casey hadn't tasted Sierra Pale Ale in ages. She used a bottle opener, then carried both beverages to the loader. Jimmy was on his feet, wiping his hands with a rag.

He pocketed the cloth and sat down on a nearby hay bale. On the other side of the big yellow Cub Cadette, her father's utility tractor, was a green metal pen. The smell and sounds told her this was Mother the Pig's current home. Normally, she loved to watch the baby piglets root for their mother's teats, but at the moment she was too upset to care.

"Is my father crazy?"

Jimmy laughed, nearly spewing his soda. "Depends on what you mean by crazy."

"What gives him the audacity to assume that I will agree to head this committee with your wife? A woman I haven't spoken to in fifteen years. He's insane."

"Maybe it's his way of helping you and Sarah mend fences."

Casey took a drink of beer. "As if it were that easy. Did Sarah agree to this? I wanted to ask her, but she disappeared before we could talk."

He nodded. "Her regular monthly doctor's appointment. I used to get to go along, but now she won't let me be there. I told her I planned to be in the hospital when the baby was born, but, knowing Sarah, she might not even call me until it's over."

He sounded both mad and sad.

"What happened to you two, Jimmy?"

He looked at the can of soda in his hand. "A lot of things. Nothing major. Your dad says that's what life is. A lot of little things—good and bad—strung together like a puzzle. If you believe Sarah, most of the bad ones were my fault. And you probably should. She's a saint, remember?"

His bitterness was obvious, but he did have a point. When they were friends, Sarah Myerson had been Casey's exact opposite. Shy, quiet, studious, a regular teacher's pet. The kind of girl who participated in Job's Daughters, a Catholic society that Casey had always wanted to belong to but her father refused to even discuss. Sarah was the one who got asked to babysit for the principal's kids. Casey always figured Red had encouraged the two girls' friendship hoping some of that sweetness would rub off on Casey.

"I'll have to take your word on that, but we all know I'm not perfect. I could see Red asking Nathan to spearhead this group, but not two women."

Jimmy's teasing grin made him look sixteen—and just as sexy as she remembered. "You may not know this, Case, but your dad's turned into a real liberal. He's talkin' about convertin' the old Ford into a bio-diesel."

Casey couldn't help but laugh.

More seriously, he said, "Sarah may look sweet and quiet, but that woman has a will of tempered steel."

Casey could respect that, but fifteen years of not speaking didn't just go away overnight. Did it?

"Even if I wanted to help out, I don't live here. I'm not even completely unpacked, but Red insisted he needed me to come down today. I do have a life, you know."

He shrugged. "You're telling the wrong guy, Case. But we both know you'd have a better chance convincing him that Wednesday was Tuesday once Red has his mind made up."

She took another drink. The beer had a stronger bite than she remembered but it was full of flavor. "You're probably right, but…"

She knew she should be back in San Francisco talking this out with her husband, but lately their conversations made Casey feel as if she and Nathan were on different planets. She'd mention her father and he'd reply in lawyer-speak.

"How bad is this going to get?"

Jimmy didn't answer right away. When he did, he spoke slowly, carefully. "I've known Red Buchanan for a long time. I'm a hell of a lot closer to him than I was to my dad. And I can honestly say this is the first time I've ever seen him scared."

"Scared?"

The taste of beer on her tongue turned sour. Her father was invincible, fearless. And he'd called her to help. But was she up to the challenge? And what would this mean to her plans to reconnect with Nathan and make a baby?

The word *baby* brought to mind Sarah's silhouette. "Jimmy, it's none of my business, but if you need a friend—"

Jimmy stood up. "We *were* friends, Casey. A hundred years and a thousand gallons of water rushing under the bridge ago. Now, we're old acquaintances with a shared past."

Casey was surprised by his fatalistic tone. "I guess you're right, but from the way my dad talks about you, you're practically an adopted son. That would make us siblings, wouldn't it?"

His lips twitched. He was still a handsome man, despite the deep tan and a few lines she read as loss. "So, sis, what do you want to know? Why my wife kicked me out?"

Casey frowned. She'd assumed whatever happened in their marriage was mutual. "Hey, marriage licenses don't come with any money-back guarantees."

He sucked in a big breath of air. She could tell he didn't want to talk about his problems. "Guess that explains why I'm living here, instead of the house I'm paying the mortgage on."

Casey looked through the barn doors to the small, but stylish guesthouse her father had built around the time she'd graduated from law school. Although he'd never come right out and said so, she'd always known he'd built the place for her.

"Red used to have a couple who ran the nut company living there, but they decided they wanted to be closer to their grandchildren and moved to Texas. He has a new manager, but she's got a place in Madera. It was sitting empty till I moved in."

"He made your move sound temporary."

"I know. He feels funny since it's your house and I'm the reason he sent you away."

Casey's jaw dropped open. "That's not true. I'm the reason he sent me away. He was afraid I was going to turn into some kind of loose woman," she said, trying to mask the old hurt.

"You were the prettiest girl I'd ever seen. I used to have to bust other guys' jaws on a regular basis just for looking at you wrong. Red knew if it wasn't me, it would be one of the other no-good cowpunchers who sweet-talked you out of your innocence. He just wanted to protect you."

"Because he couldn't trust me."

Jimmy shook his head, but Casey didn't want to discuss the old chicken-egg dilemma. "He did the right thing. I have a great life." *Except that my marriage is suffering from some strange affliction neither Nathan nor I can bring ourselves to talk about.* "Um, just out of curiosity when did you know things were in trouble between you and Sarah?"

"Who said I knew? Everything seemed fine until one day I found all my stuff sitting on the back step."

Casey's ability to catch a "tell"—the giveaway in poker that subtly announced whether or not a person was bluffing—had always served her well in the courtroom. She knew he was lying when he looked away rather than meet her eye. But she let it go. This wasn't any of her business.

"Okay," she said. She swirled the last dregs of beer around in the bottle. "I guess I'd better get back to the house. At some point, Red is going to have to talk to me. Right?"

"I'm not the person who should be giving you advice, Case, but one thing I know about your dad is sometimes you gotta listen real hard to hear what he doesn't say."

Casey looked at him a moment then chuckled. "Wow. That was almost metaphysical. I had no idea you'd turned into such a philosopher." She included a wink to make sure he knew she was kidding. His returning smirk made her insides go soft and mushy. She didn't feel any lingering spark of attraction for Jimmy beyond that which she'd have for any good-looking man, but he'd been her first love and would always have a special place in her heart. She wondered if there was any chance they could be friends again?

Impulsively, she leaned in and kissed his cheek. Well, she'd intended to kiss his cheek. But somehow their lips wound up touching.

She pulled back, flustered and embarrassed, and jumped to her feet. As she turned to leave, she saw Sarah standing a few feet away. She must have parked at the nut company and walked to the barn since neither Casey nor Jimmy had heard her car.

"Well, damn," Casey muttered, hating that her cheeks were probably bright red. "That must have looked like something it wasn't."

Sarah's chin lifted and her eyes narrowed. This wasn't the Sarah Casey remembered. This was a very angry Sarah. "Really? It looked like you were kissing my husband."

"Looks can be deceiving," Casey said defensively. "If I didn't know better, I'd say you looked jealous. But how can that be since you kicked Jimmy out?"

Jimmy stepped around Casey. "What's wrong now, Sarah? Is the pilot out on the water heater?"

She crossed her arms belligerently, as if to say she wasn't talking while Casey was present. Casey put up her hands and made a wide detour. "I'm out of here."

"What's new there?"

"Sarah," Jimmy said with a sigh. "Don't start. Casey, ignore her."

As if Casey would turn away from such a blatant challenge. "What's that supposed to mean?"

"Isn't that what you do? You leave."

"Because my father made me go. And the minute my back was turned you swooped in like a vulture and gobbled up my boyfriend."

Sarah crossed her arms over her belly. "That is such a lie. First off, he was only your boyfriend because you said so. One kiss in a hayloft does not automatically make you his girlfriend."

"It was more than that."

"Fine. He touched your breast. Big deal." She looked at Casey's chest. "Well, not very big, but you get my drift."

Casey's mouth dropped open. She wanted to shriek in outrage, but instead she started to laugh. She honestly didn't have a comeback. This was Sarah—the girl who traded training bras with Casey before either of them had anything to put in one. And now, thanks to the baby on board, Sarah's size triple D bosom made Casey look flat-chested by comparison.

Tears filled Casey's eyes, she was laughing so hard. Sarah looked suspicious. Jimmy obviously didn't know what do to, but his lips were pursed as if he was trying not to smile.

Choking on laughter, she finally said, "At least, you filled out…and then some."

That was all it took for Sarah's severe demeanor to give in to humor. She chuckled, then sputtered. "No. Don't make me laugh. I'll pee my pants. I can't even sneeze anymore with this tank sitting on my bladder."

"Come on," Jimmy said, taking his wife's elbow. "I cleaned the shop bathroom this morning."

Casey watched them walk away, undecided about whether to head back to the house or wait. But Sarah's accusation—*You leave*—seemed to linger in the air.

She looked around until she found a bin filled with empty bottles, then returned to the bale of alfalfa where she and Jimmy had been talking. She took a deep calming breath and tried to prepare herself as she would have if she were headed into court. Nathan lived for the thrill of publicly outsmarting his opponent. Casey could live the rest of her life without such a challenge, but she'd never tell him that. After all, he'd married a lawyer.

Jimmy and Sarah returned a few minutes later. Casey was the first to speak. "I haven't laughed like that in a long time."

"Me, either," Sarah said softly.

Jimmy appeared to take her admission as criticism because he made a sound of disgust and walked away.

Both women watched him until he reached the gated yard of "Casey's" house. "That is one unhappy man."

"I suppose you're here to fix that, too," Sarah said, waspishly.

Casey scooted back on the bale, drew her legs crossways in front of her. "You used to be the sweet one. What happened?"

Sarah crossed her arms atop her protruding belly and gave Casey a look that said we will never be friends. Casey had seen that look before. They'd gotten in fights as kids— huge, name-calling, hair-pulling fights—but they'd always made up. The idea that they could get over this chasm of bad feelings made Casey a little light-headed.

Casey held up her hand before Sarah could speak. "Wait. Before you yell at me for whatever it is you think I did in the past, I want you to acknowledge that your marital problems have nothing to do with me. And a peck on the cheek between old friends does not constitute cheating. Okay?"

Sarah glared at her. "Jimmy would never cheat on me."

"I didn't say he would."

"Especially not with you."

"What's that supposed to mean?"

Sarah put a hand to her temple and rubbed. "It means he thinks of Red as a father, which would make you his sister."

"Oh," Casey said, smiling again. "Is it me or is this

conversation a bit surreal? We haven't talked in more than a dozen years and we're still talking about boys."

Sarah's lips did a start-stop smile but she quit pacing and sat down where her husband had been earlier. "When I went back to the ranch and Red told me you were here, I started imagining the worst."

"Me and Jimmy in some incestuous embrace?"

Sarah blushed.

"I overreacted. Your dad blames it on hormones. He told me your mother once kicked him out when she was pregnant with you."

"Really? He never told me that."

"I see him every day. He hired me to help him organize his office. He bought a computer years ago but threatened to put a bullet in it so many times the poor thing finally just gave up and died. And about the same time my doctor said he didn't want me standing on my feet at the feed store for eight hours a day, so Red put me to work."

"That was nice of him."

Sarah looked at her sharply. "You're jealous."

"What? Me? No way."

Her eyes went wide as if suddenly figuring out a puzzle. "You are. You think I somehow managed to horn in on your life, even though you completely cut ties to everything and everyone back here."

Casey jumped to her feet. "I told you, I didn't leave by choice. Red railroaded me out of here."

"But you could have come back after high school. Or college. Or any time for longer than a holiday or two."

Casey took a few steps on the straw-littered concrete floor. Words, explanations, excuses raced through her mind as she tried to form a rebuttal, but nothing held together because every choice she ever made was tied to emotions she'd never really dealt with—shame, grief, feelings of unworthiness.

She looked at Sarah. "I didn't think anyone wanted me back."

Sarah stood up with surprising speed and approached her. She put one hand tentatively on Casey's shoulder. "Oh, Case, how could you think that? Your dad loves you. He talks about you all the time. When he heard you were moving back to the state, he called an architect to start drawing up house plans so you and Nathan could have your own place."

"What?"

Sarah's lips formed a little round O. "Oops. My bad. He probably plans to wait until all this turkey stuff gets settled before he tells you about that. Sorry. Forget I said anything."

Casey shook her head, which felt mushy and completely overwhelmed. "Between that beer and my residual jet lag, I suddenly don't feel well. I'd like to go back to the house and lie down. Do you have a car or could I borrow Jimmy's truck?"

"I'll drive you. We still need to talk about the committee."

Casey groaned. "Red was serious about that? What makes him think you and I can work together?"

"I asked him that. Believe me, I wasn't wild about the idea, either. But you know Red. Once he gets his mind made up, it turns to hardpan." Casey pictured the rocklike substrata of soil that could turn a simple job like putting in a garden into a major effort that required a backhoe.

"So, do you think we can work together?" Casey asked once they were seated in Sarah's compact minivan.

Sarah started the car. As she backed up, she sent one lingering glance toward the house where her husband currently lived. Casey read a lot of longing in that look, but she didn't say anything.

"Well," Sarah replied, once she turned onto the main road that led into town and eventually to the highway, "that depends on you."

"Me?"

"Are you going to have to be boss? Miss College Educated Lawyer lady? I won't be your flunky for Red or anybody."

Casey chuckled softly. She liked this woman. Sarah had always had a strong will beneath her sweet demeanor, which was partly why she and Casey had been so close. "How 'bout if I be your flunky? Truly. I still have a ton of boxes to unpack and a husband who is settling into a new office in a city four hours away from here. Doesn't it seem logical that you would be the point person for this operation?"

"Yes, it does. That's exactly what I told your father, but he's worried that I'll do too much and jeopardize my pregnancy."

Of course. Casey understood, and for the first time since she arrived in the valley, she was glad to be here. She could help. She was needed. And maybe, just maybe, she and Sarah could be friends again.

"How far along are you?" she asked.

"Seven months. My doctor says I'm healthy as a horse and the baby is doing great."

"Do you know what you're having?"

She shook her head. "We could have seen at the last ultrasound, but since Jimmy wasn't there, I didn't think it was right that I knew and he didn't."

Neither spoke until Sarah put on the blinker to turn into Red's driveway, then she said, "I kicked Jimmy out because I was tired of coming in last on Jimmy's list of priorities. Work, hanging out with Red, helping a friend build a demolition derby car to run at the fair this summer. Every night he'd come home and drop into bed, exhausted, smelling of smoke and beer and parts cleaner." Her nose wrinkled with distaste. "When I told him the smell was making me sick, he started sleeping on the couch. That's when I lost it."

Casey wished she knew what to say, but since her marriage wasn't on the most solid ground, either, she kept her mouth shut.

Sarah pulled the van to a stop beside Casey's car. She didn't look at Casey. "I can't believe I just spilled my guts to you, but I guess if we're going to work together we need to start somewhere, right?"

Casey unfastened her seat belt and turned to face her old friend. "I'm sorry things aren't perfect between you and Jimmy. Aunt Meg used to say that marriage is always a work in progress."

Sarah glanced her way and smiled. "Are you and Nathan happy?"

Are we? "Most of the time, but moving isn't easy."

Sarah inhaled deeply. Casey's gaze was drawn to the mound that practically touched the steering wheel. *Sarah's pregnant and I'm not.* Those old, familiar feelings of inadequacy started to surface, but Casey pushed them back down. "So, I guess I'll tell Red that I'll be part of this... What did they decide to name the committee? N.O.T.T.?"

Sarah made a face. "Neighbors Opposed To Turkeys. Could have been worse, I guess."

Casey opened the door and got out, after checking for dogs. "You have my cell number, right?"

"I'll get it from Red. Are you staying long?"

She hadn't decided. First, she needed to talk to Nathan. "We'll see. 'Bye."

As she watched the van turn around and recross the bridge, Casey let out a long, heartfelt sigh. What was her father thinking? Surely there was a better choice to head this committee than a pregnant woman and an out-of-work lawyer who lived four hours away.

She turned toward the house but stopped abruptly and swore. "Damn." Her father's truck was gone. "Red," she muttered as she trudged to the door. "You can run, but you can't hide forever."

CHAPTER FIVE

THE WEEKEND COULDN'T arrive fast enough to suit Nathan. Although he talked to Casey daily, he had yet to hear her say when she was coming home. Apparently some new problem that required her presence at the ranch cropped up every day. He found little satisfaction in the fact that she felt totally overwhelmed by her father's expectations.

"'Wave your magic wand, Casey T. Make it all go away'," she'd said last night, mimicking Red's voice. "Dammit, Nathan, did you forget to pack my magic wand?"

He'd smiled, but that single little quip had a secondary effect. It served to remind him how much he loved her sense of humor. For four days she'd faithfully reported in, telling him about her day. Apparently she'd reached some kind of détente with Sarah Mills, the woman Casey at one time had likened to Benedict Arnold. She finally managed to get all the dogs' names straight, but they still didn't listen to anyone but Jimmy, about whom, Nathan had noticed, Casey said very little.

She went into great detail, however, about an ancient pig that seemed to produce babies through immaculate conception. "We're thinking of naming a religion after her. The holy order of Mother the Pig."

And when she mentioned her father's backhanded compliments—"Pretty fancy car for a ranch, but I guess that husband of yours has got folks he's out to impress and this one ought a do that."—Nathan could hear the hurt in her voice, even though she tried to mask it.

Nathan's rental car was no Lexus, but he'd splurged on a Cadillac. Red couldn't find fault with that, could he?

Nathan had been to the ranch twice since he and Casey had married, and had no doubt that he could remember how to find it. After all, the Willow Creek ranch was on a prominent secondary road, which was one of the main draws to the turkey growers—high accessibility.

Gwyneth hadn't been too happy with the stacks of files he'd handed her, but Nathan refused to let her pretty pout get to him. She'd asked for the chance to shine and how better than as second chair to the company's largest client?

He'd called Eric Mathers and Gwyneth into his office to discuss the potential problems that could occur *if* the turkey growers were forced to fight the county planners in court. No one expected the county to turn down the landowner's application for a conditional use permit that was in keeping with existing zoning, but in this age of environmental controversy, it paid to be prepared. He also spelled out his involvement. "My father-in-law isn't the type to back off from a fight, and he's trying to drag Casey into this."

Gwyneth, showing off for Eric, quoted a line from a 1979 decision, *Yarn v. Superior Court.* "Few precepts are more firmly entrenched than that the fiduciary relationship between attorney and client is of the very highest character."

"Which is why from this point on I don't want to see any copy about this case cross my desk, nor will you discuss it in my presence. Eric, if you want some sort of written disclosure for your clients, I'd be happy to provide it. I don't want them to think we're hiding anything."

"They're business people, Nathan. They might not like that your wife's father wants to prevent them from setting up shop, but at least Mr. Buchanan isn't our client, too. Now *that* would get tricky."

Nathan was steadily coming to appreciate Eric's intelligent humor and pleasant disposition. What he found curious was that Eric seemed totally impervious to Gwyneth's sex appeal. How that was possible, Nathan wasn't sure. "Maybe there's a vaccine," he muttered, easing his foot off the accelerator.

Was it cowardly to duck out on his sexy young colleague and leave her alone in an unfamiliar city after just a few days of acclimation? Probably, but he'd rather be a coward than a cheat. He owed Casey—and himself—every chance to fix whatever was wrong with their marriage.

Nathan spotted a familiar road sign and turned off Highway 99. Five miles farther and he turned on Buchanan Road. Casey's maiden name. Her full name—much to her chagrin—was Casey Tibbs Buchanan. "Who in their right mind names a daughter after a long-dead rodeo star?" she once complained.

Nathan couldn't give her an answer. He probably

hadn't spent more than forty-eight total hours in his father-in-law's company, but Nathan knew Red Buchanan stood out as a unique figure. Big, brash, irreverent. Almost a caricature, but of what, Nathan couldn't say. Red wasn't a true redneck, but he was no Renaissance man, either. And though he touted Christian values, he wasn't a Bible-thumping conservative. He lived life the way he wanted and didn't apologize to anyone.

Not even to his daughter. Not even when he was wrong and she deserved a simple, "I'm sorry."

"Don't hold your breath waiting for that day to come," Casey once told him. "Remember that sappy line from the movie *Love Story? 'Love means never having to say you're sorry'*? My father takes that literally."

Minutes later, Nathan drove beneath the arched gate of Willow Creek Ranch. A dozen or so cars and trucks were scattered about, including his less-than-pristine silver Lexus. At least he assumed it was his, since it still had dealer plates, but through all the mud he couldn't be sure.

He turned off the engine and got out, pushed his sunglasses to the top of his head and stretched. "Hello," he called. "Casey?"

There was no answer, but a sound, like a cackle or a snort came from the barn so he headed that way.

CASEY TOOK as shallow a breath as possible and bent over to peer through the opening that had been cut in the side of the barn. Roughly the size and shape of a large doggie door, the portal provided access to the outside for the animals in the barn.

In this case, Mother and brood. Red in his esteemed wisdom had decided the porcine family needed to visit the great outdoors. Casey had never had much luck moving pigs, which although smart, possessed quirky personalities that often defied logic. Mother was notoriously lazy. She wouldn't move without persistent prodding, so Jimmy had elected to ride herd, so to speak, while Casey opened the exterior latch and wooed the sow with fresh feed.

"Come 'n get it, piglets," she called, trying to see into the building.

She shook the metal pail so the pellets would slosh from side to side.

Nothing happened.

"What's going on in there? Where's the pork?"

She straightened up and looked around. What if this was her father's idea of a prank and he was secretly filming her with a video camera hoping to catch her falling on her butt in a pen six inches deep with mud? She'd had to borrow rubber boots that were almost too tight to fit over her tennis shoes.

"We're trying, Case," Jimmy called, his voice echoing in a peculiar way inside the barn. "Mother wants to nap."

A series of high-pitched squeals alerted her to the fact that the children were up and moving. She stepped to one side lest a wave of four-legged beasts overran her.

It was a beautiful morning. She'd probably have enjoyed the experience, if it wasn't the smell. That and the fact her husband hadn't answered the phone when she'd called this morning. She wanted to think he was out jogging, but last night he'd been particularly evasive about his plans for today.

"I have something to tell you but I'd prefer to do it in person," he'd said. "It's business, not personal."

She wondered if that was true. She'd find out soon. Red had asked her—begged her actually—to stay through the weekend, but Casey couldn't stand another night away from Nathan. Despite the uncertainty of things between them lately, she missed him. She was going home this afternoon. Or early in the morning at the latest.

Leaving wasn't as easy as it should have been. Red had found excuse after excuse for her to stay—right down to helping him move the pig. "You used to love helping with the animals, Case. Mother One…or was it Mother Two…used to follow you around like a puppy, remember?"

Vaguely. In truth, Casey did love the farm and the animals, but she'd blocked her memories of that time so completely, the whole experience could have happened to a character she'd seen in a movie.

She shook the pan again, then stepped closer, figuring the sound wasn't reaching the ears that needed to hear it. "Yoo-hoo, piglets…"

A sudden wave of small pink objects made her step back too fast. Her boots stayed in place, but momentum took Casey backward. Her right foot came loose, and she went down hard with her left foot still stuck. The grain in the bucket went airborne and pelted her like hail in a brief but fragrant shower.

She was too startled to be mad. The mud oozed around her brand-new, still-stiff jeans, which she'd picked up the day before at the feed store in Chowchilla. "You can't help it if all you have is city clothes," Red had insisted, urging her to charge whatever she wanted to his account.

Before she could figure out a way to rise without putting her hands in the mud, her father's voice called out through the hole, "Here comes Mother."

Casey's eyes grew wide. "Oh, crap," she muttered, scrambling to get out of the way. Mother's eyesight wasn't the best and she might accidentally run over Casey, injuring them both.

She tossed the bucket and grabbed the boot straps, trying to break the seal that had been created. Her foot was stuck in her tennis shoe, which was not coming out of the boot. Cursing under her breath, she pushed on the heel of the boot with her bare foot.

"Casey?"

Her head popped up. "Jimmy," she cried, trying not to sound hysterical. "Go back in and stop Mother. I'm stuck here."

Her words were lost to the growing volume of grunts and snorts erupting from the doggie door.

Panic surged through her veins, and she renewed her effort to break free, but the heavy mud held her fast. A second later, a pair of arms locked around her chest and a tug-of-war ensued.

"Oh," she exclaimed when her foot popped free. It happened so suddenly she'd been unable to give her rescuer any warning. Together, they fell backward in a heap.

"Hurry," Casey urged, rolling off him. "Mother's coming."

Jimmy didn't hesitate. He grabbed her hand and pulled her to the fence, his boots slipping and sliding exactly like Jerry Lewis on roller skates.

The cold mud soaked through her white socks, but the chill wasn't the only reason a fierce shiver passed through her limbs. A heartbeat later, Mother—two hundred-plus pounds of pissed-off pig—charged out the opening. Squinty eyes flashing with displeasure for having been separated from her brood, she headed for the only non-oinkers in sight.

Hands squarely on her bottom, Jimmy boosted Casey over the wooden rungs, then swung over himself, dropping to the ground with a noisy "Umph." He remained on one knee, drawing in quick breaths while Casey tried to make sense of what had just happened.

"You saved my life," she said.

"Naw." He looked up, mud streaking his face like war paint. "Mother might have roughed you up a bit, but she's not mean."

Casey knew that wasn't completely true. She was so moved by emotion, she reached out to touch his shoulder. The contact—the very male heat and substance—made her realize how much she missed her husband.

"Casey?" a familiar voice said from behind them.

She drew back her hand as if burned and spun about on her mud-encrusted socks. "Nathan?"

NATHAN HAD ALWAYS prided himself on being impervious to petty emotions like jealousy. He'd seen too much of it as a kid. Nathan still remembered hearing his mother complain about "those women" at his father's workplace. Whether or not his father had ever given her any reason to be jealous, Nathan didn't know, but in an effort to avoid the door slamming and loud arguments of his childhood, Nathan strived never to raise his voice—except in court.

"What's going on?" he asked in well-modulated tones. Nothing in his manner could have betrayed the sudden tension—and some other emotion—that made him clench his fists. "I thought your fight was with turkeys, not pigs."

Casey stepped away from the stranger she'd been touching in such a tender manner. Of the two, she was by far the muddier, but her cohort wasn't unscathed. His cowboy boots were coated with disgusting sludge that reminded Nathan of changing his younger brother's diapers.

"Jimmy just rescued me. I was trapped in quick-mud. Is that a word? The same devouring properties of quicksand, but the consistency of mud."

She talked fast, her tone brighter than he'd heard lately. Obviously, Casey was nervous, flustered. Guilty?

Nathan took a step closer and held out his hand. "I owe you my sincere gratitude then," he said.

The stranger wiped his hand on a clean patch of denim. He was an inch or two shorter than Nathan but broader across the shoulders. Hatless, he squinted against the bright sunlight. He glanced at Casey as if waiting for an introduction before returning the courtesy. Quick. Solid. A man's handshake. "No big deal. I mean, she's a big deal, but I didn't really do nothing."

"You're wrong, Jimmy," Casey insisted. "Red always said not to be anywhere near a mother pig when she had a mad on."

Jimmy. As in Casey's old boyfriend.

"I don't believe we've met. I'm Nathan Kent, Casey's husband."

Casey smacked the heel of her hand to her forehead, sending a shower of drying mud flakes across her nose. "Sorry. I'm discombobulated."

Jimmy looked Nathan in the eye and nodded. "Jimmy Mills. Red's foreman." Then he stepped back and said, "Case, I'll grab your boots after Mother has time to settle down. I don't want to provoke her any more right now." He glanced at Nathan and said, "Nice meeting you. I'd better get back inside and help Red muck out the pigpen."

Only years of rigid self-control kept Nathan from reaching out and pulling his little woman to his side in a display of machismo. What the hell was wrong with him?

Casey shifted from foot to foot, either uncomfortable from the wet mud or embarrassed to have been caught in a private moment with her old boyfriend. Or both. "There's a bathroom in the barn. Follow me. I'd better wash some of this stinky stuff off or I won't dare drive your fancy car."

His car. Not, their car. When had they gotten to the point where their possessions held individual ownership? He'd first noticed the term crop up in the move when Casey pointed out his weighty collection of law books. "*Your* library is going to put us over the weight limit. *Mine* on the other hand is going to the senior center to be redistributed among the faithful." Faithful romance readers, she meant. For the past couple of years, Casey's taste in literature had turned escapist. That, too, made Nathan uneasy.

"Do you want a ride?" he asked. "Piggyback."

Her expressive lips curved up in a wide smile. "No pun intended, I'm sure." She swiped at a patch of drying mud on her cheek and shook her head. "No, thanks. I can walk. I don't want you to have to shower, too."

There'd been a time when a joint shower was a good thing, not a bother, but Nathan followed when she started toward the massive building. He'd been on his way inside when he'd heard the sound of her voice. He'd arrived on the scene only moments after Jimmy had jumped over the fence and rushed to Casey's rescue.

Would I have known to do that? Nathan wasn't sure. Casey hadn't looked in jeopardy when he'd first spotted her. In fact, he'd grinned at the sight of his wife on her butt in the mud. Dressed in stiff-looking jeans and a man's long-sleeve shirt, she looked wholesome, fresh and about sixteen years old. But that smile had disappeared when her frantic movements telegraphed fear. He'd started forward the same instant the cowboy had rounded the barn and vaulted over the fence, but Nathan's knees hadn't cooperated. The legs he'd used that morning to run two miles suddenly forgot how to work.

Seconds later, the huge black-and-white sow had bounded down the little ramp—its sharp hooves punching holes in the imprint his wife's body had left in the mud. In the space of four or five seconds,

Nathan's emotions seesawed from amusement to flat-out panic to jealousy, and now, Casey was strolling away as if nothing had happened.

He wanted to grab her arm and shake her. Or kiss her. He wasn't sure which would calm the turbulence still humming through him.

"So, what the heck are you doing here?" she asked, motioning for him to keep up. "This is a major surprise. I tried the apartment and your cell phone this morning, but when you didn't answer I figured you were at the office. Didn't you tell me you had to work this weekend?"

"That's where I should be, but something's come up and I thought we should discuss it, face to face."

Casey stopped abruptly. "What?"

He took her elbow—making an extra effort to keep his grip neutral—and urged her forward. "Nothing that can't wait until you're clean and dry. That wind is a bit cool and your lips are turning blue."

She made a face but didn't argue. Her lips were bluish, but still the same kissable shape he had once dreamed about when he should have been studying. He used his free hand to loop a fairly clean swatch of hair behind her ear and said, "I bet you were cute when you made mud pies."

She smiled uncertainly. Nathan didn't blame her for being puzzled. He couldn't remember the last time he flirted with her. His life was all about work, hers all about getting pregnant. Somewhere in that equation, they'd lost sight of each other.

"I'll be back in a jiff." With a flicker of her fingers, she dashed into the barn.

Nathan followed, but he hadn't gotten four steps when she reappeared. "I don't suppose you brought clothes, did you? I can't put these back on."

"Actually, I did pack a bag. Just in case…" He let the words trail off. He'd left San Francisco with no real purpose in mind other than breaking the news that Gwyneth was in town and his company was representing the turkey growers. But perhaps on a subliminal level, Nathan had hoped he and Casey might spend some quality time together. Now that idea seemed not only advantageous but imperative.

He'd been at Willow Creek for less than fifteen minutes and felt like a defendant arriving in court without the slightest hope of clearing his name. Hell, he didn't even know for certain what the charges against him were, only that he was probably guilty.

CASEY HURRIED through her shower. Something was up. Nathan didn't make surprise visits. He was all about schedules and purpose. He didn't joke about mud pies. Something was wrong, and her gut told her it was bad.

She pulled on Nathan's soft gray sweatpants and Boston U sweatshirt. Both were too big, of course, but not as bulky as they would have been on someone as petite as say…Sarah—pre-pregnancy—or the lovely Gwyneth.

After wiping a clear patch in the steamed-over mirror, Casey towel-dried her hair. She shook her head, making the shoulder-length locks bounce. Thanks to Ricardo, her hairdresser in Boston, the clever cut gave her more body and style than she'd thought possible.

Growing up, she'd never cut her hair and had stubbornly resisted her aunt's suggestion to visit a stylist. But shortly after the doctor predicted that getting pregnant wasn't going to be easy, Casey had decided she needed a change.

"Run with it," she'd instructed Ricardo. "I'm ready for a new me."

He'd immediately snipped and clipped. Then he'd freshened up her ordinary blond sameness with some jaunty highlights.

As their friendship grew, Casey had felt comfortable admitting that as a child growing up she'd hated her hair color. Not because of the inevitable blond jokes, but because she'd been one of the few non-Hispanic children in her class. Plus, her landowner parents employed many of her classmates' parents or relatives. She was smart, blond, motherless and had no siblings. All strikes against her.

Ricardo, who was gay, overweight, half Puerto Rican, half Irish and lived with his mother, had helped Casey find humor in her past. "We are who we are," he used to tell her. "Your job is to love who you are."

Nathan once suggested that getting her hair cut was like cheap therapy. Casey couldn't agree more, and as she combed her fingers through her damp locks she realized she needed a trim, and suddenly felt very alone, which, she knew, was a terrible thing to admit when her husband was waiting outside for her.

After hanging the towel on the shower door, she went in search of Nathan. She could tell by the raised voices that her father and Jimmy had followed Mother and the piglets outside. Nathan had promised to wait nearby so they could ride back to the house together. Presumably, Casey thought, so he could tell her the news that was so important it couldn't be discussed over the phone.

Her nerves humming, she looked around until she spotted him squatting beside the pen that until a few minutes earlier had been Mother's home.

She tiptoed carefully, hoping to keep his white tube socks from turning black. When she was a few feet away, she saw why he was down on one knee. A dead piglet lay pushed up against the fence, its tiny body posed as if in slumber.

"Mother's a good breeder, but she always loses a few each litter," she said frankly.

When he looked at her, Casey could tell he was upset. Nathan was a master at hiding his emotions, but she'd been playing poker since she was five. Nathan's tell was a little nerve that flicked in his cheek when his jaw was tense.

He started to say something but apparently changed his mind. He swallowed and looked away, then rose in one fluid motion. Too fast. And in the wrong place.

His head struck the edge of the uplifted bucket on her father's tractor just as Casey cried out for him to stop. He looked momentarily surprised then his eyelids fluttered and his knees gave out. Like a great tree chopped at the base, he toppled to the floor before she could move.

"Holy cripes," Casey cried, rushing to her husband's side. "Oh, my God, Nathan. Are you okay?"

He moaned once then went silent, his face bloodless. Casey jumped to her feet. *"Daddy! Jimmy!* Help. Somebody call 911. Nathan needs an ambulance."

CHAPTER SIX

"GET A BAG of peas from the freezer," Red said, once they had Nathan's body stretched out on a nearby hay bale. "There's a couple in that old fridge over there."

"I will not," Casey said with passion. "You already moved him against my wishes and now you want to treat him with frozen vegetables? Where the hell are the paramedics?"

"It takes them about twenty minutes, Case," Jimmy said calmly. "Peas make a great ice pack and will reduce the swelling."

That made sense, but she gave her father a fierce frown before dashing away. She wanted to point the finger of blame at Red. What kind of irresponsible tractor operator left the bucket in that position? Even she knew to lower it, and she hadn't driven a tractor since she was fifteen.

Ignoring the shiver that raced through her—she was still running around in stocking feet, she yanked open the door to the freezer and pawed through the frosty parcels until she found the peas.

Nathan hadn't regained consciousness. He'd moaned something unintelligible when Jimmy and her father had moved him, but not a peep since. Casey's panic level had not subsided. She knew who the real culprit behind this accident was: her. What was she doing here, anyway? Trying to fix a past that was beyond repair? Attempting to recapture her youth? Good lord, why would she want to do that? She'd been a lonely little tomboy with no fashion sense, no communication skills and no dreams beyond pleasing her father. She should have been home with Nathan trying to make a baby, not trying to get her father to love her. Again.

"The past is the past," she muttered under her breath as she raced back to the hay bales.

She couldn't deny that she'd enjoyed herself this week. The slower pace, reconnecting with the animals, cracking through a couple of layers in her father's stubborn shell had felt rewarding, even though she knew it was unlikely that Red would ever admit he was wrong to have sent her away.

And what good would an apology do anyway? She was an adult. She had a great life. Yes, she had some regrets about missing out on knowing her father for all those years, but she was perceptive enough to admit that she shared some of the responsibility. As Ricardo had pointed out more than once, "The door swings both ways, missy." But pride was inherited, and she was definitely her father's daughter when it came to stiff-necked perversity.

"He's breathing, isn't he?" she asked as she handed the peas to her father, who was sitting near Nathan's hip. Jimmy stood at Red's shoulder, his brow lined.

Casey sat down where she'd been a moment earlier,

at Nathan's head. His hair was pushed back from his forehead. An angry red gash ran from the hairline to his temple, but it hadn't broken the skin except for one small nick. His chest barely rose and fell, prompting her question.

"'Course he's breathing. He's tougher than he looks."

Casey would have responded to her father's back-handed compliment, but the trill of a cell phone distracted her. She knew by the tone it was Nathan's. He didn't often carry the phone with him, but a short hunt through his pockets revealed his brand-new RAZR—another company perk.

She hadn't used it before, but after a moment of scrutiny pushed the right button. "Hello? Uh, Nathan Kent's phone here."

Red leaned forward and applied the frozen peas to her husband's wound. Nathan made another moaning sound. His lips moved but no words came out. Casey's stomach twisted and she felt a touch of bile rise in her throat. Even as a child, she'd toss her cookies when faced with a medical emergency—human or animal. She'd planned to be a veterinarian—until she'd figured out she'd never be able to do the work because she'd be running to the bathroom.

The voice on the other end of the phone came through crisp and clear as if the person speaking was in the next room. "Casey? Is that you? I'm trying to reach Nathan. This is Gwyneth."

Of course it is, Casey thought a bit hysterically. *The barracuda has psychic abilities.*

Touching Nathan's shoulder made her feel a bit more

grounded. "He's unavailable at the moment, Gwyneth." *Why are you calling my husband's cell on a weekend?* "Would you like me to give him a message?"

"When will he be available?" Gwyneth asked.

To you? Never. "I can't say for sure." Judging by how long Nathan had been unconscious, she realized there was a chance he might be out of action for days. "As long as I have you on the phone, could you do me a favor and let his office know that he might not be in on Monday? I have the number, but I'm a little tied up at the moment."

"Casey, what's going on? I'm calling from San Francisco. I'm certain he'll want to speak with me as soon as possible."

Gwyneth was calling from Nathan's office? The barracuda was transferred, and my husband didn't tell me?

She looked down at Nathan's face, which currently appeared as innocent as a babe, and had to jump to her feet to keep from grinding the bag of peas against his wound. She paced on the cold concrete, not looking at the two men she knew were watching her.

"He's…busy." *Give nothing away,* a little voice cried. *This woman is not your friend.*

"He's okay, then?" Gwyneth asked. "Good. You had me worried."

"My dad's with him. They're bonding. Tractors, pigs, peas—it's a guy thing."

"I beg your pardon?"

Casey was a terrible liar. "Hey, nice talking to you, Gwyneth. I'll give Nathan the message as soon as we're able to grab a few minutes. It's kinda hectic around here."

The wail of a siren could be heard in the distance. She muttered an expletive under her breath. "Gotta run."

She flipped the lid closed to end the call.

Gwyneth. In San Francisco. She would be a huge asset to the company and could help Nathan whip the place into shape, but Casey suspected that Gwyneth had another agenda, as well. And the goal was to whip Nathan into divorce court.

A few seconds later—before Red could ask her about the phone call—three paramedics arrived on the scene. They discarded the bag of peas and took Nathan's vital signs.

Questions started to fly. Answers—which to Casey's ear sounded silly and not plausible—followed. But everything came to a halt when Nathan suddenly opened his eyes and tried to sit up.

"Nathan," Casey cried, rushing to his side.

The young EMT scuttled sideways to avoid getting knocked over.

"Stay still, please," the man said. "Ma'am, are you his wife?"

"Yes," Casey said with more force than necessary.

"Can you please keep him still while I get this printout of heart activity?"

She dropped to her knees and put her mouth close to Nathan's ear. "Honey, you have to lie still. You bumped your head on the tractor and you've been out cold for almost twenty minutes."

He turned his chin to see her. His eyes had a sleepy, unguarded look. Her heart turned over, reminding her of why she wanted to have his baby. She loved this man. She couldn't lose him—to an accident or the barracuda. Or to the nameless, faceless ennui that had fallen over their marriage.

The moment ended when the EMT did something that made Nathan close his eyes and let out a soft groan.

"Hey, take it easy," she snapped fiercely.

Her father appeared at her side and took her elbow, pulling her to her feet. "Casey, let them do their job. You're the one who insisted we call 'em."

Jimmy joined them a minute later with a fleece jacket, which he slipped over her shoulders. Casey hadn't even realized she was cold, but as the warmth hit her, her teeth began to chatter. She looked down and saw her toes curled up in the oversize, very dirty socks. *Nathan is gonna kill me,* she started to think, but then stopped and looked at her husband who was now sitting up and arguing with the two medics.

He could have died. When you're young and busy, you never stop to consider how fragile life is. She loved her husband. Their marriage wasn't healthy at the moment, but that didn't mean it was beyond saving.

She decided right then that not another day would pass without some kind of resolution. They were going to talk about whatever it was that had made them strangers in the same house.

Even if the problem is five-foot-five with black hair and a law degree?

Casey set her jaw and took a breath. Even then.

TWO HOURS LATER, Nathan looked at the spread of food on the table. He knew what every item was—fried chicken, a tub of mashed potatoes and another of brownish goop that was undoubtedly supposed to represent gravy. There were dinner rolls in a basket and a stick of butter on a plate. And a festive-looking green-and-orange mixture that was no doubt coleslaw. His mind worked fine, but the other three people at the table obviously didn't believe him when he told them he was okay. Each watched with an air of uncertainty as he took a bite off the plate that his wife had dished for him.

"Um…good," he said, chewing some of the coleslaw. The sauce was too sweet but he could stomach it.

Tears welled up in his wife's eyes. "Nope. That proves it. There was brain damage. He's not the same Nathan I know."

Nathan stopped chewing. He glanced from Red to Jimmy, who both eyed him as if suspecting that aliens had taken over his body the exact moment he hit his head.

"Nathan hates fast food," Casey declared. "He would never compliment KFC."

Nathan looked down. He hadn't eaten all day that he could remember. The medic who sat down beside Nathan on the straw bale and talked to him for a good fifteen minutes said some short-term memory loss could be expected with a slight concussion. So, it was possible Nathan had eaten and didn't recall it, but his stomach said otherwise.

"I'm hungry," he said, taking a bite of chicken.

The crispy coating on the outside gave way to moist meat that tasted just fine. Sure, there was too much salt and additives or whatnot but at the moment he just wanted to fill his belly, which seemed empty beyond reason.

"Jeez, Casey, let the man eat. Maybe he was only picky because you're a food snob," Red said.

Jimmy grabbed a chicken leg from the bucket and started to eat, too. He didn't talk much, Nathan had noticed, but the look in his eyes was intelligent and often highly amused. Nathan wondered if they might have been friends had circumstances been different.

Not that Nathan had many friends. Okay, any. He knew a great many people and he socialized with some who might be considered friends, except that all any of his acquaintances talked about was work. And money. Even the few pals from college had disappeared from his life after he married Casey. Mainly because she'd become his best friend.

Which might explain why he felt so lonely. His best friend had gone AWOL.

"I called Doc," Red said. "He's gonna drop by on his way home from the office and check you out."

Nathan stopped chewing. "You know a doctor who makes house calls?"

Casey groaned.

Jimmy said through his smile, "He's a vet."

"A skull is a skull," Red returned. "He set Casey's broken arm when she was nine."

Nathan looked at his wife, who had yet to eat a bite, but had managed to shred a bun into little white morsels that she'd balled up like spit wads. "I didn't know you had a broken arm…did I?" He added the last as a joke, but regretted it when he saw her color fade.

"Daddy, I need to take him to the hospital. He should

have an MRI. What if there's a slowly leaking blood vessel filling his brain with blood even as we speak."

Her voice bordered on hysteria—not something he'd witnessed in his wife before. He was absolutely positive about that. "Case, I was kidding. That was a joke."

She slumped back in the chair. "If he dies in his sleep, I plan to sue."

Nathan choked on a bite of chicken. Jimmy reached around behind Nathan and firmly whacked him on the back. Nathan's head started buzzing again and he quickly took a drink of water to avoid another helpful assault.

"Casey, you can't sue your father, and besides that, I ran into the tractor, not the other way around."

"It was negligence," she said, her tone severe. "Nobody leaves a bucket in the air like that."

Jimmy coughed this time, then waved his half-eaten bun. "Uhh, that was my fault. I'd intended to grease the arms, but the grease gun was empty and I had to pick up some more grease from town. But, Casey, as you know because you were along, they were out."

Casey made a face. So did Nathan. He didn't like the idea of his wife cavorting around the countryside with her high school flame—grease or no grease.

"Still—" she started to protest, but Red interrupted.

"Aww, Casey, let it go. Jimmy apologized. Nathan is fine. Look, he's eating like a prisoner who just got out of jail. As soon as Doc checks him out, you can rest easy. We got enough suing going on around here without you adding to the ruckus." Red looked at Nathan. "Did she tell you about the turkey con-sort-tee-um?"

Nathan turned his attention on his meal, digging into

the potatoes with gusto. They tasted quite potato-like, but the gravy had a peculiar iridescence that unnerved him. He decided to stick with butter and salt and pepper. "Uh-huh," he answered, hoping that would suffice.

Casey leaned forward, giving him a serious look. "Nathan, can you remember what I told you?"

Nathan would have rolled his eyes, but the motion hurt. He knew because he'd tried it earlier. "There's a land use battle brewing between turkey growers and the landowners in the area, but I don't want to talk business, if you please. I'm eating."

She threw up her hands. "See? It's not him. Nathan talks law anytime, anyplace. And over a heck of a lot better food than this."

Her declaration went unchallenged because a knock on the door and Red's bellowing "come in" provided a diversion. A few seconds later a gray-haired man wearing bright-yellow coveralls walked in, his knee-high black rubber boots making a squeaking sound on the tile floor.

"Don't anyone get up. It's just me. I know where the whiskey is and that's all that matters."

Red laughed. Jimmy smiled, and Casey sank down in her chair with a groan. She reached under the table and squeezed Nathan's leg, just above his knee. "I won't let him touch you. I promise."

Nathan was too startled by the effect Casey's touch had on him to worry about a crusty old vet. Her fingers massaged his thigh in a tender and caring manner—not the least bit suggestive, but Nathan's reaction was immediate and hot.

He eyed the half-eaten chicken leg in his hand suspiciously. Was fast food an aphrodisiac? Surely not. There would have been a lawsuit somewhere that he would have read about.

"So, I heard there was a little excitement around here today," Doc said, drawing up a chair between Nathan and his wife. Casey had to move back to make room for the man. Nathan couldn't decide if that was a good thing or not. He didn't want to broadcast his horniness in front of three strangers, but he wanted more of her touch.

"So you're Casey T.'s mister," the man said, transferring his highball glass to his left hand. "I'm Doc Kelly. Everyone calls me Doc because my mother was being patriotic when she named me and I prefer not to use my given name."

Nathan couldn't not ask. "Which is?"

"Jefferson Monroe."

"Could be worse. Mine's Nathan Augustus."

"Your mother was into Roman history?"

"One would think, but Nathan was her grandfather's name and Augustus was a teacher of hers that she admired and wanted to honor."

Doc tossed back the remainder of his drink then looked around the table and said, "He's fine. Nothing wrong with his head. Eyes are clear and focused. Memory sharp. He's eating. My work here is done."

Casey sat forward. "Do you really think so? Should we run into town for a quick x-ray? The medics wanted to take him to the hospital, but—"

Doc interrupted. "That's their job, but I guarantee

your husband is fine. He's gonna have one hell of a headache for the next couple of days, and I don't want him behind the wheel today because the sunlight and reflection on other cars isn't going to help his pain. No reading, either. Just take it easy."

"Oh, please," she said with passion, "not that. Nathan doesn't know how to relax."

She was right, of course, but he wasn't a workaholic by choice. If he didn't keep the money rolling in, who would supplement his mother's lifestyle, underwrite his baby brother's next degree and bail out his sister when her whacko husband lost his current job?

"Hey, I *can* do nothing. I've just never had a chance to try."

Casey rolled her eyes. "Yeah, right. You'll be climbing the walls by noon tomorrow."

He wiped his hands on a paper napkin. "Wanna bet?"

Red let out a hoot. "Now, this is getting interestin', and here I thought you two had a white-bread relationship."

Nathan wasn't sure what that meant, but he guessed it wasn't a compliment. Before he could respond, Jimmy pushed back his chair and said, "I've seen my share of marital squabbles lately, so if you folks will excuse me, I've got a tractor to grease."

Doc gave Casey a peck on the cheek then squeezed Nathan's shoulder with his huge paw of a hand. "I know for a fact Red's got some illegal painkillers around here, if the drumming inside your head gets too loud. But, don't worry, even the headaches will be gone in a day or two."

Nathan decided he liked this man. "Thank you for stopping by."

"No *problema,*" Doc said, rising. "Red buys only the finest whiskey, and I promised my late wife I'd never buy another bottle," he added with a wink.

"Which is why I never remarried," Red said. He stood up and escorted his guest into the adjoining room. "Can't abide somebody—dead or alive—telling me what not to drink."

Alone, Casey and Nathan sat in silence. He pushed his plate away and turned to face her. "I think he's right. I'm fine."

She lifted her chin to look at him. Her eyes were luminous with tears. Nathan's heart turned over and a tender feeling made him reach out to close the distance between them—until she said so softly he almost missed it. "But we aren't, are we?"

She didn't wait for an answer, before adding, "Gwyneth called while you were unconscious. She said she's in San Francisco, working on the assignment you gave her."

Nathan stifled a groan. This wasn't the way he'd planned to tell her this news. "I need her help, Casey. I'm short-staffed and she's very good at what she does."

She didn't say anything, but her expression said a lot.

"She's part of the reason I drove down here today. To tell you in person. I know you're not wild about Gwyneth, but she's a colleague. That's it. She's not an issue where our marriage is concerned, okay?"

Normally, his wife's face was the most open and easy to read of anyone he knew, but she'd learned to play poker at a very young age and could outbluff many men—Nathan included.

The sound of Red's barking laugh in the distance made her look away. "Wrong time, wrong place for this discussion."

His relief was tangible—until she placed his phone in front of him and said, "She wanted you to call her back. I'll give you some privacy since it's about business. Besides, I want to check on Red. Did you notice that he didn't eat more than a couple of bites? If I can catch Doc, he might tell me what's going on. Red won't, that's for sure."

She cleared their plates and hurried into the kitchen. The men had moved outside, but Nathan could still hear the murmur of their voices. He wondered what Casey had seen other than Red's apparent lack of appetite that caused her to worry. His father-in-law seemed his same garrulous self to Nathan. Older, of course. And thinner. His hair was solid white now and his deeply tanned skin more wrinkled, but he still commanded everyone's attention—even the paramedics had backed off when Red told them Nathan wasn't going into any hospital.

"If the man ain't sick now, he will be when you get done with him," Red had growled. "I called you here for Casey's sake, not the boy's."

The boy. Nathan couldn't remember the last time anyone had referred to him as a boy. Certainly not since he was seventeen—the year his father had died and Nathan became "the man of the family."

He looked at the red and silver, ultrathin phone but didn't pick it up. Gwyneth had called as he was loading his bag into the rental car. "This is Mother's Day weekend, you know. I usually spend it with my father back in Boston and instead, I'm here. Working," she'd said, her complaint obvious.

"Be sure to call him. Since this is our first Mother's Day in the area, I'm sure Casey's made plans to take my mother out for brunch," he'd told her. "We'll probably swing by Sacramento on our way home." Liar. Casey hadn't said a word about going back with him. Nor had she mentioned his mother, which really wasn't like her.

Her question echoed in his head. *But we aren't fine, are we?*

At one time, Nathan would have scoffed at the idea that their marriage was anything but ideal. Now, he had to agree. At the moment they seemed just like every other married couple he knew—they were in trouble.

CASEY WASN'T SURE what was wrong with her—or Red. In her case, she couldn't remember ever feeling so edgy and nervous around Nathan. Even on their first date, when one of Meg's friends brought her son's roommate to dinner instead of her son, who had come down with food poisoning, they'd fallen instantly into like with each other. None of the usual awkwardness she'd experienced in the past when her aunt tried to set her up.

Because they were both lawyers, they'd approached their relationship realistically and dispassionately... well, until the passion started.

"We're good together. Ying and yang. Hot and cold," Nathan had said.

She'd agreed, at first. Now, she was worried that

each opposite had canceled out the other, leaving them with nothing. But Casey wasn't a quitter, and she'd focus on their issues just as soon as she finished picking Doc's brain.

She peeked around the door and waited until she saw Red head toward the dog kennel on the other side of the garage. She could tell by the howls of excitement that his herd of canines couldn't wait to be released from prison. Jimmy had locked them up to keep them from returning to the barn while the EMTs were there.

"Doc," she called, racing out to the dark-red mobile veterinary clinic on wheels. She'd changed into jeans and running shoes the moment she'd gotten back to the house.

"Hey, Casey, girl," Doc said, pausing beside the open door of his vehicle. "Are you still worried about the mister?"

She shook her head. "No. Well, yes, but I trust your judgment. What I'm really worried about is Red. He's at least fifteen pounds lighter than the last time I saw him. Doesn't he look gaunt to you?"

Doc's bushy brows furrowed above his nose. "He's had a lot on his mind lately."

"I know. The turkeys. But he barely touches his food. If it weren't for the calories he gets from the whiskey, I don't know how skinny he'd be." She said the last lightly, but, in truth, Red's drinking worried her, too.

Doc let out a troubled sigh and looked toward the house. "You need to be asking your dad, Casey, not me. If he hasn't told you—"

"Told me? Told me what?" she cried.

Doc got into the truck. "Ask him."

"No, wait. You know Red. He never tells me anything. Please, Doc, I'm worried sick here. Is something wrong with him? Is it his heart? His liver? He used to smoke. Please tell me it isn't lung cancer. I watched my aunt die of cancer, Doc. I don't think I can do that again. Oh, God—"

"It's his prostate, Casey. Most men have to deal with this at some point in their lives. Red's known about it for a while, but you know your dad. Told his doctor he had to put off treatment until the ranch was out of danger."

Casey grabbed hold of the open door to keep her balance.

"How bad?"

"I've said enough. He's probably gonna come after me with a shotgun as it is," Doc said. "Ask him. And while you're at it, maybe you can make him get on the stick and let those doctors do what they want to make it go away. You wait too long and…well, you know."

She did. Too well. Even with an annual mammogram, by the time doctors discovered the lump in her aunt's breast, the cancer had spread to a point that made it difficult to be sure they'd gotten all of the tumor. Meg had had a radical mastectomy, radiation and chemo. The bad cells had gone away—for a few years. The second round of treatment bought them a little more time, but not nearly enough.

Casey couldn't lose her father. Not now. Not yet. But she knew the only way Red would ever agree to back off from this fight with the turkey growers and seek the medical attention he needed was if she agreed to jump into the fray, heart and soul. Not a war she could wage from her apartment in San Francisco.

What would happen to her marriage with Casey staying at the ranch and Nathan working in the city by the bay? Especially when there was a barracuda in the water?

CHAPTER SEVEN

NATHAN PICKED UP the empty cardboard bucket and paper napkins and walked to the kitchen in search of a trash can. He was checking under the sink when he heard the sliding glass door open. He assumed his wife had returned.

"Your dad doesn't give his dogs chicken bones, does he?"

"Hell, no," Red answered.

"Didn't think so— Whoa," he exclaimed, pressing his back against the counter when a dog he'd never seen before charged toward him. "Good lord, what is that? A dog or a moose?"

Large was too euphemistic a description of the animal with a head the size of a beach ball, from which strings of white drool swayed like moss on a cypress tree. "Stay. Back. Down. Help." The last came out an octave higher when the animal thrust its wet black nose into his crotch.

"Betsy, be polite," Red scolded. "Remember what the trainer said about inappropriate behavior."

Nathan, who hadn't for a second taken his eyes off the dog, could have sworn he saw the animal sigh with regret just before she backed away and sat down, almost ladylike, in front of him.

Nathan let out the breath he'd been holding. "Thanks, Red, I owe you. My life was just starting to flash before my eyes."

"Aw, Betsy's harmless. She's fifteen. Her previous owner was a lady friend of mine whose children decided she needed to downsize to one of those independent living places. No room for Bets, though, so I brought her home with me." He patted the dog on her broad head and she gave Red a worshiping look in return. "She spends most of the time back in my room 'cause the other dogs don't like her much." He leaned in and whispered, "She doesn't know she's a dog."

"Pretty big for an indoor dog, isn't she?"

Betsy made a whimpering sound and walked to the far corner of the room where an oversize faux-sheepskin dog bed sat. She collapsed with a loud sigh.

"She's sensitive about her size," Red said reproachfully.

"Sorry. I didn't know."

"But she'll forgive any slight if you rub her belly and tell her she's beautiful."

It took Nathan a moment to realize that Red meant that as an order, not an explanation. "Now?" Nathan croaked.

"What better way? Come on. She won't bite. I can't make that same guarantee about a couple of the yard dogs, but Betsy is a sweetheart. Aren't you, girl?"

The dog rolled to her back and stretched out her neck, making her look like a drowned scuba diver.

Nathan swallowed. He knew he had every right to refuse, but that would label him a coward in the eyes of his father-in-law, so he walked to the hearth and sat down—within arms-length of Betsy-the-moose.

He slowly reached toward her. "Hi, there, Betsy. Sorry we got off on the wrong foot. Which I'm sure you could take off in one bite if you wanted to, couldn't you?"

The dog stopped wriggling, her amber-brown eyes following his every move.

Nathan wasn't a dog person. His mother had never allowed animals in the house or in the yard for that matter when Nathan was growing up.

Taking a deep breath for courage, he placed his hand on the dog's chest. Betsy's hair wasn't overly long and he could feel her warm skin, the pointy nubs of nipples and the fast thud of her heart beating. The smell of warm dog was in the air, and Nathan found he didn't mind it. He rubbed his hand in a slow circle. Betsy squirmed, her head canted back in a way that made her upside-down jowls look as though she was smiling.

The sensation wasn't unpleasant. Who knew something so simple could be so gratifying?

"She's a good dog, isn't she?" Red asked.

Nathan looked up, a bit surprised. "Yes."

"Do you want a puppy? Betsy's granddaughter had a litter a couple of months ago. I heard there are two left. A couple of the cutest little critters you've ever seen."

"No," Nathan said reflexively.

"Yes," a second voice said from the doorway.

Casey appeared like a magical wraith on a fresh breeze. Her hair was messy from the wind, her cheeks pink. Although she had a wide smile on her face, Nathan could tell she was upset about something. "We've had this debate ever since we got married," she told her father. "Nathan's not a dog person."

Nathan didn't like the way Red's bushy brows came together—as if she'd just announced her husband was the leader of a cult or something. "We live in the city," he stated. What was wrong with his ears? Why did that excuse suddenly sound so lame?

"I'll admit that's not the best place to raise dogs or kids, but that can be fixed," Red said, pushing to his feet. "I've got a special piece of land set aside. It was the original homestead. The people Casey's mother and I bought the ranch from wanted something closer to the road so they tore down the old house and built this place. All that's left out there is a crumbling old foundation, but when I was at the planning department a few weeks ago checking on the turkey thing, I asked whether or not you and Casey could build on it."

Build on it? Nathan looked at his wife, who was obviously as surprised by this announcement as Nathan was. "Dad, we need to talk. I appreciate the gesture, but don't you think—"

Red cut her off. "I bet you don't even remember where it is, do you? Come on. Let's go for a drive. I'll show you both." He stood up before either could respond. "Betsy, let's show 'em what paradise looks like."

The lethargic animal scrambled to her feet and charged to the door, her paws slipping on the tile like Bambi on ice. Nathan recalled the image all too well because he and Casey had babysat for a friend's toddler one afternoon and that movie had been their saving grace.

Casey didn't follow with nearly as much enthusiasm. She reached up as if to touch the wound on his forehead but stopped her hand. "Maybe you should stay here and rest. I don't know if knocking around in a truck will be good for you."

Her obvious concern made him feel better, but he wasn't about to sit here alone while his father-in-law tried to lure Casey home with promises of free land and a building site.

"No, I'll go. Didn't the paramedic say people with head injuries aren't supposed to sleep right away? Besides, I came here to see you, and we've barely had a minute alone." He didn't mean to sound so whiny.

Casey covered her face with her hands and let out a deep sigh of frustration. "I know. And it's only going to get worse."

Her dire tone made him frown, but she didn't give him time to ask her to explain. She put her arm through his and tugged him toward the door. "Come on. Maybe if you're with me, Dad will give me some straight answers. You're a guy, after all."

I am. A guy who hasn't made love with his wife in nearly two weeks. Casey had taken the last doctor they'd spoken with at his word. "Step off the fertility roller coaster for a few months," the man had suggested. "Give your bodies time to rebuild, reposition and renew the lust that you feel for each other."

Lust. An odd choice of words, Nathan had thought

at the time, but now he understood. The pressures of packing, tying up loose ends at work and moving had robbed both Casey and Nathan of any desire to make love. The time change had interfered with Casey's sleep pattern and she'd taken some over-the-counter pills to help her get back on track while they were settling into their apartment. Then she'd come to the Valley for a visit. The days without sex had piled up.

Following after his wife as she led the way to her father's monster truck he couldn't get his gaze off her bottom displayed quite nicely in a pair of tight jeans. She was a knockout in a power suit with her hair up in a twist, but this wholesome cowgirl image had its own appeal. And Nathan wanted her. He only hoped this trip down memory lane was a short one.

CASEY SAT in the backseat of her father's four-door Dodge truck so Nathan could ride shotgun. The Powerslide rear window was open, affording Betsy the opportunity to pop her massive head inside and drool on Casey's shoulder any time she liked.

"Red, shut this window."

Her father glanced back at her. "Naw. Betsy's feelings would be hurt."

Casey undid her seat belt and moved forward on the seat so she could wedge her upper torso between the two men. "Fine, then I'm sending you my laundry bill. What's in that drool of hers? Slime?"

Her father laughed. He seemed happy and relaxed and…healthy—unless you looked closely at the grayish tint to his skin around his eyes. Why hadn't she noticed sooner? I should have visited more often. What kind of daughter am I? *A self-absorbed one,* she thought, guiltily.

"So, Red, where are you taking us? I don't remember another house on the property." She wanted to ask him about his health but decided to hold off until she could look him in the eyes.

"Like I said, there's not much left. Just some old footings and a depression where the well was. But you can see the outline of the yard by the trees that remain."

A memory made her say, "You mean where the two palms are? That was a homestead? Really? High school kids used to go out there and party, you know."

"Yeah. Got to be such a nuisance I put up a good fence. They kept leaving their garbage around. No respect for the land and private property," Red muttered.

"You might have been looking at some liabilities issues, too," Nathan said. "Even if someone trespasses, the landowner can be held responsible if someone gets hurt. The culpability goes down if you can prove that you made a reasonable effort to keep them off your property."

Casey listened to her father and her husband debate the inequities of the current legal system. Nathan's sharp legal mind proved an interesting challenge for Red's practical but equally quick wisdom. Before she knew it, they'd reached the far corner of her father's property.

Opening her window, she put her head out and took a deep breath of spring. "Can you get the gate, Casey T.?" her father asked.

Her running shoes sank in the soft soil and dense weeds beside the green metal gate. She walked it inward and hooked a wire loop over the post to keep it in place until they were ready to return. A low braying accented by sharp yips told her the rest of the dogs were following not far behind. Normally, Red took the animals with him wherever he went, but apparently Betsy got special treatment.

Red drove through the gate and stopped under a fully leafed-out California buckeye. She reached the truck just as Red was helping the old dog to the ground. "Good girl," he said, patting her head.

Casey hated the tiny burst of jealousy she felt. How pathetic was it to need her father's approval so badly she was envious of a dog?

"So, Red, what's this about—"

"In a minute, Casey T. I want to show Nathan the place before the other dogs get here. I know he's not a dog person, and they're gonna be excited."

Stifling her frustration, she joined the two men on a faint path that led between the two palm trees. Casey didn't know the species, but the two weren't the tall, skinny Dr. Seuss type that she associated with L.A. These were thick, stately pillars, at least four feet in width. Their fronds provided a deep green canopy that spread evenly in a circle so wide the two orbs almost touched.

Beyond the trees was a slight knoll. Casey hadn't realized this section of land was at a different elevation from where the main house sat, but as they climbed past jagged chunks of crumbling concrete she saw the view change dramatically.

"Wow. I don't remember this place being so cool. You

can see the foothills from here," she said, turning Nathan's shoulders so he could look where she was pointing.

"Last night's wind blew the smog away," Red said. Betsy had moved to Red's side, but her attention was directed toward the road where the barking was growing in volume.

Red made a sweeping motion with his hands. "Your mother and I kinda hoped one of our children would build out here someday."

One of our children. A cruel reminder of just how unfair life was. Red had lost his wife and son on a day much like this. Sunny. Beautiful. Spring bursting forth in all its glory.

"Hold on to the saddle horn and don't let go, Casey T. You slow me up and your mother could die. Do you understand, little girl?"

As if he could sense her inner turmoil, Nathan put his arm around her shoulder and pulled her close. She was five-eight, but his extra inches made her feel small and protected.

She pushed the haunting voice from the past out of her mind and said, "It's a lovely spot, Dad, but I'm so mad at you at the moment I wouldn't move here if it was the last place on the ranch that you could stand and not smell turkey poop."

Red's mouth dropped open. "What are you mad at me for now?"

His emphasis on the word *now* reminded her that they'd never really settled their other issues. Casey could feel Nathan's shock, too, but he didn't say anything.

"When were you going to tell me about your prostate?"

Red's mouth closed as soundly as the tailgate of his truck. "That's nobody's business but my own." His eyes narrowed. "Doc blabbed, didn't he? Damned old fool."

"He's a kindhearted fool who could see I was worried about you. Why didn't you tell me? I'm your daughter. Don't I have a right to know when you're not well?"

He stomped toward the truck. "I feel fine. Just 'cause it takes me half an hour to pee doesn't mean I'm on death's door. I'll last till I git these dang turkeys out of my hair." He whistled for Betsy, who was sniffing around the base of one of the palms. She trotted to his side and he helped her into the cab of the truck then hopped in, started the engine and slammed it into reverse.

Casey and Nathan started toward the truck, but it made a quick turn, nearly getting stuck in a muddy furrow. Red stepped on the gas, and the four-wheel-drive transmission dug in, sending a shower of mud in every direction.

"Red," Casey cried, throwing up one arm to dodge the hail of sludge. "Wait for us."

How he heard her over the roar of the engine was anybody's guess, but Red rolled down his window. "You can walk back. Do you both some good."

A second later he was gone. Casey and Nathan stood shoulder to shoulder, watching as the taillights glowed for a moment. Not to let them catch up. No, her father had paused to permit the dogs that had been following them to jump in the back, courtesy of the tailgate that had been left down.

"I don't know about you, Case, but I'm thinking Red doesn't want to talk about his health problems."

Casey looked at her husband. She wasn't sure whether to laugh or cry. So, she did both.

CHAPTER EIGHT

EXCEPT FOR the soft sniffles made by Casey—muffled somewhat by his shoulder—the thing that struck him most was the lack of sound.

As he comforted her, he looked around at the palette of greens, blues and browns. Real earth tones, he realized. Not the designer kind.

He expected to feel anxious, put out—even worried. After all, it was a long walk back and he was supposed to be resting, but, instead, he felt…glad to have his wife all to himself for a few minutes.

"It's okay, Casey. He'll calm down and either come back or send someone to get us." She looked up, her eyes wet with tears. "Won't he?"

She frowned, obviously wanting to disagree with him, but after a few seconds she nodded. "Probably. I don't know why I'm crying. He makes me so mad, but I know beneath that bluster he's afraid."

"Afraid of dying?"

"No. Afraid of living," she murmured. "Meg used to say Red was like the Cowardly Lion. All roar and no nerve."

Nathan didn't believe that. "Casey, you don't accumulate this kind of wealth—and make no mistake, this land is worth mega bucks—by not taking risks. And didn't you tell me Red was one of the first to plant pistachios in this area? That took guts when nobody knew for sure if there was a market."

"That's business. I'm talking about emotional risk. Like the fact that he sent me away rather than deal with my growing up."

She had a point.

"And how come he's never remarried? He's mentioned a few lady friends over the years—like Betsy's previous owner, but they never seemed to last very long."

Nathan tucked a strand of honey blond hair behind her ear and said, "I don't know. My mom hasn't remarried, either. Maybe they just never found the right person."

She looked up at him and smiled. "Are you suggesting we try fixing them up with each other?"

Nathan pretended to be horrified. "Good lord, no. Wouldn't that make you my sister?"

She snickered softly. "I was only kidding. Can you picture your mother living on the ranch? She's more of a city person than you are, and we both know you'd be lost without a Starbucks within walking distance."

He couldn't argue with that.

"Plus, what would your sister and brother do without your mother around to mooch off?"

He frowned. That wasn't a fair question. Nathan was sure there was some give and take in his mother's arrangement with his siblings, although he had to admit both Kirby and Christine seemed inordinately needy for their ages, but obviously his concerns had tainted Casey's attitude toward his family.

"Do we need to talk about them right now?"

Casey shrugged. "What do you want to talk about?"

They both knew what they *should* address—the state of their marriage—but the niggling ache in his temple made Nathan reluctant to tackle such a serious topic. He looked around, taking stock of where they were. A small island surrounded on all sides by mature pistachio trees.

"Are we in the middle of nowhere?"

"Pretty much," she said with sigh. "I didn't think to bring my cell phone. Did you?"

He shook his head. "It's just us. Alone. Incommunicado."

Something in his tone must have alerted her to his intentions because her eyes opened wide. "You can't be thinking what I think you're thinking."

"Why not? The sun is warm. The ground looks soft." *A blanket would be nice....* His gaze returned to the object he'd noticed earlier beside the gate. "That isn't a saddle blanket, is it?"

She turned to look over her shoulder. A few feet from the spot where the truck had been parked was a box of some kind with a red, green and white blob draped across it. Casey marched over to it. "Oh, for heaven's sake," she said with a groan. "Red, that's it. I've had it with you. I'm leaving this afternoon. I swear I am."

Nathan followed after her, curious to see what Red had done this time. A folded tartan throw rested atop the arched handles of a wicker picnic basket. He picked up the blanket and opened the lid to find a bottle of wine, a corkscrew and two glasses.

"Curious."

Casey, who was squatting beside the treasure, sighed. "More than you know. Red doesn't drink wine."

"What's under the bottle? It looks like house plans."

"For the house he and my mother were going to build for *one of their kids?*"

Nathan could tell that she was on the verge of crying again, so he tucked the blanket under his arm and took her hand. "Come on," he said, taking the picnic basket in his other hand. "Let's have a little wine before we start back. You don't have to look at the plans."

A few minutes later, they were both stretched out on the blanket in a clearing not far from the twin palms.

"You shouldn't drink."

"A sip or two won't kill me. I promise." He held up his glass to clink with hers. "To our first moment alone since I got here."

She smiled apologetically. "You must think this is a loony bin, not a ranch."

He tasted his wine. A Sonoma Shiraz. *Not bad.* "I'm a lawyer, not a judge."

Her snicker made him grin.

"If you want to know the truth, when I first stepped around the side of the barn and saw you and Jimmy laughing and covered in mud, my initial reaction was— 'Who is that gorgeous cowgirl? And why do I hate the guy with her?'"

Her cheeks turned a dusky shade of pink. "No way. You don't get jealous, remember?"

"Apparently I do when the guy is my wife's old boy-friend."

Her lips made an attractive moue. Her studious pout, he called it. A kissable pout. "Jimmy and I are friends… barely. More like people who knew each other when we were kids and really don't have time to know each other again."

"Would you like to know him better? If you had the time?"

She lowered her glass. "Are you asking if I'd get involved with him? The answer is no. Not if I had a hundred years. I'm not the same person I was back then, and he's not the same boy."

"Good answer."

"The truth."

"I know. You're the most honest person I've ever met."

Something changed in her eyes. An awareness of him. Of them. A sexual frisson that had been missing between them lately. "Red might come back."

"We'll hear the dogs, won't we?"

"Good point," she said after downing the last of her wine. "Very good point. Brilliant even." She set her empty glass on the wicker basket and moved to her knees. "Have you been saving up like the doctor said?"

Nathan poured the rest of his wine on the ground. "You don't honestly think I have something going with Gwyn—"

She shushed him with her finger across his lips. "I meant…you haven't been taking extra long showers without me, right?"

He let go of the guilt he felt about the occasional pull

of attraction he had toward Gwyneth and took his wife into his arms. Together they rolled back on the cushion of soft, thick weeds, bird and insect sounds serenading them. The sun and breeze on his bare skin contributed to the keenest arousal he could remember.

Casey stripped off her clothes without shame or hesitation. Nathan moved a little slower because his fingers felt clumsy and thick. He was pretty sure the blame lay in his powerful need, not some residual effect from his head injury.

As if reading his frustration when his buttons refused to cooperate, Casey reclined in a sexy, cowgirl goddess way, her toes skimming his hard-on. "You can always leave your shirt on, you know. It's the pants that count."

"You could help. I have a concussion, you know."

Her bottom lip poked out. "Aw…poor Nathan. Should I kiss it and make it feel better?"

Before he could reply, she was kneeling before him, both hands working to remove his belt. He gave up on his buttons and reclined on his elbows to watch. She unzipped his pants and bent down to drop a kiss on the tip of his penis, which was concealed by his navy-blue underwear.

"Feel better?"

"Not quite, but I'm getting there."

"Me, too," she said, eyelids lowered in a sexy, indolent way that turned up the flame of his desire another degree or two. She nudged him on to his back and stretched out on top of him.

His hands couldn't touch enough of her fast enough. "You feel amazing."

"Not quite, but I'm getting there." Her quip was accompanied by a kiss.

Tongue and breath became one. The blood rushing through Nathan's head brought pain with it, but he didn't care.

Casey wasn't sure what was going on in her head. One glass of wine did not turn a relatively conservative person into an uninhibited exhibitionist, but she had to acknowledge there was something powerfully erotic about making love to her husband outdoors in the middle of the day. She hadn't felt this turned on in way too long. Thanks to their baby-making regime, sex had turned into a programmed effort.

"This is fun, isn't it?" she asked, leaning forward to give Nathan access to her breasts.

"Uh-huh," he mumbled, tasting first one then the other. "Fun."

She ran her fingers through his hair and dropped her forehead to his. "I love you, you know."

"I know. And that makes me the luckiest man in the world."

She closed her eyes and kissed him. "Good answer."

His hands moved down her waist to her hips and he made her lift up enough to accommodate his hard-on. Smiling, she wiggled playfully, feeling the heat and desire build in her core. They'd picked up a lot of tips and techniques over the past months, but this wasn't the time or place. They both knew what they wanted and couldn't wait.

Nathan guided his penis in place as she lowered herself on him. His gratifying moan of pleasure made her sit back and grind her hips in circles, slowly picking up the pace.

His release came before hers but she didn't stop, and when his fingers touched her most sensitive spot she let out a sharp whimper. The shivers of pleasure that followed eased her back to reality as she collapsed on his chest. "Oh, my goodness. Wasn't that lovely?"

His chuckle was warm and soothing, like his hands that stroked her back and her hair. "Fabulous. I like this place. Maybe we should build a house here."

The words were surprisingly rash for Nathan. She wasn't sure what to say. But the reminder of their unsettled situation brought her back to reality in a hurry. Her father's health had changed things. Even if Casey wanted to walk away and leave things in Sarah's hands, she couldn't.

"Today doesn't come with any guarantees you'll have time to fix things tomorrow, Casey," her aunt had said at the end of her life.

It was time to talk. The sun warmed her shoulders but just thinking the word *cancer* chilled her from the inside out. She quickly drew on her clothes. "I shouldn't have yelled at him. He's right. It is his business, but I panicked when Doc told me. Red's always seemed invincible."

"I know. I'm really sorry, Case," Nathan said, sitting up.

"I suppose that's my little-girl memory talking. But living so far away I never got to watch him age. Seeing him for the first time in—what? Nine or ten months?— believe me, it was a shock. He actually looked his age.

I thought it was just worry about the great turkey menace. I never dreamed he had prostate cancer."

"You know it's highly treatable, right? Janelle's husband had it, remember? His doctor used robotic arms and computers to remove the tumor. Very high-tech."

Casey vaguely recalled his former secretary talking about her husband's speedy recovery, but Janelle's hubby was at least ten years younger than Red.

"She also said most patients don't have to rush into treatment because this is a slow growing cancer."

"Knowing Red, he's had the symptoms for years and has toughed it out. Doc said Red went to Stanford for a second opinion and those doctors told him the same thing—surgery, but Red has put off treatment until this turkey thing is resolved."

Nathan pulled on his pants. "Um…about the turkey thing…"

Casey got to her knees and started cleaning up. "I know. A complication we don't need at the moment, but, obviously, I don't have any choice. I have to stick around and help."

"'Stick around'?"

"Dad wants Sarah and me to head the antiturkey committee. We're not against turkeys, of course, we just don't want them setting up shop across the road. I know my father, and Red will never start treatment if he thinks he has to micromanage a war."

Nathan didn't say anything as he tied his shoelaces, so Casey added, "I wasn't sure if I could work with Sarah. I know this sounds childish, but a part of me resented her because it's almost as if she ended up with my life. She married my high school sweetheart. She's the only person my dad seems to listen to. Plus, she's pregnant and I'm not. Doesn't seem fair, does it?"

She jumped to her feet and answered before he could. "Silly. I know. Ridiculous. Especially given Red's health. I'm just going to have to suck it up and be a team player, right?"

When she looked at Nathan, her knees started to wobble. The brooding expression on his face was one she associated with the courtroom.

"I...I know this isn't what we planned. I'm supposed to be getting us settled in our new apartment, but I can come home on weekends."

"You can't do it, Casey," he said flatly.

She stepped back. "I beg your pardon?"

"There were two things I wanted to tell you in person. One was that Gwyneth is in town, and the other pertains to the firm's client list. GroWell, the company that plans to build across from your dad, is one of our clients. One of our biggest clients. I've already taken steps to distance myself from the case, but you know the rules of professional conduct as they pertain to conflicts of interest as well as I do. Every client is entitled to feel that he or she has the undivided loyalty of his or her lawyer until the case is settled."

"But isn't every parent entitled to feel the same loyalty from a child he or she raised, supported, sent to college so he or she could argue in court any case that might adversely affect the quality of said parent's life?"

"This company pays my firm hundreds of thousands

of dollars each year to make sure they are allowed to build on land they own. Land that is already zoned for agriculture, I might add."

She struggled to control her temper. "The land is surrounded by acres and acres of row crops like tomatoes and peppers. My father has invested hundreds of thousands of dollars in nut trees that would be ruined by the pollution your client's company gives off."

"That isn't true. I only had time to glance at Eric Mathers's notes before I figured out that this was the same company your father is trying to drum out of town, but I remember seeing the facts on the projected pollution—"

Casey stopped him. "Oh, please, Nathan, don't start. You know as well as anyone that you can't believe the figures a company like that gives to the planning department. Of course they're going to make them look innocuous. Haven't you listened to anything I told you while I was working at the land trust?"

His shoulders went rigid. "You haven't asked your old boss for help, have you?"

Casey crossed her arms. "Didn't you just tell me I'm not supposed to discuss this matter with you?"

"I said you can't be actively involved."

"Right," she said, the wine roiling in her stomach. "I'm just going to walk away and let my father, who may be dying of cancer, handle this alone."

His posture softened and he held out his hand. "I didn't mean... Of course you... I..."

Casey could see the frustration on his face, but she couldn't work up any sympathy. She'd never appreciated anyone telling her she couldn't do something. Heck, that was one reason she'd become a lawyer, because her father was against the idea.

"You'd better hope Gwyneth is as good as you think she is because nobody down here wants your client to move in next door, and we're prepared to do whatever it takes to keep them out."

"We?"

"Yeah. Me and Sarah and all the members of NOTT. That stands for Neighbors Opposed To Turkeys."

CHAPTER NINE

NATHAN LEFT the next morning with no true sense of where he and Casey stood on anything. They'd hoofed it back to the ranch house in silence. Red had left a note saying he was taking a nap and would be at his lodge meeting that night.

Nathan didn't see his father-in-law again until Red delivered Nathan's rental car, which had been sitting at the barn since Nathan's run-in with the tractor.

"Drive safe and come back soon," Red had said cheerfully as if his snit in the field had never happened. "And think about that offer of a pup. They won't last long. They're real cute. Just like their grandma," he'd added, lovingly stroking Betsy's broad, shaggy head.

"I will," Nathan had said in return. *Drive safely.* The puppy was not an issue. The city was no place for a dog like Betsy—even if she did have soulful eyes that seemed to offer unconditional love.

His wife's love, he'd decided last night, came with conditions. They'd slept in the same bed, but sleep was all they'd done. Nathan's hope for a repeat performance of their lovemaking had been dashed when Casey told him, "I found two kinds of painkillers in Red's medicine chest—horse-pill size and regular. They both say may induce drowsiness."

He'd opted for the smaller, but as she'd predicted he'd been sound asleep not long after swallowing it. He'd made a halfhearted effort to talk her into accompanying him to Sacramento in the morning, but she'd shot down the idea.

"I have a mother, too, you know," she'd said. "I plan to take flowers to her grave and have a serious talk with my dad about his health issues. I bought your mother a card and a very pretty robe when I was in Merced the other day. I got it at a department store that has branches in Sac so she can exchange it if she wants something else. The gift receipt is taped to the inside of the card."

The beautifully wrapped box was sitting on the passenger seat beside him, making him feel guilty. Casey was a good wife. He could always count on her to help him out in little ways he never really gave her credit for, but now that he needed her help, she appeared to be taking her father's side.

"When are you coming home?" he'd asked after Red and Betsy walked away to greet Jimmy, who had followed Red from the barn in his mammoth truck.

"I'll probably be back to the apartment before you."

"Really?"

"The cemetery is only about half an hour away. Dad and I plan to go to church then drive up together. We'll have a late lunch at a little restaurant he likes then I'll take off. I should miss the worst of the traffic."

Then she'd kissed him goodbye. A quick peck on the lips that could have meant she was still mad at him or might have had something to do with the fact Red and Jimmy were watching.

He heaved a sigh. This was not how he'd seen his weekend unfolding. And now, he was on his way home, without Casey, to who knew what kind of reception. Of course, his mother would be glad to see him. When he'd finally gotten around to calling her last night, Joan had squealed in delight.

"I told Christine you wouldn't miss Mother's Day now that you live so close. She said you'd already been here over a week and hadn't come to see us yet, but I know how busy you are."

Thanks, Chris. At one time, Nathan and his sister had had a much more friendly relationship. But then she'd married a man with big dreams and a short attention span. Every new business venture brought more debt and crises that only Joan could help them get past. Finally, Nathan, who was helping his mother put her financial affairs in order, put his foot down. "Mother isn't a bank, Christine, but if she was she'd have foreclosed on your overdue loans years ago."

Chris hadn't really talked to him since.

"Will Casey be with you?" his mother had asked.

He'd explained about them having two cars and Casey's desire to visit her mother's grave. "But you'll see her soon," he'd promised...and hoped.

Joan Kent had made it clear from the start that she didn't approve of Casey's independent style. "When I was a young wife, I gave up my career to support my husband and raise our children," she'd said more than once. "I know that's not a popular position these days, but unless you need to work to put bread on the table, you're depriving your children of the best child care in the world."

"We don't have any children, Joan," Casey had replied.

"Will you stop working once you have kids?" his mother had persisted.

"Isn't that when the real work begins?"

Nathan smiled as he recalled his wife's answer. Casey's quick wit and diplomatic ability had always come in handy—whether with family or entertaining people from work.

A sudden idea grabbed him. Maybe Casey was feeling left out of the loop. She'd only met the people in the San Francisco office when they'd flown out to look for a place to live. Perhaps if she felt more like part of the team, she'd be less inclined to work for the opposition.

"A dinner party," he murmured. "We could host a dinner party so she can get to know the people from the office." Which included Gwyneth, he realized. That took a bit of the gloss off his idea.

He hadn't been completely honest with Casey. True, he wasn't seeking any kind of relationship with Gwyneth, but she'd made it clear she would welcome one with him. That kind of raw intensity was hard to resist. Plus, she had the body of a lingerie model. Every man in the Boston office had lusted after her.

He spotted the green sign indicating his exit. I-80 East would eventually take him to Reno. Hell, it went all the way to Chicago, where he could hook up with I-90 and before long he'd be back in Boston. He'd driven that route right after college, filled with dreams and ambition. His primary goal had been to make enough money to pay back his school loans, help his mother and siblings when they needed it and build the kind of security his father had never been able to provide for his family.

His journey had brought him full circle. He'd made it. Almost. Once he was a full partner in the firm, he could breathe a bit easier, but Nathan knew that offer wouldn't come if Casey wasn't on his side during this upcoming confrontation. He had a feeling logic and bribery weren't going to help. Which left guilt, and that meant asking advice from a master—his mother.

CASEY WOUND UP following Red to the cemetery.

"It'll save you driving all the way back to the ranch," he'd told her.

He had a point, but she'd been planning on using the time together in the truck to pin him down on the specifics of his illness and treatment options. Now, that discussion would have to wait until they were at lunch.

She wasn't looking forward to their upcoming talk, but she really needed to know how bad things were for him. She'd never felt more torn. Did she help her father or stand behind her husband?

She hated the way she and Nathan had left things this morning. Nathan probably felt betrayed because she hadn't immediately jumped ship once he'd revealed his firm's interest in the fight. But Casey had inherited more than a bit of her father's stubbornness. And being told she couldn't do something really irked her.

They had enough problems right now without a lack

of loyalty being added to the mix. They were infertile, newly moved to a city she loved to visit but had no desire to call home, and then there was Gwyneth. Casey hadn't brought up the subject with Nathan again because she didn't want to seem jealous. But, darn it, the woman undermined Casey's self-confidence faster than Red did.

She'd spent most of the night watching Nathan sleep. How could they make love with such tenderness and passion one minute then wind up yelling at each other the next? This wasn't the way they operated. How had they gotten so far off track?

But by the time morning had arrived, her brain had been too tired to tackle such tough questions. She planned to get back to their apartment early enough to take a nap. Knowing Nathan's family, he'd be tied up with his mother's clinginess and his siblings' minidramas until early evening. Maybe by then, she'd have figured out some kind of compromise they both could live with.

She returned her attention to the present when she saw her father's blinker indicate it was time to turn. The metal gate was open so she followed the big white truck to a familiar spot in the far corner of the cemetery. The tiny graveyard was so radically different from where her aunt was buried in a centuries-old mausoleum surrounded by perfectly trimmed green lawn she almost laughed.

But she didn't. Her mother and her aunt had been very different people. A wildcat and a lady, she'd privately called them. The two sisters had been born in Cheyenne. One went west with a cowboy who barely had two coins to rub together. The other went east to marry into old wealth the likes of which still boggled Casey's mind.

Her aunt had provided abundantly for Casey in her will, but the vast majority of the Merryweather estate had gone to charitable causes that Meg and her late husband had supported.

"If I were in Boston, I'd be putting flowers on Meg's grave," she said as she joined her father in the shade of a scrubby oak. "It feels wrong to admit, but I miss her a lot more than I ever remember missing Mom."

"You missed your mother real bad to start out. There were some days all we both did was cry. But you were six. You can't be expected to remember that."

She remembered some events from her childhood clearly. Too clearly. "I think a lot of my memories come from photos you've shown me. And I sorta recall her rubbing rose petals on my cheeks, but I could have made that up."

Red gave a low humorless chuckle. "Abby always had the prettiest gardens wherever we lived. Most of her roses are gone, though. I didn't know how to take care of 'em, and by the time I got around to figuring it out, they weren't worth saving."

"They used to grow along the fence, didn't they?"

He nodded. "She wanted to be able to see them from the kitchen window. All summer long she'd bring in fresh-cut flowers to put on the table."

Casey brought the bouquet of peach roses she carried to her nose and inhaled. They smelled fresh but not particularly fragrant. She'd bought them at Costco the same day she'd shopped for Joan's gift. "I'm glad I chose roses. There were so many pretty flowers available, but this color reminded me of Mom for some reason."

She let Red lead the way since she hadn't been to the cemetery in years. A scattering of large oaks kept the enclosed area fairly shady. The weather was starting to warm up and several of the other visitors to the grave-yard were dressed in shorts. Casey still had on the denim skirt and two-piece sweater and tank that she'd worn to church. The only dressy clothes in her suitcase. She'd have to bring some business suits with her next time, if she was going to handle the land use case.

If... Did she really have any choice? Her father had never asked for much from her. He needed her now. How could she turn her back on him?

"I...I was real sorry to hear about your aunt, Casey T.," Red said after clearing his throat in an embarrassed way. "Meg and I might not have always got along so hot, but she was a good woman."

She looked at him and smiled. "Yes, she was. And she pretty much said the same about you—being a good man, I mean. When she was dying she asked me to do something for her. Do you know what that was?"

He shook his head.

"To take care of you."

Meg's exact words had been: "Take care of Red, Casey. Your mother would have wanted you two to be close. I got a little greedy and kept you here with me, but you need to go home at some point.

"We all do," she'd added cryptically.

Red frowned. "I'm sorry I didn't make it back for her

funeral. I figured I'd just be in the way since you had your husband. And I've never been very good with women's tears."

Maybe that explained why it was so hard for her to cry. She'd grieved deeply but privately when Meg died. She'd kept her sadness out of the public eye—even hidden from her husband.

"Meg had everything planned just the way she wanted. There wasn't anything you could have done," she told him. Which was true. Meg and Red had never been close even though they had—in essence—shared a daughter. To hear either of them speak, she was an uppity society broad and he was an illiterate cowboy who hadn't deserved a woman like her sister. For the first time, Casey wondered if there was more to their story than either let on.

"I'll give you a few minutes alone with your mom. Abby and me talk all the time. You know the way to The Bon Ton, right? It's not fancy, but they make good pie."

As Red left, Casey started to miss Nathan so much tears clustered in the corners of her eyes. He should be here with her. She should be at his side when he faced his family. She'd never felt more alone in her life.

She brushed away her tears with the heel of her hand, then stepped close to the headstone that bore the inscription: Abigail Dawson Buchanan and son, Roderick Buchanan, Jr. Too soon taken, but never forgotten.

She couldn't look at her brother's name without feeling a peculiar sense of envy. *Junior.* Why did that sound so appealing? So romantic? She knew the thought didn't make any sense. Maybe she needed to see a psychiatrist.

Meg had suggested taking Casey to a therapist not

long after Casey moved to Boston. The "threat" had been enough to shake Casey out of her deep despair. Somewhere along the path of growing up she'd embraced one truism: Buchanans didn't talk to shrinks.

"No, we just slowly go crazy on our own," she murmured.

And her father was completely and utterly bonkers if he thought she was going to drop the issue of his prostate cancer. The first thing she was going to do when she got back to San Francisco this afternoon was dig out her laptop. She felt naked and out-of-touch without the Internet. Red had a computer, but the modem was slow and annoying. She planned to upgrade his internet connection, too, when she returned.

Not if. When.

After some cautious snooping around Red's desk while he was retrieving Nathan's rental car that morning, she'd discovered a little business card with the date and time of his next doctor's appointment. This coming Thursday in Fresno. She planned to be there, whether her father liked the idea or not. That gave her four days to convince her husband that she wasn't siding with the enemy, she was honoring the promise she'd made to her aunt on her deathbed. "Take care of Red," Meg had said.

Casey didn't have any choice, but first she needed to spend some overdue time with her mother.

"Hi, Mom," she said, placing the flowers beside the headstone. "Happy Mother's Day."

Thirty minutes later, Casey pulled into the parking lot of the building built around the time of western explorer and politico John C. Fremont. Red was standing beside the bed of his truck messing with something in the back.

As she got out of her car, Casey heard the sound of a metal hinge being lifted. A second later, the high-pitched yip of a young animal filled the air.

Curious, she thought, heading his way across the parking lot. Red had made a point of shooing the mob of dogs away from the truck when he'd gotten ready to leave the house that morning. Not even Betsy had been invited along for the drive. Had he left her so abruptly at the cemetery to pick up a new animal?

The moment she joined him, Red whipped a small, squirming handful of animal out of the back end of the truck and held it out to her. A tricolored fuzzy puppy with a coal-black nose, big ears and huge blue eyes squirmed and whined. "Here's your Mother's Day present. 'Cause I know you're gonna be a fine one some day, Casey T."

Casey's heart got jump-started by a syringe full of hormones. The fat little beast's back legs pedalled in the air, and suddenly a stream of yellow sprayed everywhere. "Dad," she yipped, jumping back, "it's leaking."

"Oh." Red whipped the animal around and set it down in the truck bed, which was equipped with a plastic liner. The poor pup couldn't find purchase as it tried to escape back into its kennel.

Casey couldn't resist. She looped her purse strap over her shoulder and picked up the puppy. A long pink tongue attacked her. "Stop, you wild and crazy thing."

She petted and cooed until the puppy gave a long sigh and closed its eyes, burying its nose in the crook of her arm. The fuzzy ball's resemblance to Betsy was uncanny.

"Shame on you, Dad. My husband will kick us both out if I show up with a dog. You heard him decline your offer this morning. What were you thinking?"

"I was thinking you need a dog. The pup could stay down here with me when you're up in the city. That house I built for you has a fenced-in yard."

"The house where Jimmy is living?"

"Aw, that's just temporary. Sarah's going to be taking Jim back one of these days. Just wait 'n see."

"I appreciate the offer, but I'm still getting settled in the city, and my husband was right about one thing. It's not a good place for a puppy."

She handed the drowsing pup back to Red, who set her in the well-ventilated wire kennel and closed the hatch. Fortunately, the temperature wasn't ungodly hot, so the dog would be fine in the shade while Casey and Red ate.

Their lunch went smoothly because they talked about what had been happening in the area while she was away. A little gossip. Who among his friends and acquaintances had passed on. Finally, over pie, Casey said, "I'll be back here Wednesday so I can I go with you to your appointment on Thursday. Don't even think about lying. I saw the note from your doctor. I want to help, Red, and I can't do that if you shut me out."

He took a bite of pie then said, "Want me to keep the pup till you get back?"

The smart answer was yes. The answer in her heart was no. "Has she had her shots?"

"Good question. I honestly don't know. Just in case, I'd better take her to Doc and get her checked out."

Casey nodded. She tried the pie. Flaky, moist crust and the filling was rich with cinnamon. "Um…good."

"You got a name in mind?"

"For the puppy? How could I? You just showed her to me."

"Names are funny things. You know in a blink. Just like I knew you were Casey T. when you first popped out. All red-faced and madder than hops. The nurse wrapped you in a blanket and handed you to me. The second I said your name, you quit your squallin'."

She smiled indulgently. "Maybe it was the tone of your voice. You told me you used to talk to me through Mom's belly while she was carrying me. I probably recognized you, not my name."

He snorted. "Believe what you want, but I knew."

"How? Did I actually resemble this glorified bronc rider?"

"Casey Tibbs was more than that, little girl. He was my hero, the Joe DiMaggio of rodeo. My folks were dirt-poor ranchers in the west river area of South Dakota. Times were hard and one of the only forms of entertainment was the rodeo. Casey Tibbs made a name for himself long before there was a pap-a-razzi."

Casey grinned. She knew her father could pronounce the word correctly if he wanted to, but his colloquialisms were part of his style…and charm.

"You still haven't told me why you chose the name of a cow*boy* for your firstborn girl child."

"'Cause it was your name. You were a scrappy fighter and you had your own style, right from the start."

A scrappy fighter. Maybe that was what he was

counting on when it came to battling land use issues. "So, Red, there's something I need to tell you, but you have to promise to keep this between us. I mean it."

His bushy white brow rose as if asking, "Do you doubt my word?"

"Nathan's firm represents the turkey people."

He nearly choked on his sip of coffee. "Damnation."

"My sentiments, exactly. He's distancing himself from the case, but any involvement I have with the opposition might jeopardize his job. He asked me to stay out of it." *Actually, he ordered me.*

"What did you tell him?"

She sighed into her coffee cup. "We're still discussing the matter. Part of my decision comes down to your health. If your doctor says you should begin treatment right away, then, of course, I will step in to take the load off your shoulders."

"And if there's no big rush, you won't lift a finger?"

She made a face. "This is your ranch, Red. You made that clear when you sent me away. I never had a chance to learn the day-to-day operations at your side. You have Jimmy to take over when you're not physically able. If you're worried about leaving me a legacy, don't be. I'm a lawyer, not a rancher."

"You're my daughter, and Willow Creek is gonna be yours some day. All that book learnin' won't hurt when it comes to growing trees. Heck, you might even be able to teach me and Jimmy a thing or two."

Casey shook her head. "That isn't going to happen, Red. Nathan loves the city. He thrives in metropolitan areas with culture and coffee houses and the opera. He isn't cut out for this kind of life, and I've been away so long… Well, let's worry about the future once we know how long it's going to take you to recover. I lost one person I love to this despicable disease, and I'll be damned if I'm going to lose another."

"So, BIG BROTHER, here's the short 'n sweet of it. Mom's selling her house. The Realtor is going to do a multiple listing next week. Everyone says the prices in this area have peaked."

Nathan hadn't been home for even half an hour when his sister cornered him, apparently determined to tell him what was happening where their mother was concerned, regardless of any input from him. He didn't appreciate the finality in her tone.

Is this how Casey felt when I told her she couldn't help her father? He'd blown it yesterday when she'd revealed her intention to co-chair the antiturkey committee. He was determined to handle things better today with his sister.

"I've said for some time that this house was too big for her. Does she plan to buy something smaller? A condo?"

"She's moving into an independent-living center. We've visited three in the area and she picked the one she liked best. It's a little pricey, but…"

"But with the proceeds from this house she should be able to afford it," he filled in. "I don't have a problem with that."

Christine looked at Kirby in a way that Nathan remembered all too well from when they were little. Two against one.

"She also wants to give some of the profits from the sale to us kids," Chris said.

"How much are you talking about?"

Christine crossed her arms. She so resembled their mother when she would argue with their father, Nathan almost smiled. "Twenty-five thousand apiece."

Nathan couldn't prevent the sharp huff of air that was quickly followed by a cough as he tried to control his anger. "You're skimming fifty grand off the top from the sale of this place?"

"Seventy-five. You get a share, too," Kirby said.

He looked from one to the other. "Mom is in excellent health. She might live to be ninety-plus. I haven't done the math, but what if that were to change? What if she needed long-term care? She might need every dime she gets from the sale of this place."

Christine and Kirby exchanged an "I told you he'd say that" look. To Nathan, Chris said, "Nobody can predict what will happen five or ten years from now. This is now. I work two jobs to keep food on the table. A babysitter is raising my kids. Our girls have never even been to Disneyland. This money would help us now," she said with conviction. "Later on, if Mom needs help, we'll be in a better place financially to give back."

He looked at his brother. "Does that go for you, too?"

Kirby, by far the more easygoing of the two, shrugged. "It'll mean I can finish my doctorate without a huge debt load. The better the credential, the better the job. Once I start teaching, I'll be able to supplement Mom's income every month, if she needs it."

The way Casey and I do now? he was tempted to ask. But his ongoing financial support between him and his mother was a private thing. A gift, he'd tell her when she called upset because her monthly bills were more than her income. "What does Mom say about this plan?"

"Mom suggested it," a voice said from behind him.

He turned. His mother, who had been on the phone with a friend while this conversation was taking place in her backyard, looked every day of her sixty-two years. Silver hair in a short, functional bob. Casual lilac-colored slacks with a flowered blouse. The same June Cleaveresque look that had embarrassed him when he was a hip, cool college student, but now he just wanted to protect her.

Nathan couldn't help but feel a little hurt. They'd planned this all-important step in her life without consulting him, and in his opinion, the scheme benefited his sister and brother far more than it did their mother.

As if sensing his feelings, Joan took his arm and led him to a patio chair. "Sit. We'll talk about this before the kids come back." Christine's husband, Doug, and their two daughters, Rachel and Laura, were at the store buying ice cream.

"Mother, I think it's short-sighted for you to give away money that you could conceivably need while you're alive. That money should be part of any bequest you leave after you're gone."

"But the kids won't need it as badly then as they do now," Joan argued.

Nathan wasn't so sure he believed that. His siblings were perpetually tied to their mother's apron strings.

Kirby, Nathan had learned today, lived with two room-mates in a dump of a place, and Joan still did his laundry once a week. All Christine had done since Nathan arrived was complain about her husband's latest business fiasco.

"You're a generous woman, Mom, but I wouldn't be a good son if I didn't go on record opposing this idea. Sell the house, yes. But put the funds in diversified accounts and certificates of deposit that can keep up with inflation and provide a comfortable cushion in case something unexpected happens."

"Mr. Doomsday himself," Christine said.

"He's a lawyer. What do you expect?" Kirby asked.

The discussion went downhill from there. The party was pretty much ruined. Chris and her family left half an hour later after the girls, who were bright, beautiful and full of energy, inhaled dishes of their Baskin-Robbins ice-cream cake. Kirby took a call from someone at the college and wasn't seen for twenty minutes. When he did come back, it was to kiss their mother on the cheek and ask where she'd put his laundry basket.

Nathan might have jumped his little brother about his careless attitude, but his mother was quick to defend her youngest son after Kirby left. "I know you think I baby him, but the truth is helping Kirby keeps me busy. We have a schedule. I babysit for the girls a couple of days a week and I do Kirby's laundry. He takes me out to dinner when he comes to pick up his things. It's nice."

Who pays? He didn't ask. This was his mother's business and he wasn't worried about getting a piece of her estate. He just wanted her to be safe, secure and happy. He was sure that was what his father would have expected of him. And if that meant he had to play the heavy with his siblings, then so be it.

Several hours later, as he drove across the Bay Bridge at dusk, he let out a sigh. The San Francisco skyline was one he never tired of viewing, but at the moment, he was too exhausted to appreciate it. He had a feeling he was going to be facing another disgruntled person when he got home, too. Or, rather, two more disgruntled people—his wife and Gwyneth.

CHAPTER TEN

"YOU WANT ME TO host a dinner party this coming Saturday? Here?" Casey repeated, utterly dumb-founded. "Not to be crude, but what part of what I've been talking about for the past ten minutes didn't you get? Oh. Right. All of it."

Her exasperation apparently got through to her thick-headed husband. Belatedly, it crossed her mind that his obtuseness might be connected to his concussion. In the past, Nathan would never have set up a party without running it past Casey weeks in advance.

"You said Red has a doctor's appointment in Fresno on Thursday morning," Nathan repeated with exagger-ated patience. "I assumed you'd return that night or Friday morning at the latest. That would give you the rest of Friday to shop, and I'd make myself available on Saturday to help cook."

"Why now? Why so fast?"

"Because it occurred to me that you haven't met any of these people—past a cursory introduction when we were checking out the place. This is my new team, and in order for them to function as a team they need to bond. With me. And with you."

The argument was sound—from his point of view, but it didn't make Casey any more enthused about the prospect.

"I'm not talking fancy. They know we're still settling in. Just some home cooking and good wine."

Casey had arrived back at the apartment two hours before Nathan got home. Wired from her drive and her many worries, she'd spent the time unpacking and ultimately repacking, since it was obvious a great many more of her treasures were going to need to be squeezed into storage.

By the time Nathan stepped through the door, she'd perfected her current mantra: "Apartments suck. I hate apartments. This is not my home."

"And where exactly are we going to put these people?" she asked, making a sweeping motion with her hand. "Will they sit on our bed, balancing their plates on their laps? Or should I buy a bunch of TV trays? Wait. I've got it. We'll eat in shifts. Fourteen people divided by four…I'm terrible with math. Help me out. How long would I need to keep the food warm?"

Nathan's scowl told her she'd made her point.

"Fine. We'll eat out. Can you make reservations someplace?"

"Not a problem. Well…it might be a problem on such short notice, but I'll give it the old school try."

"Thank you. I'd appreciate it."

But would he?

"How's your family?"

"Busy. They're selling Mom's house and pocketing the change."

"I beg your pardon."

He shook his head. "I don't want to talk about it. Christine and Kirby have a plan and I was told about it after the fact. When I raised a few points about whether or not Mom might be giving away too much before she dies, my brother and sister basically told me to butt out."

Casey wanted to offer her sympathy, but in a way, she agreed with his siblings. Joan was no dummy—even if she leaned on her eldest son more than she needed to. Her house was too big for her. From the little she'd gleaned from listening to her father and Jimmy talk, real estate in California was going through the roof. It was Joan's house, and Joan's money to do with as she pleased. That Joan hadn't consulted Nathan probably hurt more than the fact that she wasn't taking his advice now.

"If she sells the house, where are we going to move your Mustang?"

"Hadn't even thought of that. I guess I'll rent a garage around here."

She made a skeptical sound. "Not unless I get a job. Garage space goes for premium from what I've heard. You could probably cover it up and store it at Red's. There's an empty garage at the house Jimmy is staying in."

"*Your* house, you mean."

A thought that she'd toyed with earlier came back. If Jimmy moved out of that house and she started commuting between San Francisco and the valley, she could furnish the place with all of her antiques, which were currently in storage. And there'd even be room for Nathan's car.

Somehow she didn't think that plus would be enough to sell the idea to Nathan. They dropped the subject and prepared for bed, but the number of issues between them seemed to be increasing exponentially—and now, she had a dinner party to plan.

"WHY NOT HAVE the party here?"

Nathan had accompanied Gwyneth to the company suite, which in truth was larger and more spacious than his and Casey's apartment, to pick up the files she'd *accidentally* left behind that morning.

Nathan wasn't stupid. This was a ploy to get him alone, away from the office. He also wasn't in the mood for games. He'd only agreed to accompany her because he wanted to clear the air between them once and for all—and he valued her too much as a colleague to embarrass her in front of the rest of the staff.

He'd been about to launch into his "I love my wife" speech when she'd surprised him with her suggestion. Obviously she'd overheard him ask his secretary for a list of restaurants that could handle a big group on short notice.

"Pardon?"

"You've heard the expression 'The walls have ears.'? I was in the conference room next to your office when you mentioned hosting a dinner party for the staff. If Casey doesn't think your apartment is big enough, then why not have it here?"

She made a sweeping motion with her arm.

The tenth-floor suite was lovely…and quite spacious. There was even a balcony for the smokers in the group. The formal dining room could easily sit twelve.

"I'm no chef," Gwyneth said, "but my cousin is in the catering business, and he has connections all over the country. Even last minute, I'm sure he could hook us up with something fabulous."

Hook us up. The phrase made him a little uncomfortable. "It's a good idea, but maybe I should hold off until Casey's a little more settled. She loves to entertain—you've been to some of our parties back in Boston. There's no real rush—"

"I disagree, Nathan. You're the new captain, and the crew is definitely mutinous. You're not privy to some of the conversations I've heard. And you can be sure I'm only catching bits and pieces since they know I'm your friend. You need to instill a sense of camaraderie. A nice dinner off-site with wine, relaxed conversation and a chance to show off significant others would go a long way to turning the tide."

She winced slightly. "Forgive my mixed metaphors and clichés, but I was reading case files until about three this morning, which is why I left the Hardgrave file here."

Nathan felt like a heel. So much for thinking she was after his body.

"Do you want me to call Casey and set it up? I could make a few suggestions and let her take it from there."

Nathan walked to the window and looked at the city below. The fog pretty much limited his view of the crush of buildings and rooftops that occupied every square inch of space around him. His home. His turf. He loved it here.

So why couldn't he picture Casey sitting at this table making small talk with his staff?

"Nathan? What's wrong? You haven't acted like yourself all morning. Are you sure that bump on the head wasn't worse than those backwoods doctors thought?"

Gwyneth had walked up beside him. Too close. Her perfume was intense, evocative and dangerous.

He stepped back—ostensibly to pull his phone from his pocket. Casey hated it when he carried the thing, but he'd told his secretary he'd be available. "Are you kidding? I saw the best vet in town."

She appeared truly appalled.

Nathan hit the speed-dial number he'd programmed into the phone. "This is Casey Buchanan-Kent. Sorry I missed your call. Please leave a message."

"Casey, it's me. Change of plan. We're going to have the dinner party at the company suite—the one we stayed in when we were looking for apartments. Gwyneth has volunteered to find a caterer, so you're off the hook. Hope your dad's appointment is going well. Call me on my cell if you have any questions."

His *I love you* went unuttered. He couldn't say it. Not in front of Gwyneth.

CASEY CHECKED her phone. One message, from Nathan. If she hadn't been behind the wheel of her father's massive pickup, she would have listened to it. But dodging eighteen-wheelers on Highway 99 while re-hashing what the doctor had said was more than enough to occupy her mind.

"So you're going to do what the doctor wants, right?" she asked.

Red didn't answer. He'd been uncharacteristically quiet this entire trip. He hadn't argued with the oncologist. Not once did he tell Casey to butt out. Casey wasn't sure what was going on in her father's head, but she didn't like it.

"You're not dying. You know that, right?"

"Everybody dies," Red muttered.

"I meant your death isn't imminent. Not from this. Not if we act soon and deal with the cancer. You're too young and in too good health to do nothing."

He made some kind of grumbling sound but she couldn't make out his words.

"What?" she asked, glancing sideways.

He'd tossed his cowboy hat in the backseat and for some reason the indentation in his shiny white hair made her stomach flip in an unpleasant way. Her fingers tightened around the steering wheel.

"Why am I driving?"

He'd tossed her the keys and gotten into the passenger side after they left the doctor's office.

"Figure I might as well get used to being an invalid."

"What does that mean?"

"That's what everybody will think once they hear about this. Mel Johnson had prostate cancer. Everybody joked about him needing to change his name to Melinda 'cause a certain body part never worked again." He shifted moodily. "And he grew boobies."

Casey had a hard time not laughing. She'd guessed that some of Red's reticence was tied to his masculinity and to his understanding—or misunderstanding—of the prostate's function. She'd done some research to prepare for the meeting with his doctor and she felt comfortable telling him, "I'm sure Mrs. Johnson, if there still is one, is happier to have him alive and not sexually active than six feet under. Your doctor seemed to think you'd regain your prowess with no problem. Besides, a lot of men have breasts—they match their beer gut."

His snort sounded less pensive.

"Dad, you really don't have an option. You have to be treated. I will make your life a living hell if you don't."

He didn't respond right away. "You called me Dad."

"I did?"

He nodded.

"Well, you are my dad. I don't remember when I switched to calling you Red."

"After you left for Boston. You were mad at me for a long time. That was one way to get my dander up."

Casey didn't dispute that. "I'm sure you're right. Meg didn't approve. She said it was disrespectful, but you know how stubborn I can be."

His hoot of laugher sounded like the old Red. "Ain't that a fact? Look how long it took you to forgive Sarah, and she didn't even do anything wrong."

"Who said I've forgiven her? She stole my boyfriend. Jimmy was my first love. That kind of thing stays with a girl a long time."

"Oh, pisshaw. You and Jimmy weren't really in love.

All that twittering and moon-pie eyes was just your hormones kicking in. That's why I sent you to your aunt. I figured it was a lose-lose situation. If I fired Jim, you'd see him on the sly because he was the victim. If I ordered you not to date him, you'd probably have run off together. I couldn't shoot either one of you, so I put you on a plane."

"You could have trusted me to be smart. Even if I'd have had sex with Jimmy, I would have used birth control. I wasn't dumb."

"You were fifteen. I was raised in a time when that kind of thing—con-sen-tual or not—was against the law. I know times have changed, but I haven't changed quite as fast."

"You could have bought me a chastity belt."

"We didn't have eBay in those days."

His joke was so unexpected, she laughed outright. And nearly sideswiped a FedEx van. She took her foot off the gas. "Oops."

He made a pointing motion with his index finger, indicating she should turn at an exit she'd never used before. "We'll take the back way in. Wanna show you something."

A few miles later, her nose prickled as an unpleasant odor crept in through the open vents. "Eew."

She looked around for a dairy but all she could see was rows and rows of nut trees.

"What you smell is turkey manure. It's a great additive to the soil. I use it myself, but there's no way to deodorize it. For the first couple of days, if the wind is blowing in the right direction, it's enough to make you choke."

Casey was desperately trying to breathe shallowly through her mouth, but the smell permeated her entire respiratory system and left a bad taste on her tongue.

"Now, imagine this produced daily, weekly by the turkeys your husband's company wants to put next door to me."

She stepped on the gas and once they'd cleared the offending orchards rolled down the window. "It's not Nathan's company."

Red didn't reply.

Casey knew what she had to do. She'd known before she left San Francisco to accompany her father to his doctor's appointment. She couldn't sit back and not help. She was, after all, her father's daughter.

"I'll call Sarah and set up a meeting before I leave today. I have to put on a dinner party for Nathan's staff on Saturday, but I'll be down next week to get the ball rolling."

Red let out a satisfied sigh. "Good. Then, I guess, I'll schedule my little procedure, too."

Casey was glad, but there was a part of her that wanted to cry.

CHAPTER ELEVEN

THE FOOD WAS OUTSTANDING. Crab cakes so fresh they could have come straight from Nantucket. Vichyssoise chilled to perfection. Rack of lamb with some amazing rub that tasted Middle-Eastern without being overpowering. Dessert—a chocolate raspberry torte—was too beautiful to cut, but they did anyway. Casey ate every bite and part of Nathan's.

"Gwyneth, everything was fabulous."

"Thank you, Casey. Nathan deserves the credit for picking up the tab, of course."

A few satisfied chuckles were accompanied with a toast. "To Nathan. Our new commander-in-chief."

"Here. Here."

Everyone lifted their snifters of port. Everyone except Casey. Although she'd had a few sips of chardonnay, the first sniff of dessert wine had made her stomach react most unpleasantly.

She added her water goblet to the mix and exchanged smiles with the group. Five male lawyers and their wives. Two female lawyers. One with her female partner and one who came alone. With Casey, Nathan and Gwyneth, that made sixteen. Casey stifled a shudder, imagining how crowded their apartment would have been with this group squeezed into it.

"Coffee or espressos, anyone?" Gwyneth asked. "I splurged and bought a new Breville espresso maker. Felt positively uncivilized without mine."

Casey glanced at her husband. She couldn't deny that Gwyneth was gorgeous, smart and organized to the max, but surely that comment was just a bit too much. Right?

Their gazes met, but she couldn't tell anything from the look he gave her. He'd seemed inordinately closed and tense since the moment she'd returned from the valley. Probably because she'd dropped the turkey bomb in his lap the minute she walked in the door.

"I have to do this, Nathan. He's my dad."

"And I'm your husband."

"And you're not going to make me choose between you, are you? I've been wracking my brain trying to come up with a compromise, but the best I can do is try to stay in the background. At this point, nothing has really been decided anyway. The planning department will present their recommendations to the planning commission and the public will be invited to speak. There are plenty of people who can make our position known. I don't have to do that."

"But you will."

He knew her too well. He'd picked up his briefcase and left with a "I have to go back to the office."

She'd curled up in bed and tried to relax, but images she hadn't liked much kept dancing through her fertile mind. Finally, she'd made a cup of tea and watched a little Letterman. When her eyelids felt heavy enough to stay shut, she'd returned to her big, empty bed. At last check of the clock—twelve twenty-seven—her husband still hadn't returned home.

"So, Casey," Gwyneth said, coming back into the room with a tray of demitasse cups, cream and sugar. "Nathan said your father wasn't well. I'm so sorry to hear that. Is there anything I can do?"

Casey felt all eyes turn her way. "Worry. Oh, wait, I'm doing enough for ten people." Those around her chuckled. "Actually, I feel a little more optimistic after meeting with his doctor. The statistics on curing prostate cancer are quite high."

"His prostate?" the fiftysomething lawyer across from her asked. Casey was pretty sure the man's name was Eric, but she couldn't recall his last name. His wife, Rosaline—or Roz, as she'd asked to be called— appeared to be several years younger, but she seemed friendly and very down-to-earth. "My dad had that."

Casey had heard that a lot in the short time since she'd learned of Red's diagnosis. "How's he doing?"

Eric looked at Nathan. "He passed away, but that was nearly twenty years ago. They've made a lot of advances in treatment, I've heard. Especially with early diagnosis."

Casey ignored the little flutter in her chest. She wasn't ready to be an orphan. "I was very impressed with my father's doctor. He took his time and explained each step thoroughly."

"Where is he being treated?"

When she told him the name of the facility in Fresno,

Roz let out a little gasp. "What a small world. My sister is a nurse there. I'm from Clovis. Where does your dad live?"

Casey glanced at Nathan. She'd promised to keep a low profile. This wasn't a good way to begin. "The Central Valley," she mumbled, taking another sip of water.

"Casey's father is a prominent rancher and nut grower near Chowchilla," Nathan announced loud enough for everyone to hear. "His place is in close proximity to the land one of Eric's clients wants to build a new turkey hatchery on. Just to be clear on the matter, Casey and I are both professionals and know to keep our personal and business lives separate but to avoid any *potential* hint of conflict of interest, I've made Gwyneth second chair."

Nathan stood up, lifting the demitasse cup Gwyneth had set before him. "I'd like to make a toast. To a fine group of lawyers." Casey's hand was shaking despite the fact that she was pinching the tiny handle as tight as she could. "May all of our current cases turn into wins."

She brought the cup to her lips, but her stomach was too full and too nervous to cooperate. Even one taste would probably have pushed her over the edge.

"Is the espresso not to your liking, Casey?" the ever-vigilant Gwyneth asked. "Or would toasting compromise your integrity?"

"I beg your pardon?"

Gwyneth shook her head as if the answer to Casey's question was obvious. "It must be difficult to choose where to place your loyalty—with your husband or your father. I don't envy you that decision."

The room had grown still. She looked at Nathan, whose handsome face was frozen in a mask she'd seen all too often when he was unhappy about the way a case was going. She put down her cup and stood up. The fine china made a light clatter against the saucer, which was just enough noise to attract the attention of the people at the other end of the table. "It was so nice to meet all of you tonight. I hope you'll excuse me, but I'm still getting used to West Coast time." A tragically lame excuse.

"Would you like to lie down in my room?" Gwyneth asked.

Several images—none pleasant—washed through her mind, making her slightly ill. "No. Thank you. It's been a very long and stressful week. I really need to say good-night."

Gwyneth started to stand up to, but Nathan beat her to the punch. "Stay. Everyone. Please. I'll be right back."

She grabbed her jacket—a puffy, quilted silk the color of fine champagne. The nights in this city, more often than not, were downright cold when the misty fog rolled in off the Pacific.

"I'm sorry, Nathan. My head is pounding, and I really don't feel well. Maybe the crab…"

"Are you sure you don't want to lie down here until I can leave, too?"

His concern touched her. She could tell he was worried. This wasn't like her at all. "Can't. Sorry."

Was this a smart move? Heck, no. Strategically, wimping out was playing into Gwyneth's hand, but the pulsing beat in her head said, "Bed. Now."

"Don't worry. I'll call you when I get there. I got around Boston just fine without a bodyguard. It's probably just the emotional turmoil that's zapped me. I'm sorry."

Nathan pulled her close. "Don't apologize. I was an idiot to schedule this party without taking into account what you've been going through with Red. Forgive me?"

She melted against him. How could she not? She loved him. "Will you be late?"

He shook his head and kissed her, sweetly.

As she settled back in the cab a few minutes later, it struck her that he hadn't really said when he'd be home. Whenever Gwyneth let him out of her clutches? Casey knew without a doubt that she and the barracuda were going to have words—at the very least.

"So what about the third of June?" Eric Mathers asked Nathan as they stood on the balcony, as far away as possible from the smokers.

Casey had left half an hour earlier and had just called to tell him she was curled up in bed. He wished he was with her instead of freezing his butt off trying to keep his party from crashing. He honestly hadn't realized until tonight just how much he relied on Casey's support, her wit and charm, to make a party a success.

Gwyneth had done her best, but she lacked Casey's compassion and tangible interest in the people around her. The difference in the two women's styles had never been more apparent.

"Sorry, Eric, you lost me. What's the third of June?"

"The first Saturday of the month. Weather permitting, Roz and I would like to take you and Casey out in our boat. There's a group that gets together once a month for a little social cruise."

"Sounds great. I did some sailing with college friends, but don't think I've been out on the Bay except once when my parents took us to Alcatraz."

"Excellent. I'll go tell Roz. She really likes Casey." He hesitated. "Um, I hadn't planned to tell anyone about Casey's dad, but it was probably smart to get your connection to the opposition out in the open. Less chance of it coming back to bite you on the butt."

Nathan's respect for the man continued to grow. Eric was smart, levelheaded and had integrity. "Well, I had hoped that Casey would be able to stay out of the fray, but her father's illness pretty much torpedoed that idea."

"Completely understandable. You're both going to be under a lot of stress in the next few weeks, which is why you're going to love getting out on the boat." Eric grinned. "We like to tell people we're taking them on a *three-hour tour.*" He walked away humming the theme song from *Gilligan's Island.*

Nathan was still chuckling when he opened the door and walked inside. "What's so funny?" Gwyneth asked.

Nathan decided not to mention the invitation Eric had extended. The last thing he wanted was to have Gwyneth and Casey on the same boat—those three hours would seem more like forty. "I'm surrounded by smart and witty people," he said. "You did an outstanding job tonight, Gwyn. I really can't thank you enough."

She ran the tip of her finger around the rim of her

brandy snifter and gave him a patently sexy look. "Oh, you could probably come up with a way if you thought about it."

He swallowed and glanced sideways to see Roz Mathers watching, just a few steps away. His blush felt like one of those hot flashes his mother had complained about last Sunday. "Um…people are starting to leave. I'd better play host." To Roz, he said, "We really haven't had a chance to talk. Do you have a minute?"

With a wide, genuine smile that reminded him slightly of Casey, Roz took his arm. "Sure."

As they strolled toward the entrance, he said, "Eric probably told you we have a tentative date to go boating. I have to check with Casey, but if it works out, be sure to call her and let us know what we can bring."

Roz made a hand gesture that said, "Don't worry." As he helped her into her coat, she said, "You know, I'm an Okie by birth. My parents did the *Grapes of Wrath* thing, only thirty years later. Eric hates it when I tell people that, but I'm proud of my heritage. People who grow up poor see things differently. Money. Looks. Possessions. You can hold on tight to any of them, but in the end, what do you have when you're ready to cross over? Family."

Nathan nodded, not exactly sure he understood the point behind her message.

"Just tell your wife that if she needs a hand on the antiturkey picket line, she can call me."

"Won't your husband be upset?"

"Of course, but it wouldn't be the first time we didn't agree on something and it won't be the last. Doesn't mean we don't love each other."

Her words were still in his head when he let himself into his and Casey's apartment two hours later. For the first time in a week, he felt optimistic that he and Casey would get through this ordeal in one piece.

He hung up his coat and changed into slippers—the tile floor was bone chilling at times, then tiptoed to the bedroom to check on Casey. She was sound asleep. Sitting partially upright with her open laptop resting on a pillow atop her knees.

"Oh, sweetheart," he murmured softly, kissing her brow.

Once he picked up the computer, she gave a little groan and fell over sideways to curl up in her usual sleeping position. Her regular breathing told him she was out for the count, so he carried the laptop to the small antique secretary that Casey had set up in the corner of the bedroom. She claimed it was bad Feng Shui, but the lack of space was just one of her many complaints about the apartment they'd settled on.

Casey's lack of enthusiasm about this move had been apparent from the start, but Nathan had been certain once they got back to California, she'd feel more at peace with things. To his surprise, Casey seemed to have made the adjustment more quickly and with considerably more grace than he had. She and her father were getting along swimmingly, while Nathan felt more disconnected from his family than he ever had.

Impulsively, he carried the unit into the living room and sat down. He touched the mouse pad, intending to log off whatever Casey was working on and check his e-mail.

The image that filled the screen was a ball of speckled white-and-gray fur with pale blue eyes and a shiny black nose. The pup appeared to be smiling for the camera. His mind couldn't help jumping to certain conclusions.

His guess was confirmed when he closed the little X in the corner of the page and found the original e-mail that had included the photo as an attachment.

Casey T,
Doc says she checks out just fine. A few worms. Took care of that and got her shots. Still needs a name. Have you told your husband, yet? Shake a leg, girl. She's your dog. Whimpers every time I say your name. Gotta go.
R

Nathan shook his head and sighed. He needed an antacid tablet but was too tired to get up and find the bottle. The rich food, liquor and the fat cigar someone had pushed on him had definitely done a number on his stomach. Now, he had to figure out what to do with a dog.

"Damn."

He switched to his e-mail and scrolled up until he found his sister's online name. Her e-mail voice was just as rushed as she was in person.

N
Mom got an offer on her house today. Sounds good. Will keep you posted.
C

Double sigh.

He signed off and got up. Although restless and cranky, he decided to go to bed. He slipped between the sheets slowly to avoid disturbing Casey, but she woke up with a yawn so wide he could see her tonsils.

"Glad you're here," she mumbled, holding out her arms as her eyes closed again.

He went happily, inhaling her smell, absorbing her warmth. She was back asleep within seconds, but he nuzzled her neck, tasting her. As he closed his eyes, his mind flashed to his mother telling him, "Big boys don't need fuzzy rabbits to sleep with, Nathan. Give Mr. Bunny to me."

Maybe she'd gotten tired of washing the dilapidated thing. Or sick of patching its threadbare wounds. Nathan didn't know, but he'd given up his best friend without so much as a murmur. He was glad his mother didn't have any say in his current sleeping partner. Casey beat the heck out of a security blanket. He didn't plan to give her up without a fight. He just wasn't sure who he was fighting: Red? The turkeys? Or himself?

CHAPTER TWELVE

"IN THE NEXT SLIDE, you see the angle of drainage the proposed application hopes to correct if you change the designation from Rural class 11B to Rural Class 1," the speaker, one of the three planners at this monthly meeting of the planning commission, said. Her monotone delivery was so dry Casey had to fight back a yawn.

The woman, who had given her name just as Casey slipped in the back door of the Board of Supervisors room where today's public hearing was taking place, was facing the six members of the planning commission. Four women and two men. The disparate group sat behind individual microphones on a raised dais.

Casey wondered if behind the impressive oak-paneled desk the commissioners were tapping their feet as impatiently as she was.

The huge assembly hall was mostly empty. At most twenty people were present, sitting together in small clusters awaiting their point on the agenda. It was easy to pick out the lawyers. Three men in suits. None from Nathan's office that she could tell, but that didn't surprise her since this was just a preliminary application review probably designed to test the local waters and scope out what kind of opposition GroWell would be up against on the board—and from local residents.

As the turkey application went to the next stage in the approval process, the conditional use permit, the fighting could be expected to escalate. That was where Casey and her team of determined NOTT volunteers would rally the troops, the media and any activists interested in joining their cause. She'd already e-mailed a few feelers to Earth First and PETA. In the case of the latter, this collaboration came with certain risks given the fact her father raised hogs that were given to kids who sold them for top dollar to be slaughtered, but she wasn't going to worry about that right now.

"Wouldn't you hate to have her job?" Casey murmured under her breath.

"Actually, the pay isn't bad and the benefits beat any job I've ever had," said Sarah, who was sitting beside her in the surprisingly comfortable theater-type seats. "She's a nice person, by the way. Takes her job seriously."

Why? Casey almost asked, but her cynicism hadn't gone unnoticed by her fellow NOTTers.

"This is still America, Casey," Jimmy had complained the night before at a gathering in Red's kitchen. "Every vote counts, and every man—or woman—has a say."

Casey wished she could agree with him, but in her job at the land conservancy, she'd watched greed win out over environmental concerns nearly every time. Those with the most to lose often had little or no say in the actions that sent them packing.

"If that's true, then I'd better see every one of you at the meeting when the battle begins in earnest. You can get your toes wet tomorrow. Who's coming with Sarah and me?"

That's when the excuses started flowing, of course.

Casey looked around. Neither her father nor Jimmy were present, but she hadn't been expecting them. Red was scheduled for more tests, and he'd been adamant that he wanted Jimmy by his side this time.

"You know where you're needed most," he'd told her over breakfast.

Here. With Sarah and half a dozen familiar faces. Casey sat down in her chair tucking the ample material of her denim skirt around her. She'd dressed with care that morning, topping her patchwork mosaic of denim with a lace blouse and one of her favorite vintage linen jackets. It showed its age a little, but she figured she'd blend in with the crowd better. The Bettye Muller boots she'd bought at a consignment shop were four or five years old, but the soft leather made her feel extravagant.

"When is it our turn?" She leaned sideways to examine the printed handout Sarah was holding. "Where'd you get that?"

"Pays to come early," Sarah said, not offering her copy of the agenda to Casey. "Or even on time would be refreshing."

She and Sarah still had a long way to go on the concept of teamwork, but Casey couldn't really blame her for being upset. With one foot in the city and one in the valley, Casey wasn't always present when some important issue came up, which left Sarah doing more than her share of the work.

Casey leaned forward to peek over the shoulder of another NOTT member. According to the boldface print, their item was last on the agenda, of course.

At the rate these people were droning on, this would take hours and she'd left the puppy alone in the fenced yard of Jimmy's house for the first time. Casey knew she'd be fine, but she was worried just the same. *What if Jimmy gets back before I do and leaves the gate open? She could wander out to the road and get hit by a car.*

"Why do I care about any of this?" Casey groaned, slumping farther down.

"You don't." Sarah's emphasis on the word *you* made the statement sound like a real dig.

"What's that supposed to mean?"

She looked straight ahead and didn't answer.

"I'm sorry I'm late. I had to call Nathan and it took a while to get through, then I had to drop off the puppy at Jimmy's…er, the little house."

Still no answer.

"Come off it, Sarah. What is your problem?"

Sarah puckered her lips together so tightly Casey could see little vertical lines where her lipstick stuck in the crevasses.

"Tell me."

Apparently her demand caught the attention of the planning department woman, who turned to look at Casey. Sarah's face filled with an unhealthy scarlet hue. She stood up to leave, which meant Casey had no choice but to get up to let her out of the row.

Since she was already standing, Casey followed Sarah up the aisle, feeling a bit like a groom çhasing after a runaway bride.

"Sarah, what is going on? I thought we had this conversation and decided we could put our differences behind us and move on."

"I thought so, too, but I was wrong."

"Why?"

"Because Jimmy and I are supposed to be working on our communication skills, but when we're together all he can talk about is you. 'Casey this. Casey that.' Is the man completely obtuse or what?"

"He's a man, Sarah. He was born with the obtuse gene. My father's just as bad. I was ready to kill him last night. He went over every talking point ten times. Doesn't he trust me to do this right?"

"He trusts you. He's not here today."

"Only because he had a doctor's appointment he couldn't miss. If Jimmy weren't the one taking him, I'd worry that Red was hanging out in a bar somewhere between here and Fresno."

Sarah smiled, for the first time looking approachable enough for Casey to ask what had been on her mind since Red told her the news. "Is it true that Jimmy is moving home? You're taking him back?"

Sarah waddled with more grace than most unpregnant women walked. She sat down on a wooden bench a few feet away from the door. Her color was high but she still looked like Sarah—serious, focused and worried.

"You are the world's worst—no, make that best—worrier," Casey had once told her friend. "I bet you'd

worry about running out of things to worry about."
They'd been about ten at the time.

"I don't know what's going to happen to us—
marriage-wise—but I finally had to admit that I can't
do this pregnancy alone." Her tone was defeated, almost
apologetic. "You could, but I'm not you, even if Jimmy
wishes I were."

Casey shook her head in astonishment. "Me? What
do I have to do with this? Jimmy loves you, not me."

"But he admires you, Case. Everyone does. Red is
so proud of you. He tells everyone about your work at
the land conservancy, taking on companies that would
carve up the wilderness. It's hard to compete with that
when you're a part-time clerk at the feed store."

Red bragged about her? "But you have your degree.
Why didn't you work some place else if you didn't
like your job?"

"It was convenient and close to home. Jimmy said
he'd worry too much if I was commuting every day."

*Does Nathan worry about me driving back and forth
from the city?*

"And now, I plan to be a stay-at-home mom. This is
my choice and I'm not apologizing. I've saved nearly
every dime from my job so we could afford for me to
have this time with the baby, but your coming back...
Well, I guess you undermined what little self-esteem I
thought I had." She lifted her chin. "You look great, you
know. Classy. Smart. That same get-out-of-my-way
attitude you've always had."

"You used to say that if we were one person instead
of two, I'd be the body and you'd be the head."

"Now, you're both. My head is filled with hormones. This morning I cried over the fact that my toothpaste tube was too neat, instead of squished in the middle the way Jimmy does it." She rubbed the left side of her belly. "And my ribs feel bruised from the inside out because this baby plays soccer all night."

Casey's fingers itched to touch her, to feel the baby move, but at the same time, she was slightly repulsed. Being around Sarah had churned up that old need that had prompted three tries at in vitro, but being home had brought other memories to the surface. Her mother had died in her last month of pregnancy. What if history repeated itself?

Casey took Sarah's hand and squeezed it supportively. "I'm glad Jimmy's moving home. He needs to be there with you and the baby. Maybe the closer proximity will mean you two can't hide from your problems."

Sarah didn't look convinced.

"And we're still a pair, Sarah. Only, now, you're the body and I'm the head. I'll argue our points, but if things start going badly, you can pretend to go into labor. That ought to get us a couple of sympathy votes, don't you think?"

Sarah's tentative smile turned into a grin. They were both laughing when the door opened and one of the NOTT volunteers who had been at Red's the night before looked out. "We're next," the woman said, motioning them to hurry.

Casey jumped to her feet and pulled Sarah up, too. As they made their way to their seats, Casey thought about what Sarah had just told her. With Jimmy moving home, the little house her father had built for her would be empty.

The first thing she'd move out of storage was her aunt's four-poster bed. Sarah wasn't the only one suffering from sleep deprivation. Between the lumpy mattress on her childhood bed, her father's nocturnal pacing and the dogs barking at every coyote, squirrel and owl in the area, Casey felt exhausted before she even climbed out of bed.

Plus, her puppy would be safe from the pecking order Red's dogs enforced. Casey still hadn't named the poor little thing. She didn't know why. *Probably because naming her would really make her mine.*

And Casey wasn't ready to deal with the repercussions that declaration would have on her marriage.

The screen to the right of the podium went white.

"The next item on the agenda is the application by GroWell Farms for a conditional-use permit to build a turkey facility on parcel number…" The planner paused to locate the long string of numbers that had at one time been the Booth ranch.

Casey looked at Sarah and nodded. "It's showtime."

"I KNOW YOU'VE distanced yourself from this case, Nathan, and GroWell seems okay with that, but I'm concerned about what might happen if the media figures out the connection between you and Casey," Gwyneth said passionately.

She and Eric had spent the morning in the conference room with representatives from GroWell. As promised, Nathan had kept his distance, even though it had nearly killed him. He shouldn't even be talking to them now, but he'd stopped them in the hall to ask how the meeting had gone.

"As I said before, this becomes a moot point once we win," Eric said, his tone frustrated. "Are you hoping for a scandal?"

Gwyneth shot her co-counsel a severe look. "Of course not, but I've seen Casey in action before. She's not above using the media to paint an unflattering picture of our client just to win a sympathy vote."

Nathan didn't point out that Gwyneth had used the same tactics herself a time or two.

"None of that matters," Eric insisted. "Historically, this particular county planning commission has voted on the side of agriculture eight out of ten times."

"When it's in their best interest and there's little or no community opposition," Gwyneth countered.

"It's your job to make sure the planning commission approves GroWell's application without requiring a full environmental impact report," Nathan said. "An EIR would pretty much kill GroWell's interest in the project, and that would probably cost us half a million in revenue. Failure is not an option. Understood?"

Gwyneth hesitated a second, then took Nathan's arm and pulled him into her office. She motioned for Eric to follow. "I know you're keeping your distance where this case is concerned, but this affects you, too."

Nathan looked at Eric to see if he knew what she was talking about. Nathan wasn't sure what he read in the other man's eyes. Sympathy? Resignation? Regret?

She sat down at her desk and opened her laptop. "I

arranged for an acquaintance of mine to attend the planning commission meeting this morning. He's going to send me a streaming video feed."

"I don't remember authorizing any travel expense," Nathan said.

She nodded. "Because I didn't ask for any. If you'd have turned me down for economic reasons, then later we learned that our being there could have helped our case, your motivation might have become suspect. So I took it upon myself to send someone."

Nathan checked his watch. Casey had called before leaving Red's for the courthouse. "Sarah says today is just a see and be seen day. No public input," she'd told him.

He sincerely hoped that was the case.

That was about all they'd had to say to each other—thanks to the fight they'd had before she left for the valley. He'd asked her about the e-mail photo of the puppy on her laptop. She'd immediately turned defensive.

"Do you see a puppy here? No. That's because the animal in question lives at Red's. Would I like to keep her? Yes. But knowing your extremely rigid stand on the matter, I told Dad we weren't interested in acquiring a dog at this time. But you know my father. Red does what Red wants, and he wanted to buy me a puppy."

"But I clearly told him 'No dog.'"

"And he told you, 'No turkeys.' Neither of you seems to give a fig what the other wants, which leaves me—and a very sweet little pup—caught in the middle."

Her complaint echoed one that had come up in conversation the day before with his sister. "Christine, you and Kirby are thinking of what's good for you. I'm looking after Mom's interests, and she's caught in the middle. All of this haggling can't be good for her."

Christine had taken his complaint personally and hung up on him. Then half an hour later, his mother had called. "Kirby is going to be in the city tomorrow for some kind of meeting. I think the two of you should meet. Maybe you could go out to dinner since Casey isn't home."

Dutifully, Nathan had left a voice message with Kirby asking him to call. He was about to excuse himself to check with his secretary when Gwyneth's cell phone rang. Her choice of ring tones—the "Ride of the Valkyries"—didn't surprise him.

"Gwyneth Jacobi."

She listened intently for a moment, and then typed something into her laptop. "Got it. Thanks. I owe you a drink."

Nathan wondered if Gwyn's volunteer detective thought he was going to get lucky tonight. Not that he cared. Did he?

He was saved from any personal interrogation by Gwyneth's sharp inhale. "Casey's at the podium. Where's the volume?"

Nathan and Eric both hurried to stand behind her. The grainy image on the screen showed Casey in profile, shaking her finger at someone beyond the scope of the camera phone's lens.

"This is a public forum and I am a member of the public who went to some effort to attend this meeting," Casey told whomever she was addressing. "The least you could do is give me the courtesy of listening to what I have to say."

Offscreen a man said in reply, "I don't have to look at you to listen."

"By what standard of politeness? Your mother may have failed to teach you manners, but at least your fellow board members appear to look interested in what I have to say."

Nathan groaned. He couldn't help himself. Casey's aunt had been a stickler for manners. One of Casey's favorite Meg stories was the time her aunt had done something outrageous to a cab driver who, in Meg's opinion, had acted snotty.

Gwyneth shook her head. "Someone should tell her that's not exactly the best way to win people over to your cause," she said. Grinning, she looked over her shoulder at Nathan. "Maybe I was wrong. Maybe Casey really is on our side."

Nathan stepped back. "If you'll excuse me, I'm going to my office. This is your case and I'm not involved, remember?"

Ten minutes later—after two unsuccessful attempts to reach his wife, he settled for leaving a recorded message. "Give me a call when you get this. I…I'm going to the gym after work, then I'll probably head back to the office after that."

He started to add, "I love you," but a knock on his door made him hang up the receiver. "Come in."

Gwyneth. With two mugs of coffee. "A peace offering."

He pointed to the chair opposite his desk. He didn't want coffee. He wanted his life back, for starters, but he wasn't sure how to get it. "Not necessary."

"I was gloating in there. It was unbecoming and unnecessary. I don't need Casey's help—inadvertent or intentional—to win this case. And I certainly didn't send someone to that meeting to ambush your wife. You believe me, don't you?"

Did he? Did it matter?

He didn't know, so he didn't answer.

Gwyneth stood up and walked around his desk. She pushed his phone out of the way so she could rest her bottom where it had been sitting.

"Can we talk frankly? You know why I agreed to take the number-two seat on this case, right? Because you asked me to. You need this win, Nathan. Without it, your control of this office—and your future with this company—will be seriously at risk. I want to win this case for you, and I think you know why."

He didn't want to hear her say the words he was afraid she was going to say. "You want to win it because that's what you do, Gwyn. Your take-no-prisoners attitude is what helped you climb the corporate ladder so fast."

She acknowledged his allegation with a nod. "True, but I also believe that you and I have a chance together. I'm not a sweep-me-off-my-feet, fall-in-love kind of woman. You need me, and I want you. That is an equation that works for me."

You need me. He found the statement jarring but before he could ask her to explain her reasoning, she added, "But your time is running out, Nathan. Once I prove myself with this case, I want a yes or no from you. It's me or Casey. I'm my own mistress, nobody else's."

Nathan started to say that he would choose Casey no matter what happened, but she stopped him. "Don't say anything now. You're loyal to the nth degree. I get that. I respect it, but you're savvy enough to know when that loyalty is misplaced. Casey's got another life going, Nathan. One you don't fit into. Can you actually picture yourself in Hicksville settling property disputes between men in overalls? Please."

She uncrossed her shapely legs and stood up. "I have to get back to work. By the way, it wasn't me, but you should know that the home office is aware of your wife's involvement in the turkey matter."

"Of course, they are. I told them myself." But her comment implied someone had tried to sell him out. His ship was rife with spies, but who? Maybe he could find out from Eric when they were on his boat.

His phone rang. He snatched it up.

"Nathan? It's me."

Kirby.

"Hello, little brother. Mom said you were in town. Do you want to meet for a drink?"

A pause followed—long enough to make Nathan wonder if they'd been cut off, then Kirby said, "My meetings may run late. How 'bout I drop by your place?"

"Sure. Great." He gave him the address and some quick directions. "Are you driving? Parking can be a bear, but if you try around the corner on—"

Kirby cut him off. "No. I took BART over. I'll take the bus and walk."

"I'd pick you up, but Casey has our car. Damn, I should have had you drive my Mustang over from Mom's."

Kirby's choking sound told Nathan his brother

hadn't been expecting that suggestion. "Are you nuts? Mom would never let anyone but you get behind the wheel. Believe me, I've tried. The royal chariot is not for use by the common folk."

"I never told her not to let you use it."

"Never?"

Nathan felt his cheeks heat up. "Well…when you were in high school, but what do you expect? The thing is hell on wheels and you were a kid. You're a grown-up now. You have my permission to take it out any time you're in the neighborhood."

As an afterthought, he added, "Although you better make it soon. I might be moving the car to Casey's dad's place if Mom sells her house."

"Why store it anywhere when you could be driving it?"

"I don't think the salty air would be good for it over here, and from what I hear, garage space in San Francisco is at a premium."

Kirby didn't comment, but Nathan knew what he was thinking. Both of his siblings thought Nathan was overly frugal. "So what time tonight? Should I pick up takeout?"

"No. They're feeding us here. I wouldn't mind a beer, but I can get by if you don't have any."

"Beer it is. See you later, then."

He made a mental note. Workout. Dinner. Beer. Another action-packed night in the life of a married single guy.

He looked up. He'd forgotten about Gwyneth. She was looking at him as if waiting for an invitation. He cleared his throat. "Sorry about that. My brother's in town for a meeting."

"I didn't even know you had a brother. Is he cute?"

Nathan frowned. He needed to clear things up between them. Now, not later. "Gwyneth, you're an amazing lawyer. I consider you a friend, but my life is with Casey. And that isn't going to change." *Not if I can help it.*

She shrugged. "If you say so, but you might want to check with your wife to see if her agenda has changed. According to my guy on the scene today, Casey seemed pretty chummy with the locals. He overheard her asking somebody about a moving company." She left a few seconds later with a satisfied smile that made him uneasy.

Did Gwyneth know something about his wife that he didn't?

CHAPTER THIRTEEN

"I CAN'T BELIEVE you said that."

"He was in the wrong, not me."

"But you reprimanded an elected member of the planning commission. In public. On the record."

Casey looked at Sarah in the passenger seat. They'd left the meeting a few minutes earlier—after Casey's apparent faux pas—and were now headed to a restaurant. Casey was starved. She couldn't remember ever feeling so empty inside. "Was it on record? Good. Maybe this will make them all take note and pay more attention in the future."

"Or maybe, they'll take note that you're the kook with the turkey opposition, and they'll do everything in their power to help the growers."

Casey frowned. She'd lost her temper. She'd reluctantly approached the podium after no one else in their group would get up. All she'd intended to do was make the board aware of the community opposition to the project. She'd spoken at hundreds of similar forums. She was comfortable in front of a microphone and she believed firmly in her right to be heard. The members of this elected board were paid by her taxes—or in this case her father's taxes—which meant they had an obligation to listen to her provided she followed their rules.

They gave her ten minutes.

She stated her name and the fact that she was representing her father, who had a doctor's appointment today. She gave the ranch as her address. Then she started to explain about NOTT. "Neighbors Opposed To Turkeys is a grassroots movement that quite honestly isn't opposed to turkeys, but firmly believes that good agriculture comes from conscientious placement of agribusiness concerns that create public health issues, such as water pollution, noxious odors and traffic congestion, in areas that are not presently serving a good-sized population."

Five of the six members of the board appeared to be following her calm, thoughtful delivery quite intently. The sixth—a man in a gray wool, western-cut suit—was slouched so low Casey could barely see him, but what she could see led her to believe that he was either text messaging someone or working a crossword puzzle.

She knew she could have handled what happened next differently, but for a moment, she'd felt as though she was channeling her Aunt Meg, who would never have stood for that kind of rude behavior from anyone.

"At least there weren't many people in the audience," she said, pulling into Farnesi's—a venerable truck stop on Highway 99. "And no press."

She shuddered to think what Nathan would have thought if he'd been there to see her lose her cool.

"But you can be sure Red will hear about it."

Casey didn't want to think about that. "Can we not talk about what happened? I'm starved."

Sarah gave her a shrewd look.

"What?"

"Nothing. Are you headed back to the city after you drop me off?"

"I'd planned to, but Red rather sneakily managed to make an appointment for me to take my puppy in to get fixed."

"Isn't she too little?"

Casey held the door open for Sarah and followed her in. The smell of truck-stop food was curiously repelling and mouthwatering. The hostess led them to a booth by the window.

"I don't know. Red just said he and Jimmy wouldn't be back in time and since it was my goddamn dog I could take her in."

Sarah snickered. "You do that well. Mimic Red. He's a sweetheart and I love him to pieces, but I've really never envied you your relationship with him. He's too…big. When I was a kid, I thought he'd have made a great Oz—only the real thing, not a little man pretending to be great and powerful."

Casey and Sarah had probably watched that movie twenty times together. Casey now had it on DVD. Somewhere. She really had to finish unpacking. Was there some deep psychological reason she still had several dozen boxes sitting around her apartment? She didn't want to think about it.

They were nearly done eating—Casey had devoured her oversized plate of chicken-fried steak while Sarah toyed with her Chinese chicken salad, when Sarah suddenly let out a little peep and pointed over Casey's shoulder.

Casey turned to look. Red and Jimmy walked in and headed straight to their table.

Red sat down beside Sarah and put his arm around her shoulders to give her a one-armed hug. "Hello, little miss mother-to-be. Don't you just glow. Look at her, Jim, she might be the prettiest pregnant lady in the whole county."

Sarah's "glowing" cheeks went up in wattage.

Jimmy was left with no choice but to sit beside Casey—something she was sure he'd prefer only to sitting in a dentist's chair.

"How'd your appointment go?" she asked, scooting over as close to the window as possible.

"Same ol', same ol'. Took some blood. Filled out papers. Got weighed. Made me feel like a lamb going to slaughter."

The image quelled Casey's appetite and she pushed her mostly empty plate away. "Are you ordering? I have to take the pup to her appointment in half an hour. Hey, wait. You're here. You could do it."

Red looked at Jimmy. "Told you she'd say that."

"The doctor gave your dad some pills to take. He's supposed to start as soon as he gets home. He's not supposed to drive or drink alcohol."

"Might as well shoot me now and get it over with," Red muttered.

Casey looked at Jimmy. "Which means he needs supervision. I get it. Well, I don't think Nathan was expecting me, anyway."

She pulled her purse to her lap and pawed through it until she found her phone. There were two missed calls and one message. From Nathan.

"How'd the meeting go?" Jimmy asked his wife after ordering a burger and milkshake. Red settled on a bowl of soup.

Casey looked at Sarah as she pressed the button to retrieve her message.

"It was interesting."

"Did the turkey people show up?"

She shook her head.

"Anybody from our side talk?" Red asked. He was looking at Casey when he spoke and she felt a sinking sensation pass through her body. *He knew.* Of course, he knew. This was the age of instant communication.

Casey listened to her husband's voice. "Casey, it's me. Call me when you get this...."

Did he know, too? Something in his tone said, yes.

She snapped the phone shut and sat forward. "Okay. Here's what happened. The commissioner was a jerk and I very politely pointed out his rude behavior. Maybe in hindsight that wasn't the most politically correct thing to do, but—"

To her immense surprise, Red laughed. "Oh, Casey T., you're finally back. Does my heart good. I never liked that guy, either. Don't know how he got elected. He cornered me at some fund-raiser. The man's got halitosis like you wouldn't believe. Made me think a gopher crawled down his throat and died."

"Ew," Casey and Sarah exclaimed in unison.

"Excuse me while I go throw up."

"That is so gross, Dad."

Not Red. *Dad*. She'd been slipping up and using that word more and more often.

Red stood up to let Sarah out, but not before Casey spotted a tear in his eye. Her heart, already bruised from being pulled in two directions, suffered another blow. Her father's tears. Just not something she could handle.

NATHAN STARED at the mostly empty shelves of his refrigerator and shook his head. With Casey gone, he'd been eating out or grabbing power shakes at the Jamba Juice around the corner. Instead of healthy food, three different brands of beer—amber microbrew, dark imported and a popular pilsner—took up a majority of the space. His shoulder still ached from lugging the six-packs home.

He wasn't sure what Kirby drank, and Nathan didn't like what that said about him. "I don't know my brother," he muttered, pulling a chilled green bottle from the collection. "Why should I feel guilty about that? Kirby was just a goofy little kid when I left home."

He opened the beer and took a drink. In truth, Kirby had never been easy to know. Quiet, bookish, obsessed with bugs and dinosaurs. At family gatherings, Kirby would often disappear after a few minutes. Usually, Nathan would stumble across him later, outside digging in the dirt or hidden in some corner with his nose in a book.

He swallowed a second gulp, savoring the complicated blend of yeast and hops. The clerk at the store had recommended the brand, although Nathan had never heard of it before. The bitter effervescence tasted better than he'd expected. He changed his mind about digging through a box to find a proper stein and walked into the living room.

The numerous boxes sitting around made getting from point A to point B a bit like walking a labyrinth. He kept telling himself he was going to get home early and tackle a couple of boxes, but Casey had promised to do the chore. Since she was kinda picky about what went where, he told himself she'd just redo anything he accomplished, so why bother?

He sank into the comforting softness of their loveseat. The matching couch was in storage, but when they'd lived in Boston, his and Casey's nightly routine had included at least an hour together on this cocoa-colored double recliner. Shoulder-to-shoulder, they'd watch a little television, read or just plain talk. Had that happened even once since they moved? He didn't think so.

A buzzer sounded. "'Bout time, little brother," he murmured, hurrying to hit the button that would open the exterior door. "Come on up. Beer's cold," he said into the old-fashioned intercom system.

He opened the apartment door and rested his shoulder against the jamb, his attention focused on the elevator. Behind him, the click, click, click of footfalls on the stairs made him shift to the other foot and look toward the stairwell. His brother was a lab geek who lived in Birkenstock sandals. Who had he let in?

"Gwyneth," he exclaimed a moment later. "What's going on?"

"I heard there was cold beer," she said, not the least bit breathless.

Hot. That was the only way to describe her outfit. The stretchy black skirt was barely wider than the angled belt with shiny brass grommets that canted downward from her left hip. Dark patterned hose and shiny patent leather boots with four-inch heels made her almost Nathan's height. Her hands were stuffed in the pockets of a distressed leather jacket and her purse, dangling on a skimpy strap, hung beside her knees.

"My date dumped me. He said I intimidated him. We were at a restaurant a few blocks from here and I was too pissed off to go home. I overheard you talking to your brother and I thought I'd take a chance you hadn't drunk all the beer yet. Got another one of those?" she asked, pointing to his beer.

She walked past him without waiting for an answer. A second later, the elevator opened to release his brother.

"Hey, Nathan. The outside door was open so I just came up. Everything cool?"

Nathan blew out a sigh. "One of the attorneys from the firm just showed up unexpectedly. She's helping herself to a beer. Date problems. Come on in."

Kirby, who was dressed awfully casually to have been in business meetings all day, smiled agreeably. "I know all about dating disasters. Is she hot?"

"She's thirtysomething."

"Great. I'm really into older women."

Nathan couldn't tell if Kirby was teasing or not, but the thought of Gwyneth and Kirby together was enough to make the beer in his belly curdle. Gwyneth would chew Kirby up and spit out the bones. Just like…well, a barracuda.

He closed the door and hurried after his brother, who dropped his canvas satchel on top of a box marked Nathan's junk, and turned left into the kitchen with a, "Hi, there, I'm Kirby. Nathan's brother. I bet he's told you all about me, so you already know I'm the brain in the family."

Nathan missed Gwyneth's reply but he reached them in time to witness a hug. Gwyneth hugging a complete stranger? He was almost too shocked to speak.

"Nathan, shame on you. You didn't tell me you had a little brother. What a cutie."

The conversation pretty much spiraled downhill from there, in Nathan's opinion. Gwyn was on some kind of antimen campaign, but she was far too skilled at political double-talk to come right out and tell them that she hated their sex. No matter how often Nathan tried to steer the topic to another direction, she would return with one more example of how annoying men could be.

"I met Jack in the coffee shop a block from the office. I told him what I did for a living. He asked me to dinner, not the other way around," she stressed. "Then halfway through the meal, he tells me that historically the number of lawyers in society correlates to that society's imminent decline. X number of lawyers, Rome crumbles."

"What does he do?" Kirby asked.

He'd joined her on the loveseat, leaving Nathan the recliner a few feet away. Both were tossing back bottles of Guinness at a rate that made Nathan nervous.

She took another chug. "Stockbroker. Like that qualifies him for sainthood."

Nathan and Kirby exchanged a look. Nathan was a little surprised by the wise humor he read in his brother's eyes. Although Kirby was giving Gwyn his full attention, he clearly hadn't been swept off his feet. If anything, he felt sorry for her.

That tiny insight rattled him. Gwyneth was gorgeous, successful, driven. She and Nathan shared a lot of similar likes and dislikes, including a passion for law, but, he was beginning to see quite clearly, they loved it for different reasons.

As if tuning into his thoughts, Kirby asked, "Why'd you become a lawyer, Gwyneth?"

She burped behind her hand before answering. "I'm an only child of Jewish parents. I had two choices: doctor or lawyer. Medical school would have taken longer, and then you have to deal with sick people," she said, laughing as if that statement were incredibly clever and original. "Not that some of the people we have to talk to aren't mentally off, but we don't have to look under their clothes." She gave a full-body shudder that made her breasts shimmy in a way that for the first time caused Nathan to wonder if she'd had a breast job.

Kirby looked at Nathan and nodded, his grin suggesting he'd come to the same conclusion.

Nathan stood up. Gwyneth was a colleague. A friend. She was also drunk and making a fool of herself. He held out his hand. "I think you've had enough, Gwyn. Let me make you a cup of coffee and call you a cab."

"I could stay here," she said.

"Kirby's already claimed the sofa. Sorry."

Kirby's brow lifted in question—they hadn't discussed his staying over—but he kept his mouth shut. A little over an hour later, she was gone and the brothers finally had a chance to talk.

"Sorry about that. I really didn't see that coming."

"You should have, brother. She's got a hard-on for you."

Nathan, who'd switched to coffee, too, set down his cup. "There's nothing going on between us."

"Didn't say there was, but the chick, fine though she is on the outside, has the soul of a newcomer. You gotta be careful around them."

"What's a newcomer?"

"Someone who is in a corporal body for the first or second time. They haven't learned a lot of the lessons the rest of us have, and they're dangerous—to themselves and to others who want to help them but often wind up getting burned."

Nathan chuckled. "Ah, yes, the West Coast woo-woo mentality. I'd almost forgotten about that."

Kirby didn't appear to take offense. He smiled and polished off the last of his beer. "Easy to do when you're stuck on the east coast with a bunch of stiffs who are afraid to access their inner child."

They laughed together in a companionable way that surprised Nathan and made him a little blue. He wasn't sure why. "Enough about Gwyneth. I really want to hear what's happening with you. What was your conference about today? Can you spend the night? I should have asked you before."

Kirby looked at his watch. The band was made of some braided fiber. Hemp, Nathan assumed. His brother's clothes were a mix of Banana Republic and Joe College. Clean, slightly rumpled and good quality. Kirby either shopped at high-end thrift stores or Joan was supplementing his clothing budget.

"Might be a good idea if I crash here. The last train leaves in about half an hour. I'll just call my house and leave a message. My roommates don't really care, but they might need to borrow the car in the morning."

"You guys share a car?"

"One guy, one girl. They used to be an item. Now, they're not, but we're all still friends. Don't ask me how."

"You're all old souls?"

Kirby laughed. "Yeah, maybe that's it. Or we're all so focused on our thesis projects we don't have time for relationships."

After his brother made the call and hung up the phone, Nathan asked, "What exactly is your thesis project?"

"My major is environmental studies with an emphasis on what effect climate change and man's encroachment has had on vernal pond ecosystems. Historically, vernal ponds, which collect spring rains and runoff from foothill streams, have nurtured an amazing number of species and microspecies that play a major role in the health of the soil. Overgrazing, urban sprawl, more traffic and air pollution has changed these unique environments—for the worst. We're losing species at a rate that would make Darwin roll over in his grave."

"Microspecies?"

Kirby slumped down in the cushion. "Yeah, I know. Not exactly the most glamorous cause. Hard to get people excited about saving a bull-nosed spotted salamander." He brightened slightly. "But we did have some luck getting the public behind the plight of the fairy shrimp when a new university was going to be built in the Valley."

"Did you stop it?"

"No," he admitted. "But we raised awareness. A little. It's an ongoing battle. People want their conveniences. Longtime ranchers can make a fortune by selling to developers. Pollution and the extinction of fragile ecosystems take a back seat to progress every time." He used his fingers to put quote marks around *progress.*

"You and Casey have a lot in common. She used to work with a consortium dedicated to saving open space." He named the group. "Have you heard of them?"

"Who hasn't? My thesis advisor used to teach with one of their board members. Somehow my name came up and he asked if Casey and I were related. Dr. H. said the consortium was sorry to lose her, but that she was planning on taking time off to have a baby. I was going to ask Mom about that but figured if you hadn't announced anything maybe your plans had changed."

Had their plans changed? Nathan wasn't sure. He still wanted a child—at least, in theory. But if they couldn't agree on whether or not to have a dog, what did that mean to their parenting agenda?

"Casey's helping her dad at the moment, but once we get back on track, we'd like to start a family."

"Cool. I like being an uncle."

They talked family for a while, then both decided it

was time to turn in. After Nathan located the extra sheets and blankets, he turned to leave. "Um, Nathan, one question. It's none of my business, but how come there are so many boxes around?"

"This thing with Casey's dad came on kind of fast. First, the land use issues, then Red's health. He has prostate cancer. Although I'd never tell Casey this, I think Red is milking his illness to keep her around."

"Very manipulative. Sounds like something Mother would do."

Kirby said the last with a laugh, but there was an edge to the chuckle that told Nathan he was serious.

"Explain."

"Naw. It's late. She's our mother. She does my laundry. Only a real jerk would complain about the little mind games she plays, right?"

"Why does Mom do your laundry?"

"Because she gets upset if I don't bring a basket with me when I come to see her. She'd probably offer to do yours if you lived closer. And didn't have a wife." He shrugged. "One of the reasons I thought it would be good for her to move into one of those senior complexes is that it would give her more social outlets." He spread a fat caterpillar of toothpaste on the spare toothbrush Nathan had found him. "Plus, they have to use communal washers and dryers, which might make her less inclined to obsess over my dirty clothes. But we'll see. The woman is bound and determined to take care of some man. I think she sees that as her lot in life."

His brother's remark stayed in Nathan's mind long after he turned off the light. His mother was a caregiver, but that devotion came with a price. For years, Nathan had paid his dues with money while his siblings shared the emotional burden.

He made a mental note to call his sister in the morning and tell her he appreciated everything she did for their mother.

Just as he was slipping off to sleep, the thought crossed his mind that Kirby's understanding of environmental causes and issues might be something that could benefit Casey's group. If there were vernal ponds filled with endangered species on the land that his firm's clients were planning to build their hatcheries on, Casey might have sufficient grounds to demand that the planning department require a full environmental report.

He rolled over and punched his pillow. Dangerous thinking. That kind of information would require him to choose sides and he didn't want to think about that. His goal was finally in reach. If he lost his job, he and Casey would have to start over somewhere else. That would mean moving again. Moves cost money. Having a baby cost money. He needed his job, and its health benefits.

This is best for both of us, he told himself. Only his conscience whispered, "Liar."

CHAPTER FOURTEEN

CASEY HEFTED the strap of the soft-sided cooler over her shoulder and trudged out of the elevator to the door of their apartment. Their day on the Bay had been wonderful, exhilarating and more than anything, it had served as a reminder of what a special place San Francisco was. For the first time since their move, Casey was actually glad to be living here.

She dropped the cooler beside the door and rearranged the coats, sweaters and extra shoes she was carrying to find her key. It took two trips, but she finally hauled everything inside, beating Nathan, who was parking the car, by five minutes.

"Damn," he said, rushing in as she put the last of the leftovers in the refrigerator. She'd been a bit shocked to find so many bottles of beer on the shelves last night when she'd returned home, but she'd figured Nathan had stocked up for their outing today. "I had to park eight blocks away. Maybe we should look into renting a garage."

She ignored the suggestion. "Why is there so much beer? I only saw you and Eric drinking wine today."

"Yeah, I know. I bought these for Kirby. I didn't

know what Eric drank, so I included a couple in the cooler. Do you want one? The pilsner is really good."

"No, thanks. I'm still getting my land legs."

She loved sailing and had really enjoyed being on the water today, but the first couple of hours had been challenging for her, stomach-wise. She blamed the smell of the diesel exhaust. In Boston, she'd only been out on sailboats.

Fortunately, Eric and Roz's boat had a fly-bridge, or second story, that allowed her to escape to the fresh air once they'd exited the marina. The crisp ocean breeze had done wonders to clear her head and settle her stomach. By noon, she'd been able to sample every bit of Roz's delicious picnic lunch.

"Plus, I swear I'm still full. Roz is an amazing cook."

"I know. Eric says her dream is to open a deli once the kids are through college. He plans to work for her when he retires."

"That's what she told me. She said they were headed to Grass Valley tomorrow to look at some property. They can't wait to leave the Bay area, even though they love it here. Funny, huh?"

Nathan shrugged. "The price of real estate drives your overhead up so high you have to kill yourself to make ends meet. That's not Eric's idea of retirement, but he said they both love the water too much to give it up entirely. He thinks they might wind up in Oregon or Washington."

He'd picked up a little sun today, too, she noticed. His cheeks had a healthy glow and the wind had whipped his hair in a way that made him look like a pirate. She skated across the too-white tile in her stocking feet to hug him. "I had fun today. Thanks."

He set his beer on the counter to put both arms around her. "It was my pleasure. You looked like that actress from *Pirates of the Caribbean* when you were up top today. The wind streaming through your hair."

She'd had it pulled through the back of her cap most of the time, but when they'd stopped just below the Golden Gate Bridge, Casey had taken her hat off to wave to the tiny people who were calling and gesturing from high above them.

The water had been, in Eric's words "unusually flat." And except for a large regatta of sailboats, sporting colors as vivid and diverse as a spring flower garden, they'd only encountered a few other yachts and the usual "working" vessels, like the tour boats that took visitors to Alcatraz.

"Wasn't it fun cruising past the wharf? I have to say, seeing the city from that angle made me want to get out and play tourist. I can't believe we haven't been to Pier 39 since our initial scouting trip."

He nuzzled her neck in a way that was guaranteed to make her weak in the knees. "That's because you're never here, remember?"

A little dig. Certainly one he had a right to, but…she pushed the thought away and looped her arms around his neck. They had a lot to make up for and today had been a nice break. She planned to make the most of it.

"I'm thinking a quick shower to wash off the salt spray and residual seagull stuff. Wanna join me?"

He pulled back and gave her a dubious look. "We're not in Boston anymore, Dorothy."

Her mind flashed to the mini-coffin/tub and shower—again done in miniature black-and-white tiles and white grout—in their bathroom. "You're right, Toto. Shower, then sex."

"Speaking of dogs…"

She shushed him with her index finger across his lips. "We could, but then I'd have to kill you. Let's play, instead."

His smile wasn't quite as carefree as it had been earlier, but he nodded in agreement and followed her into the bedroom. The sight of the many unpacked boxes made her feel guilty, so instead of turning on the overhead light, she walked to the bedside table and pulled the chain on the lamp. An amazing find they'd snagged at an antique store in Mystic, Connecticut.

Nathan sat down on the bed to remove his socks. Casey grabbed her silk, boy-cut Victoria's Secret undies and a lacy tank that she never had the nerve to wear under her business suit. What if she got hit by a bus?

As she lathered and rinsed, her mind wandered back to the conversation she'd had with Roz. Although only ten or so years older than Casey, she possessed a wisdom that reminded Casey of Meg. Mostly, they'd talked about family, the weather and the differences between the east and west coasts.

Only once had they focused their discussion on business. Casey shivered recalling the piece of insider information Roz had deliberately dropped. "I like you, Casey, and I'm telling you this because sometimes a person has to choose people over profit. GroWell lost its soul years ago. Eric told me the company is using the parcel by your dad's ranch as leverage to broker a better deal with another county."

"They don't plan on building here?"

"Only if the other county's tax breaks fail to meet their expectations."

Casey knew how damaging this revelation would be. No county would ever trust GroWell in negotiations again. But even if she could come up with documented proof, she couldn't use the tantalizing tidbit. Someone would surmise that the information had been leaked by a person close to the case. Fingers would point. If not at Nathan, then at Eric, but either way Nathan's credibility would come into question.

Nothing more was said because suddenly Roz jumped to her feet and pointed out a stately taupe-and-white Victorian perched atop a small island. Its dark red roof, ornate trim and widow's walk caught one's eye, even without the operative warning beacon in the attached tower. "That's the East Brother Light Station. It's a bed-and-breakfast accessible only by boat. Eric and I stayed there for our twelfth anniversary. It was so romantic," she'd said. "You and Nathan should go there. Gourmet meals. No phones. The consummate getaway."

Casey let out a wistful little sigh and ducked under the spray to rinse the conditioner out of her hair. She thought she heard the phone ringing but ignored it. If her father was calling to discuss her performance at the planning meeting, he could stuff it.

She'd blown it. She had no excuse. Nathan never would have done something that embarrassing.

Her favorite fluffy towel was peeking out of the laundry

basket, so she grabbed a lavender one that might have been used for packing. It looked clean but smelled stale.

"Nathan," she called, opening the door a crack. She liked to keep the steamy warmth around her as along as possible.

When he didn't answer, she raised her voice. "Nathan?"

With a frown, she dried off quickly, moisturized and slipped on her pretty underthings. After a superficial tango with the blow-dryer, she opened the door to the bedroom. No Nathan.

The air temp was a little too chilly to be running around in skimpy undergarments, so she grabbed her chenille robe before going in search for him.

The size of the apartment and the strength of his voice didn't make it much of a hunt. She found him sitting at the dinette, cell phone to ear. He glanced up when she walked in and his eyes widened in a totally male, *yeah-baby*—way. His lips went from pursed in thought to a tight, partly lascivious grin.

Only partly? Casey was disappointed. Had she lost her touch? Or…was something wrong?

"Your mom?" she mouthed.

He shook his head, returning his focus to the person on the other end of the line. After another minute of silence, he said, "Sounds like a real mess, but I'm not a plumber. Did you try the management people? As much as the firm pays for the suite, I'd think they could service it, weekend or not."

Gwyneth. Of course. Probably feeling put out because she didn't get invited along on the boat trip.

Feeling grouchy and not particularly charitable, Casey walked into the living room and turned on the television. She'd grab a little of her favorite news program while waiting for Nathan to talk Gwyneth off whatever make-believe ledge she was on. She turned up the volume, but a restlessness that probably stemmed from jealousy made her pick up a packing box.

The label read: Desk stuff.

Cool. Red's home office was an organizational disaster. Supposedly he'd hired Sarah to help him stay atop his bills, but she'd mentioned that Red had refused to let her modernize his system. He'd convinced himself that using a computer accounting program would invite identity theft.

Tough, Casey thought. Next week, he was scheduled to begin treatment. The doctor said Red could expect to feel pretty crummy for three or four days. Casey, although no nurse, planned on being around to help as much as Red would let her. When he was resting, she would bring his books into the twenty-first century.

She used a fingernail to open the tape. As usual, the contents had shifted during the move and several items slid to the floor before she could stop them. A clear plastic container of paper clips hit the hardwood floor and exploded, sending paper clip shrapnel everywhere.

With a resigned sigh, she got on her hands and knees. With butt in the air, she stretched to reach a couple beyond her fingertips.

"There's a view no guy would ever get tired of seeing," a male voice said from behind her.

Nathan's low, suggestive chuckle sent a shiver of

anticipation through her. She scooped up the paper clips and returned to an upright position. "Are you poking fun at my granny robe?" she asked, turning to face him.

"Didn't see the robe. Only the perfect body under it."

She adored his lies. With a happy snicker, she stood up and opened her hand to drop the paper clips back into the box. Something quite obviously not a looped piece of wire winked at her. An earring. Three pretty colored beads, gold chain and an artsy piece of wire told her this was not a cheap piece that the previous renter might have left behind. Nor did the lovely item of jewelry belong to Casey.

"Look at this," she said, turning just as he reached for her. "Any idea where it came from? Or who it belongs to?"

His low curse told her she wasn't going to like his answer.

"I think it must be Gwyneth's."

A silvery chill—the kind she associated with bad news of any kind—passed through her body.

"She was here the other night. When Kirby stayed over," he quickly added. "She'd been on a date from hell and dropped by for a beer."

"You bought that selection in the fridge for her?"

"No. I didn't even know she drank beer. I got it for Kirby, but she had a couple before I fixed her a cup of coffee and put her in a cab."

Casey examined the earring a bit more closely. A wire, not a post. In theory, it could have come out accidentally, but Casey'd pierced her ears at fourteen and she had never lost one without knowing it.

"That was her on the phone, right? Did she ask if

you'd run across a lost earring? These are nice stones. Not cheap."

He shook his head. "She's got a water leak in the condo. She wasn't sure who to call."

So she called my husband, who wouldn't know a plumber's wrench from a…a… She didn't know what. She held out her hand. "Here. Give it back when you rush off to the poor girl's aid. I'm going to bed. Suddenly, I don't feel all that sexy."

Nathan looked at the little gold earring in his palm and silently cursed. Did he stay and reassure his wife that there was nothing going on between him and Gwyneth or did he dash over to the company suite where an atypically hysterical Gwyneth seemed convinced the floor was going to fall through if something wasn't done.

"I'm the boss, Casey. I have to go. But this isn't about Gwyneth. Nothing is going on between us. You know that."

She crossed her arms. "There isn't much going on between us, either, if you get my drift. Roz told me she and Eric go on monthly dates. Just them. No kids. No work. When was the last time we even ate together?"

"Things are hectic right now. As much for you as me, but you have a point. We could get Dim Sum in the morning. Gwyn said there's a great place in Chinatown. I'll ask her—"

"Did you see that lighthouse we passed on the way back to the marina today? Roz said it's a B and B. Very romantic and totally inaccessible. Like Alcatraz only high-end."

He smiled. "And you want to go there."

"Yeah. I do. No work. No Red. No phones."

No Gwyneth. She didn't say the words. She didn't need to. He knew what she was thinking.

"Great. Book it."

"When?"

"Anytime."

"*Any*time?"

He nodded, hoping like hell he wasn't going to regret his impulsive gesture.

She scrambled off the bed and grabbed her laptop. "I'll go online right now and see what's available. Might take us a couple of weeks, even months, to get in, but I'll put our name on a waiting list if there is one." She looked up. "I'm serious about this, Nathan. We are on shaky ground, and I'm not talking earthquakes."

He agreed. And the only way he knew to shore up that foundation—sitting down face-to-face and talking—wasn't an option at the moment. Not only was Gwyneth panicky, she'd threatened to call the home office if he didn't fix things. "So, you're okay with me running over to the condo?"

Before she could answer, the phone rang. Casey snatched it up. "Hello?"

Her aggressive demeanor changed. "Oh, hi, Sarah. What's up? You're not in labor, are you?"

As she listened, the color drained from her cheeks. "D…did you call Doc?"

Nathan had turned away to reach for his running shoes, but he froze in place when he heard Casey say, "Which hospital? If I leave now, I can be there in a couple of hours."

"Hospital?"

Phone tucked between her ear and shoulder, she hopped off the bed and dashed to the highboy dresser. As she yanked clothes from a drawer, she said, "Sounds good. I'll have my cell on. Call if anything changes."

She tossed the receiver toward the bed. "That was Sarah. Red is passing blood. It scared him enough to call Doc, who said he needed to get to the emergency room. Jimmy made a delivery to L.A. today and isn't back. Sarah's going to drive him. I have to go."

"Now?"

"I have to."

"Casey, stop a minute. What would you be doing if we were in Boston? You'd pace and fret, but you wouldn't hop a plane. Sarah seems pretty capable. She can handle this."

"If you're worried about me driving there alone, then come, too. Gwyneth is an adult. A healthy, young adult. Property damage is one thing, a human life is another. I have to be there, Nathan. He's my father."

And I'm your husband.

She zipped up her jeans and looked at him. "Listen. This probably isn't the best time to bring this up, but there's something else you should know. Jimmy moved back in with Sarah. They're not calling this reconciliation, but she hasn't been sleeping well and that's taking a toll on her health, so he's agreed to move home. That means Dad's little house will be empty. I'm thinking about moving the stuff in storage down there. That way I don't have to stay at Red's. When you visit, you won't have to sleep in my little girl bedroom, and, best of all, we won't have to pay to store our furniture."

Nathan felt as if she'd just socked him in the gut. "When did you decide this?"

She shrugged and reached for a bulky sweatshirt. "Makes sense, doesn't it? And the place has a fenced yard."

"For your dog."

She heaved a long sigh and said, "I have to go. Are you coming with me or not?"

He thought about the case files waiting for him in the morning. The calls from home office that would track him down and demand to know why he hadn't handled Gwyneth's problems. And the hurt that came from hearing his wife was planning to move into a second home without running the idea past him first.

"I can't."

She took the keys from the brass bowl on the dresser. "I had a feeling you were going to say that. Don't forget to give Gwyneth her earring. 'Bye."

CHAPTER FIFTEEN

"OH, HELL, who called you?"

Casey marched straight to Red's hospital bed. Seeing the man she was certain would never die in a cotton hospital gown was almost enough to make her knees give out, but she refused to show any weakness.

"Who do you think? Someone who cares about me more than you must."

He looked wounded. "I cared enough not to pull you out of bed in the middle of the night. Good cripes, are you alone? What's that husband of yours thinking letting you drive here by yourself?"

"Let me?" She didn't have to fake her outrage. "He's my husband, not my parole officer. Now, forget about me. What is going on here? Blood in your urine. What's the doctor say?"

Red tried to turn toward the wall but was hampered by the IV in his arm.

Jimmy, whom Casey had talked to on the phone when he arrived to relieve Sarah, stood up. "He's going to be fine, Case. The catheter and IV is emergency room policy. Turns out he has a raging urinary tract infection. The nurse said she had no idea how he stood the pain, but you know your dad."

Did she? The only time she'd suffered a UTI, she'd nearly passed out before the medicine took effect.

"Are they keeping him overnight?"

"I'm right here, you know. You can ask me. It's my damn body. Even if it is falling apart," Red added with a low grumble that nearly broke Casey's heart.

"When can you go home?"

"As soon as that bag is empty," a voice said from behind her.

She spun around. The woman who had entered undetected—a doctor, Casey gathered by her white coat and stethoscope, flipped open a chart and made a few notes before looking at Casey. "You're his daughter."

Casey nodded and introduced herself.

"Nice to meet you. Your father told me you're a lawyer."

"Not practicing at the moment. I just moved from the east coast."

"Too bad. I have a patient who is being forced out of the home she's lived in for forty-four years because a development company wants her few acres for a parking lot. They've convinced the powers that be to invoke eminent domain. Poor Tessy probably has less than a year left before she'll be in hospice care, but they don't care. We need someone to help us fight the greed."

Casey felt all eyes on her. "I…um…I wish I could help, but I never took the California bar. I honestly never expected to be living here again."

The doctor cocked her head. "Really? But Willow Creek is so beautiful. I've driven past the ranch hundreds of times. And I buy all my Christmas gifts from the nut company. You must have a heck of a great life wherever you live not to want to come back to this."

"Actually, I'm going to be staying here for a while, but I hadn't decided about petitioning the Bar for temporary privileges."

Red scooted back on the bed to a more inclined position. "Judge Miller would help. He owes me big-time. Remember when his durned bull hopped the fence and went courting that herd of fancy heifers over on the Burdick place?" he asked Jimmy.

"Still got the scars to remind me," Jimmy said.

"Is it too late to call him?"

"Yes," three voices said in unison.

Red chuckled and lay back. "Well, as long as we're agreed on something. In the morning, I'll call the judge. Once he gets Casey squared away, she can do something about your patient."

Casey would have argued the point, but what was the point? Was she too busy to help an old woman? Did she want developers to run rampant over this valley that she once called home?

She quite honestly didn't know what she wanted any more. The only thing she knew for certain was she wasn't ready to let her father die, and seeing him in a hospital bed had changed the playing field. She was home—in body, if not in spirit.

"DOESN'T MATTER who's right and who's wrong when it comes to a marriage. What you have to ask yourself is, 'What can I do to get my wife to like me again?'"

Nathan looked across the table at the restaurant in

Pier 39. His mother had called that morning, waking him out of a sound sleep—the kind that came at the tail end of a restless, crummy night of tossing and turning. The kind of restless crummy night prompted by fending off the blatant advances of a woman who didn't take no for an answer.

"This would be just between us, Nathan. No strings. I promise. I don't like to admit it, but I freak out when things beyond my control start to fall apart. I just talked to my father and…well…suffice to say I need some creature comfort tonight. Stay. Please."

The "please" had nearly done him in. Casey was gone. Gwyn, who had never shown the least bit of vulnerability in all the years that he'd known her, needed him. But, in the end, he'd paid a gazillion dollars in overtime to watch a plumber replace a leaky valve under the vanity, then he'd returned home to his empty bed in an apartment his wife obviously hated.

"Thanks for the advice, Mom, but Casey and I like each other. Our current problems are more a matter of time and distance. She's helping her dad, and I have to be here. We're both too busy for our own good."

Joan looked skeptical but she didn't say anything.

"Tell me again why this sudden decision to come to town?"

"Christine and I come to the city about once a month. Today, I thought I'd get out of my rut and have lunch with my handsome son, and I'd hoped, my daughter-in-law."

Nathan sighed and looked out the window, which afforded a really stellar view of Alcatraz. Joan had made the reservation, claiming this was one of her favorite places to dine, despite the fact that it was popular with tourists, as well.

"I'm sure she's sorry to keep missing you, but as I told you on the phone, her dad had to go into the hospital. He's home now, but she has some other things to take care of and won't be back until Thursday or Friday." Apparently, the ever-resourceful Jimmy had connections with a moving company.

He hadn't mentioned Casey's idea of creating a home-away-from-home to anyone. His gut said "Bad idea." But he knew Casey hadn't been crazy about their apartment from the beginning. He'd talked her into signing the lease by promising that once she made it her own, she'd feel right at home. Unfortunately, most of her treasured belongings—antiques that had belonged to her aunt—didn't fit in the small, ultramodern apartment.

Impulsively, he decided to ask for his mother's advice.

"I don't blame Casey for wanting her things around her," his mother said after listening to his take on the subject. "Ever since I decided to sell the house, I've had more than a few sleepless nights trying to decide what to keep and what to sell. If your father was alive, he'd put the whole lot out in a yard sale and buy new. It's different for women, but your problem isn't about where Casey stores her antiques. It really comes down to how much do you love your wife?"

Nathan sat back in shock. "Me? Casey's the one who wants to move."

Joan made a negating motion with her hand. "About

a year ago, Chris and Doug were going through a rough patch. The therapist they saw cut through all the 'He said this/she said thats' to the core issue. They'd lost touch with each other."

"How?"

"Life. Both working. Two young girls with hectic schedules. Too many irons in the fire, if you'll forgive the cliché."

"What did they do?"

"They went to Hawaii. The girls came to stay with me, and Doug and Chris had a second honeymoon. Maybe you and Casey should try that."

The same advice twice in one week, Nathan thought, smiling. "Maybe we should." The red-roofed Victorian set atop a micro-island in the middle of the bay flashed to mind. Casey had been about to book a room there right before Sarah called. "I know just the place."

Joan picked up her coffee cup. "Good. Now, can we talk about my problems? Kirby wants to pay me for doing his laundry. My own son. Did you make him think I can't afford a little laundry soap? It gives me something to do and gives him a reason to come see me. What's wrong with that?"

For the first time in days, Nathan laughed. "Nothing, but he's a grown-up, Mom. He values your time—even if you don't. How much do you charge, by the way?"

Her smile made him glad he'd had his secretary re-arrange his schedule. This had meant canceling a tele-conference with Boston, but he was tired of having his every move micromanaged by the home office. If they wanted to know what was going on, they could ask their spies. He had reservations to make.

"PUT THE SIDEBOARD in the dining nook and please be careful with it. My aunt claimed it once belonged to someone famous who fought in the Revolutionary War."

At one time, she'd known that person's name. But today, she could barely remember her own. She was hot, dirty and exhausted, but her work here was almost done. This move had been a heck of a lot easier than the Boston to San Francisco leg. The movers were young men who didn't dawdle. Jimmy had recommended them and personally overseen their efforts. Casey had been shocked by his fluency in their language.

"When did you learn Spanish?" she asked when he finally paused for a second.

His shrug was so Jimmy. "I picked it up. Can't work in the Valley and not know a little. Then, a couple of years ago your dad decided everyone in a managerial position needed to be fluent, so he sent me and Marcia—the lady who runs the pistachio production crew—to immersion school. I wasn't crazy about the idea at first—you know me and school. But turns out I have an ear for languages." He blushed. "Anyway, I'm glad I did it. Comes in handy."

"I bet. I took French. Nice to have when you're ordering in a restaurant, but not much use around here, I'm thinking."

"Allí, Paquito," he called, dashing off when a young man carrying two lamps started up the stairs. "First floor, man, not the bedroom."

Casey was charmed by her new home. Not overly large, but all of the rooms seemed bigger than they were. Probably because of the nine-foot ceilings and all the windows, she thought, walking into the kitchen. Warm, earthen-tone walls and trim. The brick-colored tile was ten-inch squares with tiny grout lines. The best thing was one didn't get vertigo from looking at it.

She and Sarah had made plans to go shopping at Bed Bath & Beyond in Fresno later to pick up some everyday dishes. Her aunt's Spode was going into the hutch, but Casey's wedding dishes were in San Francisco with Nathan.

Was this what divorce felt like, she wondered? Dividing things up. *He takes half the pots and pans. I take my share?*

The thought made her a little queasy. She didn't want a divorce. She wanted the life she'd had before this move. Correction. She wanted the life she and Nathan had when they first got married. Playful, fun, passionate. Before her aunt's cancer returned. Before they'd decided to get pregnant and learned that good sex didn't necessarily produce babies.

For a while there, they'd had a great marriage. A picture-perfect marriage.

Or did such a beast really exist?

Watching Jimmy and Sarah, who'd loved each other for years, attempt to salvage their relationship had proven a revelation—and made Casey question whether or not she and Nathan had any chance of making it. Jimmy and Sarah had a baby on the way, but they were still fighting. Jimmy seemed baffled by Sarah's expectations and demands. Sarah, who admitted she was happy to have Jimmy home and could finally sleep at night, still complained that he remained "emotionally ambivalent." According to Sarah, Jimmy hadn't once touched her belly to feel the baby move.

Casey had never questioned Nathan's ability to step into the role of fatherhood. As older brother to Christine and Kirby, he'd had much more experience to draw upon than she had, but he'd seemed genuinely relieved when the specialists suggested they take a break.

Was that because of the move and his career advancement or had he ever really wanted a child? Maybe he'd only been humoring her. The man didn't even want a dog. What did that say about him?

A familiar jingle started to play. Her cell phone. Nathan's call tone. She dashed downstairs, bobbing and weaving to avoid the young men carrying furniture. She missed the call, but hit redial.

He picked up on the second ring. "Hi. Sorry. I was upstairs, purse was downstairs."

"No problem. I'm on my way to court to evaluate one of our junior legal eagles in action."

"Hmm."

"I had lunch with Mom today. She said to say hi."

"Oh. How is she? Mad that I haven't been up to see her? I feel terrible."

"No. She understands about your dad. Said to tell you how sorry she was to hear about Red and to let her know if she can help."

"That's sweet, but he's back to his ornery old self now that the antibiotics are working. He won't be able to start the chemo until the infection is cleared up, though."

"How's the move going?"

"Very well, but I'm ready to drop. You'd think I was the one carrying all those heavy pieces of furniture. Sarah and I were going to town, but I think I'll cancel."

"They call that burning the candle at both ends. I'm not sure having two places—" He stopped what was certain to provoke an argument and asked, "Are you free a week from Friday?"

She glanced at the calendar she'd hung up on the wall beside the phone. "Um…yes. Looks clear. We have a strategy session on Sunday night. Our last before T-day."

"What time?"

"They're usually at seven. Why?"

"We're going on a date. Forty-eight hours. No cell phones. No e-mail. Can you live with that?"

Could she? She swallowed. "Okay."

"Are you coming back to the city this weekend?"

"Dad's supposed to be taking it easy, and he won't if I don't nag him constantly. Could you come here, instead?"

The pause seemed filled with stuff she didn't want to think about. "I'll see if I can arrange it, but I can't promise."

She understood. All too well.

CHAPTER SIXTEEN

"THIS ISN'T HOW I pictured us spending the day, you know," Nathan said the afternoon of their scheduled trip.

So much for his great plan. He'd managed to keep their destination a secret, and he could tell Casey was both intrigued and pleased by his efforts. They'd spent a companionable evening together in their apartment, retiring early so they'd be in good shape for their romantic escapade.

Roz had called at six-thirty.

"Nathan. I'm so sorry to call so early, but it's Eric. He woke me up an hour ago complaining of a stomach-ache. I thought it was bad yellowfin tuna, but none of the OTC things I gave him helped. Then his hand went numb. I called an ambulance. It—it's his h-heart."

Nathan had jumped out of bed and started throwing on clothes. "What do you need us to do?"

Casey, only half awake, had grumbled something about Gwyneth's plumbing—until Nathan had mouthed, "Eric. Heart attack."

Apparently Eric's sister, who lived in Oakland had rushed over to meet Roz at the hospital and take the girls, but she was a real estate agent and had an open house scheduled for that afternoon. "I really hate to ask. I know you and Casey had plans—Eric told me about the lighthouse, but if you could stay with the girls, I'd really, really appreciate it."

So, Casey—by then fully awake and primed to help—had carried their already packed bags to the car while Nathan canceled their trip to the island. That had been nine hours earlier.

Casey looked up from the jigsaw puzzle she and Mariah had been putting together. Mariah was the younger of the girls and seemed really shaken by what was happening. She'd barely let go of Casey since Nathan and Casey had arrived. Even now, she'd just excused herself to go to the bathroom, but had promised to be right back. Bethany, on the other hand, had been Little Miss Hostess, filling in for her mother who was, no doubt, tearfully pacing at the hospital. Bethany was in her room writing in her journal. Nathan had been amazed by how together the young girl acted.

"I know. Bethany told me all about it while you were unloading our things. You were taking me to 'the rock.' Not Alcatraz. The other one. The romantic one." Her smile eased his disappointment. "Mariah said her mother went on and on about what a great guy you were and how much you loved me."

Nathan felt his face heat up. "How'd she hear about it? I barely mentioned it to Eric."

Casey grinned. "Women have romance radar. We can smell a potentially blissful escape the way guys know which bar has Samuel Adams beer on tap."

A phone rang somewhere in the house.

"I'll get it," Bethany called, her high, thin voice echoing down the hall.

Mariah scurried back into the room and leaped into Casey's lap, nearly knocking her backward. Nathan got up from the sofa and walked to where the two were sitting. He held out his arms. Mariah was small for her age and seemed younger than ten, in his somewhat limited opinion.

Mariah gave a small sob. "I'm so scared for my daddy."

Casey stood up, too, and rubbed her back, supportively. "I know, sweetheart, but he's in good hands."

They turned at the sound of Bethany charging down the hall. "Dad made it through surgery. Mom says he's going to be fine." Tears were streaming down her cheeks and she broke down weeping the moment Casey put her arms around her shoulders. Nathan managed to take the phone from Beth's shaking hand and put it to his ear, despite holding a sobbing Mariah.

"Roz? Are you there? Good news?"

"Oh, Nathan, the best. I thought I'd have a heart attack myself before they came out to tell me, but he's doing great. I'm not sure I got it right. One bypass and two valve-jobs or one valve and two bypasses. Don't quote me."

Her joy was clear, her relief shared. "Have you seen him yet?"

"Another hour or so, I think. I honestly didn't hear much after the part that he was going to be okay."

"You stay put until you feel comfortable leaving him. Casey and I brought our overnight bags, so we're here for as long as you need us."

"Oh, you're both wonderful. I, for one, am so glad you took over at the firm. The last guy they had running the place would have sent flowers. Maybe. You and Casey have your values straight. Thank you from the bottom of my heart."

She hung up ten minutes later after talking to Casey and both of her daughters. Nathan walked to the sliding glass door of the Concord home and stared at the small, nicely landscaped backyard. Pool, cabana, flowering plants. A comfortable life that had almost been changed forever.

You and Casey have your values straight.

Did they?

Casey maybe. She'd managed to get past her hurt feelings where her father was concerned and help Red deal with his health issues and the threat to his livelihood. Nathan, on the other hand, had barely scratched the surface of connecting with his family, and instead of supporting his wife in her cause, he was sitting on potentially helpful information that could derail Gwyneth's case.

Guilt was the true strange bedfellow. Maybe that explained why the past few times they'd made love, Nathan had felt emotionally absent.

Casey joined him. "Want to sit outside? The girls are calling their friends to tell them the good news."

He nodded and opened the door for her. They chose two glossy teak folding chairs that matched an oval picnic table. The sun was warm, but there was enough of a breeze to keep the temperature pleasant. Nathan had had a friend in college whose parents lived in Concord and he'd always liked the area.

"This is nice."

"Yes. Not a lighthouse in the Bay, but very cozy and comfortable. Roz says they bought before the huge land boom, but they still paid more than they could afford. Which is why she works at a job she hates."

"Like you."

She blinked. "Beg your pardon?"

"Oh, come on, Casey, you've never really liked being a lawyer. You were happy with the conservation group because they didn't require you to do a lot of lawyerly things, but if this land use battle with your dad goes all the way to court, you're going to be miserable."

She frowned. "I'm not you, Nathan. I'm too emotional. I speak before I think—obviously," she added under her breath. "But there are things about the law that I like. Especially when it comes to helping someone and knowing I've made a difference."

He snickered softly. "You like the interaction with people—the part of the job I'm really bad at. If we could ever find a way to work together, we'd make a good team."

She sat forward, folding her hands on the table. "So, what's stopping us?"

Nathan felt his mouth drop open. "You wouldn't last a day at Silver, Reisbecht and Lane. You're too…"

"Wimpy?" she asked, contentiously.

"Genuine. Honest. Compassionate."

He could tell his words had cooled her pique, but her frown didn't abate. "Thank you. I appreciate that, but what you're saying is that you're none of those things. And that's not true."

If you only knew....

His cell phone, which he'd started wearing attached to his belt again, rang. He recognized the number.

"Gwyneth. I was just going to call you. Good news. Eric is going to be fine."

Casey sat back in her chair and crossed her arms over her chest. Her body language said exactly what she felt about the woman on the phone.

"Wonderful. When will he be back at work?"

"Um…I have no idea. I imagine something like this takes weeks, maybe months to recover from. I don't know."

"Then that must mean I'm first chair on the GroWell case."

Was that satisfaction he heard in her voice? No one could deny that Eric's misfortune was a break for her, career-wise, but Nathan found the statement off-putting.

"We'll talk business on Monday. I have to go. Eric's daughters are still pretty upset." He hung up without waiting for her reply. He turned off the phone and looked at his wife. "Let's take the girls out for dinner. Someplace nice."

LONG AFTER the girls were in bed and Roz had returned home for a shower, nap and change of clothes, Casey and Nathan hunkered down in a loveseat, not unlike the one they shared at their apartment. She rested her head on his shoulder and gazed unseeing at the so-called reality show on television.

"That was really nice of you tonight. The girls were distracted and relieved and you made the whole thing feel like a celebration." He'd treated the two young girls like princesses and she'd never been more proud of him.

He flicked the channel changer. "We are celebrating. Eric is a great guy. I'm really, really glad to know that he's going to be okay."

She shifted slightly. "He's not out of the woods yet. And Roz is already thinking ahead. She said she spent a lot time in the waiting room doing the old 'What if…' thing. And she decided that slogging it out in the fast lane just so they might someday be able to afford to retire nearly killed the man she loves. She isn't sure Eric will agree with her, but as soon as he's well, she's going to suggest he quit SRL."

"You're kidding."

His obvious shock sent a chill through her body. "It's just a job, Nathan."

"An extremely high-paying job. They'd never be able to afford a house like this if he wasn't working for me."

"So they sell the place and move. What good is money if he's not around to watch his daughters grow up?"

Nathan pulled himself forward to get the recliner upright. "Money provides the lifestyle and advantages that his family has come to expect. What about college tuition? And retirement? And, now, health care. Good lord, if he quits, he might never qualify for another group plan."

Casey got his point, but deep down she knew he was less concerned about Eric's long-term needs than what message his colleague's quitting would send. If Eric was brave enough—or foolish enough—to turn his back on everything he'd worked so hard to achieve, what did that mean to Nathan?

Neither spoke for a few minutes, then Nathan said, "Speaking of life-altering decisions, we haven't really talked about what getting your reciprocal privileges means. Are you planning to hang out a shingle in the Valley?"

If he'd asked her that question last night, she would have been able to answer honestly, "I don't know." But seeing both the fear and the conviction in Roz's face this afternoon had been a revelation. Casey knew without a doubt that that could be her in a few years if Nathan continued on his present course.

To avoid a direct yes or no, she said, "Dad says he'd sell the ranch rather than live next to a turkey farm. So, I guess we have to wait and see how good Gwyneth is…arguing her client's case, of course."

At the moment, Casey wasn't optimistic about NOTT's chance of blocking the application. None of the so-called experts she and Sarah had contacted had been able to give them any tangible evidence to support a claim that the county should require the turkey growers to produce a full EIR. Everyone agreed that a large-scale, high intensity operation like the one planned, would foul the air and create water pollution and traffic problems, but since the parcel was already designated for agricultural use, the planners felt their hands were tied.

Nathan hunched over. "She's very focused."

And I'm not. Two homes. Two loyalties. One puppy.

As if he heard her thought, he looked at her and said,

"I'm sorry I gave you a hard time about the dog. Is your dad taking care of her this weekend?"

She shook her head. "Sarah's got her. The outside dogs pick on her, and she can't stay inside at Dad's because Betsy is jealous. I tried explaining that the pup was her granddaughter, but she didn't seem to care."

"What's her name?"

"I haven't decided yet."

Neither spoke for a few minutes, then she said, "You know tomorrow is Father's Day, right? If it's okay with Roz, maybe we could take the girls to the hospital for a few minutes to see Eric then do something fun, like Great America."

"Sounds like a plan. How does your dad feel about not having you around?"

"I'll call him in the morning, but he knows I'm not leaving here until late afternoon. Sarah and Jimmy are taking him out to brunch."

"How come? Where are their dads?"

"Jimmy's lives in Texas but they're not close. Sarah's died just before we got married. Since I was away for so long, they sort of adopted Red." A fact that bothered her more than she thought it should.

She told herself this was a made-up holiday. She had no reason to feel guilty about the many Father's Days he'd spent in the company of two other men's children. She'd never failed to send a gift. Even when she didn't have a clue about what Red might like or need, she'd dug out her credit card and ordered something... anything.

But she hadn't given him the one thing he needed

most—her time. And there was only way to make up for that.

"I bet the girls would have a blast at the ranch. Maybe I could bring them down next weekend," Nathan said, taking her by surprise.

She sat up and looked at him. "That's a wonderful idea. Roz is going to need all the help we can give her. Too bad the turkey hearing is on Wednesday or I could take them with me. Bethany said they're both out of school for the summer, but I'm going to be busy every minute strategizing our defense."

She studied her toes. "I…um…I don't know if I mentioned it, but I had a little run-in with one of the commissioners."

Nathan's brow arched questioningly.

"The guy was rude. He never made eye contact while I was talking. I shaved my legs that morning. The least he could do was pretend to listen, right?"

Nathan's bark of laughter made her relax. She'd been too embarrassed to tell him earlier. Plus, she was certain he'd lecture her.

"Shaved legs, huh? You're too much."

"What if he votes against us because of me?"

"If the guy shows flagrant favoritism or bias, you might be able to make a case in appeal that his prejudice influenced the outcome. That might win you an injunction."

She hadn't thought about that.

She leaned in and kissed him. "I knew I kept you around for a reason—your sharp legal mind." His tongue went exploring and left her breathless. "And you're an amazing kisser, too. Let's go to bed."

"Good idea, but we need to check on the girls first."

Tears blossomed in her eyes. *What a sweet, fatherly thing to say.* Another part of her mind thought that was a pretty lame thing to tear up about and wondered if she was premenstrual. Which led to her trying to picture a calendar and recall the last time she'd had her period.

How long has it been? Was it possible? No. It couldn't be.

Or was it?

CHAPTER SEVENTEEN

WEDNESDAY ARRIVED all too quickly for Casey. Eric was mending like a champ, and the girls had been a delight at the amusement park. Mariah even kept up with Nathan's thrill-seeking tendencies while Casey and Bethany watched. Eric's mother flew in late Sunday afternoon to stay for the week, which dovetailed neatly with Nathan's plan to bring the girls to the ranch the following weekend.

Now, all Casey had to do was convince a panel of people that the right thing to do was just say no—to turkeys.

Unfortunately, she'd awoken in a fog after a restless night. Probably because the tea she'd brewed for herself that morning had produced a quick, intense rush of nausea when she'd brought the cup to her lips.

"Shake a leg, Casey T. We don't want to be late."

Red had offered to pick her up, for which she was grateful.

She picked up her briefcase and purse. "Coming. How do you feel this morning?"

"Crappy. Those pills make everything taste like dog doo."

"How do you know what dog doo tastes like?"

Laughing, he opened the truck door for her. "You got a point. Are you nervous?"

"Yes."

"Did I hear tell that Nathan is coming?"

"Yes. He's riding down with the barra—I mean, one of the lawyers who is handling the case. Her name is Gwyneth."

He nodded, but didn't say anything. Which was good, because she really didn't want to think about Nathan or Gwyneth or anything outside the parameters of her arguments. At the Sunday night strategy meeting, she and Sarah had divided up the discussion topics among the faithful: air quality, water pollution, traffic, disease and decimation of property values. Casey's job would be to summarize the points that each of the speakers made to drive home their impassioned plea.

God, I hope I can do this without throwing up.

She didn't feel well. A part of her still asked the "Am I? Or aren't I?" question. She'd picked up a pregnancy test but hadn't used it because she was sure the disappointment would have been too crushing on top of what was certain to be a grim decision today.

Plus, she couldn't say what this would mean to her and Nathan. Six months ago, they'd have danced a happy dance and toasted with bubbly water. Now, they lived in two separate homes four hours apart. And although she hadn't come right out and told Nathan her decision, Casey knew in her heart, she couldn't live in the city again—baby or no baby.

She was a country girl. She loved the animals, the space, the smells, the quiet. And she felt guilty about her feelings. She'd married Nathan under false pretenses, although not intentionally. While living with her aunt, Casey had devoted herself to becoming a woman of the city. Partly to make Meg happy and partly to get back at her father, who had sent her away from the life she loved.

Coming home had brought back those feelings she'd buried, and the truth was very clear—she was no longer the wife Nathan thought he'd married.

"MUST YOU DO THAT?" Gwyneth snarled at the driver of the car in front of them. "Don't they teach you people how to drive out here in the boonies?"

Nathan looked around. Modesto was hardly a small town. They'd just turned on Highway 99 South and Gwyneth had already changed lanes four times. He looked in the backseat where Philip Kim, the junior partner who had moved into Gwyneth's place after Eric got sick, was sitting. Nathan had been impressed by the young man from the day they were introduced. A critical thinker whose mother was Japanese and father Korean, Philip's only shortcoming was his habit of thinking out loud. He never stopped talking. Oddly, Gwyneth's driving had turned him to stone. Nathan wasn't even sure the guy had blinked in ten miles.

"We're only thirty minutes away," Nathan told him.

Phil wiped a bead of sweat from his upper lip. "Good."

"Do you know where the courthouse is?" Gwyneth asked.

"Yes."

"Is Casey expecting you?"

"Yes. You and Philip can go home and I'll ride back with her."

"Even if I beat the pants off the NOTT people?"

There was a giddiness to her tone that made Nathan uncomfortable. From what Eric had told him, chances were good that Gwyneth would win, but Casey wasn't a pushover. When she felt strongly about a subject, she was known to bend a few rules to make her position known. They hadn't discussed the case directly, but he'd overheard her explaining the issue to Bethany while they were standing in line at the theme park.

"Turkeys are cool birds. Their meat is nutritious and they're easy to raise, as long as you don't expect them to think." She'd laughed in that singsong happy tone that made him smile. "But you can't raise turkeys without dealing with the by-products. Turkey poop is great fertilizer, but there's a process required to break it down. That process stinks. When the wind is right, you can smell it for miles and miles. And the runoff from holding ponds is toxic to fish and crawdads and frogs. Have you and your sister ever gone fishing for crawdads? We'll have to do that when you visit next weekend."

Nathan had never fished for crawdads, either. His father had always promised to take him fishing, but they had never seemed to find time. There hadn't been time for a lot of things.

"Damn you!" Gwyneth exclaimed, stomping on the brakes.

Nathan put his hand out to brace himself. "We're not in that big a hurry, Gwyn."

"I know, but driving is my passion. I just hate it when a few retards spoil it for the rest of us."

He glanced in the back seat. Philip was staring at his hands—the politically correct response, of course, but Nathan was certain he spotted a hint of a smile. Or a grimace.

"This is our exit," he said. *Thank goodness.*

"APPARENTLY A FEW of the citizens speaking today misunderstood the directive we as a board put forth at our last meeting. We were making an effort to bring the language in the planning document in line with similar documents, nothing more. Actual approval for the plan will come after due process and recommendations set forth by the planning department."

Western-suit Guy was talking into the microphone, his gaze zeroing in on Casey every few minutes. She tried flashing him the smile that always worked with her male teachers but his frown only deepened. *Maybe he's gay.*

The silliness of the thought—that because some man wasn't won over by her girlish charms automatically brought his sexual proclivity into question— made her giggle.

Jimmy leaned in and whispered, "Making friends wherever you go, hey?"

"Whatever."

His laugh was somehow comforting. They weren't exactly friends yet, but she hoped they might be one day, once his and Sarah's relationship solidified. Surely that would happen after the baby was born, she thought, adding a little wishful prayer.

Casey clicked her pen and doodled in the margin of her agenda while sneaking peeks across the aisle where her husband sat with Gwyneth and an associate whose name Casey had forgotten. Peter, Paul, Patrick? Something with a *P,* she was sure of it.

Her father, who was sitting beside her, cleared his throat. "Are you listening?" he whispered tersely.

"Yes."

No. She was staring at her husband like a groupie. Her mind was all over the place. *What's wrong with me?*

"We'll open the public comment portion of this meeting. Those of you who planned to talk have already signed the agenda, I trust," the sweet-faced commissioner who had smiled when Casey took her fellow board member to task said.

Casey nodded, even though the question hadn't been asked to her specifically. Sarah had been in charge of getting all the volunteers lined up and on the schedule. She looked around Jimmy to check with her.

Sarah's normally pale skin was a rosy hue that resembled a flush from too much exertion. "Sarah? Are you okay?"

She winced slightly and tried to smile. "The Braxton-Hicks contractions are really bad today."

Casey looked at Jimmy. Maybe these weren't the small, preliminary contractions she'd read about. When was their due date again? A clammy feeling in her hands made her wipe them on her good skirt.

The pregnancy question fled her mind when Gwyneth stood up and made her way to the center aisle. Granted she was wearing spike heels, but did she have to rest her hand on Casey's husband's shoulder as she edged past him?

Model-thin, black suit with a skirt short enough to draw everyone's attention to her artfully sculpted legs. Straight back, chin high. Hair in an elegant twist that made her look like a force to be reckoned with.

"Gentlemen and ladies of the board, thank you for granting this hearing. My name is Gwyneth Jacobi. My law firm represents the turkey growers, GroWell Agriculture. I have a short PowerPoint program that I'd like to run for you." She turned to look over her shoulder at Philip—Philip!—who had moved to some AV equipment near where the planners were sitting.

Casey softly groaned and slunk down in her seat. Red's eyes narrowed and the furrow in his brow seemed to fold inward another inch or two, but he didn't say anything.

Casey watched the slides with a combination of awe and mortification. If you believed Gwyneth, raising turkeys was the cleanest, most environmentally friendly occupation in the world. "Yes, there are by-products and a certain amount of waste, but GroWell recognizes its responsibility to the world at large and to its neighbors. The bottom line is GroWell is coming to your county with a viable agricultural product that it plans to raise on land that is zoned agricultural. Who could possibly find fault in this?"

Her intonation made it sound as though only narrow-minded zealots would question such a great plan. And the look she exchanged with the cowboy-suit commissioner—the man hadn't taken his eyes off her the whole time she was speaking—said he agreed completely.

Casey groaned. How did Gwyneth know to target that particular supervisor? Had Nathan mentioned Casey's blunder to her? The idea made her queasy.

Red turned in his seat—to give his back to Gwyneth and rally the troops. "Okay, now, she's a city gal with no attachment to the land. All of that falderal was easy for her to say because she doesn't have to smell the dang stink. Now, let's give our side."

Our side? Our side sounded like a bunch of whiners. Our side didn't have one supportable argument other than the fact nobody wanted the birds around.

But that didn't mean they wouldn't try.

She consulted the list Sarah had produced and pointed at an eighty-year old woman in Wranglers, boots and a tucked-in shirt. "Maude, you're first. Give 'em heck."

The white-haired woman leaned over and squeezed Casey's shoulder. "We call it hell where I'm from—just like what it's going to be around here if those flapping birds go in."

Naturally, Maude's whisper was loud enough to be heard in the next meeting room over. Casey gave her a thumbs-up, then looked at Sarah. She was going to raise the question about putting Maude first, but the look on Sarah's face made her swallow her words. Something was wrong. Very wrong.

She elbowed Jimmy who was focused on Maude's impassioned speech. He elbowed her back.

"You folks got no right to force me and my mister out of the house we've lived in for forty-seven years. He's not well now. The body is willing but the mind gets confused a lot these days. If you take away what little he can connect with—the trees he planted when our littlest was born, the tractor he still tinkers with on his good days, all the things that we built up together, you're going to be signing his death warrant.

"I got nothing against turkeys—'cept they're the dumbest animals God saw fit to put on the Earth, but our place is just eight miles from this here farm. On a still night, I could hear old man Booth yellin' at the missus. I don't need no fancy slides to tell me the stink is going to travel just as far and as fast."

Casey was pleasantly pleased by the digs Maude had gotten in, but she doubted the old woman's plea would connect with the male members of the committee. But her main concern at the moment was Sarah.

"Jimmy, your wife is in pain. Could be labor."

The words seemed to jolt him into action. He turned to Sarah and they discussed her condition in low whispers. Finally he looked at his watch then turned to Casey. "The pains are coming real regular. Five minutes apart. Maybe I'd better take her to the hospital."

She rolled her eyes. "Ya think?" She reached around him and gave Sarah's arm a quick squeeze. "I'll text Jimmy's cell as soon as we know something."

The couple slipped out the side door just as Maude was finishing up. Casey applauded—until cowboy-suit guy reprimanded her. "This is not a high school debate. Members of the audience will please refrain from emotional outbursts."

Casey's cheeks ignited, and she was unlucky enough to spot Gwyneth's smirk. Crum. She called her next speaker. Joe Morisi. Her big gun. The sixtysomething farmer could buy and sell everyone on the board, but he was also a kind, very soft-spoken fellow with a shy manner that really didn't leave much of an impact on their opinions when he was done.

And so it went until her list was depleted and it was Casey's turn. She took her legal pad and approached the podium. A slim wand stuck out of the wooden stand. She set her notes in the allotted space and adjusted the microphone to her height.

She cleared her throat.

"Thank you for affording this opportunity to the residents of the county to make their feelings known. Unlike the paid representative who spoke on behalf of the turkey growers, I was born in this county and spent my formative years here. I floated down the creek on my homemade raft. I picked wildflowers to place on our table every Easter. I have only the most delightful memories of an idyllic childhood. Then I went away to school back East. I lived in a city. I learned a different side of life and felt attuned to it, but in coming back home to help my father with this campaign to save a way of life, I realized just how much of a country girl I am at heart."

She realized that her husband was hearing this for the first time and she felt bad about that, but she followed her instincts. "As all of the speakers who went before me have said, we're not here to ask you to rule against turkeys or agriculture. We're simply asking you to take into consideration the bigger picture. Cities are expanding at unprecedented rates. Landowners are selling out to developers for unprecedented profits. The farmers who spoke to you today are a dying breed. They honor the land, they live in harmony with their neighbors and they do their best to give back to their community. The multinational company that is geared to ram a million turkeys down our throats doesn't care about any of that. They care about making a profit."

Cowboy-suit guy, who had rocked back in his chair with arms crossed defiantly, snorted.

She zeroed in on him. "Making a profit is the American way. I don't have anything against that— unless you're hurting other people in the process. Can GroWell promise that their high-tech barns won't give off a stench so horrific it won't drive Maude and Taylor off their ranch? No. Can they promise to contain the runoff from their holding ponds and not pollute the surrounding vernal pond beds? No. They assure us that they will be good neighbors, but we all know the code of a good neighbor is to do unto others as you would have them do unto you. So, as soon as the CEO of GroWell builds a house beside one of his industrialize-size hatcheries, I'll back off."

Nathan had never been more proud of his wife. She spoke with passion, with logic and with heart. And one thing she said triggered an immediate reaction in his head. Vernal ponds. Where there are vernal ponds, there might be endangered species.

Kirby might have been able to help her cause. Now, there was a good chance Casey and her group were out of luck. The decision rested on the shoulders of the planning commissioners.

Fortunately, they didn't drag out the wait too long. Before the guy that Casey had pissed off could open his mouth, one of the women on the board said, "Thank you all for coming today. This strong turnout tells me we are not dealing with an open-and-shut case. I, for one, want more information before I approve or disapprove the petitioners' request for a conditional-use permit."

"Oh, come on, Sandy," the man in the gray suit said. "A little dog and pony show doesn't mean this company shouldn't be allowed to build on the land they bought and paid for. This is ridiculous."

Sandy turned to him with a fury that told Nathan she really disliked the man and probably never agreed with anything he said. "I make a motion to postpone for one week the application regarding—" She consulted her paperwork then rattled off the parcel number.

The majority of the board members agreed, but later, when Nathan overheard Sandy address Casey privately, she said, "Bring us some meat, Casey. Give us some solid proof why we should require a full EIR. Help us help you."

Solid proof. The kind Kirby might have. But what would that mean to his future? He just heard his wife publicly espouse the benefits of living in the country. He knew Casey. She wasn't just making a case for her side. She was home—until that home was no longer a viable option. And Nathan, who flourished on exhaust fumes and coffee shops on every corner, had to decide which cause he supported—hers or his own.

CHAPTER EIGHTEEN

JAMES RILEY MILLS was born shortly after one that same afternoon. Casey and Red had been pacing in the hospital waiting room, while Nathan worked on his laptop in a coffee shop across the street, where, unbelievably, they had a WiFi hookup.

She retrieved him once they got the okay to see Sarah.

"We're going to call him Riley," an exhausted-but-beautiful Sarah said, reclining in her hospital bed. Her hair was loose and the flowery gown she had on was one Casey her given her at a recent baby shower. Her eyes glittered with triumph and love. Mostly love.

"Isn't he the most incredible thing you've ever seen?" Jimmy asked from the overstuffed rocker beside the bed, where he was holding the tiny bundle of blanket-swathed child.

Casey leaned over his shoulder. Her fingers were actually shaking when she touched the soft pink cheek. The baby turned automatically toward her fingers, his lips opening and closing like a little fish. "Absolutely. He has your eyes, Sarah. And Jimmy's nose. And my lips."

The new parents chuckled. "He likes to eat. Took right to the breast—just like his old man."

Everyone laughed.

Nathan carried the large bouquet that he'd purchased at the hospital gift shop to the extra wide casement window. A perky blue balloon with the words *It's a boy!* bounced along in the air behind him.

"Thank you, Nathan. That was really sweet of you," Sarah said.

"You're welcome. I'm really happy for you both. Um, all three of you."

"Maybe you and Case will be next," Jimmy said, his gaze never leaving his new son.

Casey looked down. *Maybe sooner than you think,* she thought, hoping her blush didn't show. She'd felt different lately. Tempting though it was to blame the myriad pressures and changes in her life, more and more she was beginning to think she and Nathan might have gotten lucky.

Casey hadn't used the EPT test yet. A part of her was afraid to jinx the outcome. Silly, she knew, but Sarah would have understood *if* Casey had confided in her.

The reason she hadn't was simple. First, she needed to discuss the matter with her husband. And she made up her mind to do that as soon as they got back to the ranch. When he'd mentioned attending the hearing, she'd asked him to stay over in her new little house. He'd agreed.

"He's a cute little tyke, but we've probably been here long enough," Red said, looking uncomfortable. Casey wasn't sure if his uneasiness came from being in a hospital or from the birth. Losing your wife and unborn son could probably leave a pretty deep scar.

"Red's right. I'll be back on Saturday. Nathan and I are bringing the daughters of his colleague who had a heart attack down to the ranch for the weekend. The girls would love to see the baby, if you're up to it. I'll call first."

They left a few minutes later—Red in his truck, Nathan and Casey in their SUV. Nathan was driving.

"So, does this make you an aunt?"

She smiled. "I guess so. In a way. Dad certainly treats Jimmy like a son."

"Does that bother you?"

"It did. For years. Seemed patently unfair that I got sent away and the boy I was in the hayloft with moved into my rightful place in my father's life, but…"

"But what?"

She let out a long sigh. "I don't care anymore. Being jealous of Jimmy seems so pointless. There's enough of Red to share." She laughed. "Sometimes I think there's too much of him. And if you think about it, Dad really did deserve a son. If not for…well, he should have had one."

They didn't speak for a few miles, then Nathan said, "I never really thought about what that must have been like for your dad. To be up in the mountains with a six-year-old. No cell phones. His very-pregnant wife suddenly collapsing. I don't know if I could have recovered from that."

Casey closed her eyes, returning to that pivotal moment in her young life. A perfect day, really. The spring sun had been so bright and warm, unlike the fog-shrouded house they'd left behind. She'd been on her favorite horse, Katie, an older, sure-footed mare that loved kids. Her mother had planned a picnic.

"We won't go far," she'd told Red as they saddled the horses. "This might be the last time I ride for who knows how long, so don't be a spoilsport."

Her father, who could deny her mother nothing, had agreed to lead the way. Casey was in the middle. They'd barely covered half the distance to the waterfall that her mother had had in mind for their picnic when Casey's mother had stopped singing.

Casey and her father had both turned to see what was wrong. Abigail had one hand—the one not holding the reins—to her head and had let out a little peep. As if confused by something. Then she'd slumped forward in the saddle.

Casey didn't know how her father got to her mother before she fell, but somehow he'd caught her and pulled her limp, very pregnant body onto the saddle with him. His horse, a big, powerful gray named Shadow, wasn't used to carrying twice the load and wasn't particularly people-friendly in the first place.

Red kept calling her mother's name, but there was no answer. Casey couldn't tell if she was breathing or not. She could barely see through her tears, and her heart had been beating so fast and hard, her chest hurt.

"We gotta ride fast, little girl," Red said, turning back the way they'd come. "You keep up, you hear. If you don't keep up, your momma might die."

Casey had tried her best, but her horse was old. Every time he'd disappear out of sight, she'd scream in panic and he'd have to wait. Once he tried taking her reins to lead Katie, but neither horse would cooperate. Shadow didn't like another horse at his flank and Katie just didn't have the speed Red needed.

Prior to that day, Casey had never seen her father cry. She hadn't understood at first that his wet face was the product of tears until they reached the cabin. He'd carried Casey's mother to the truck then dashed back for Casey. As he carried her to the truck, she touched his cheek. Hot. She remembered the tears had almost scalded her fingers.

"For a long time. Years, actually. I thought I was the reason my baby brother died," Casey admitted.

The vehicle swerved slightly. "What do you mean?"

"Red told me if I didn't keep up Mom might die. I…I slowed him down. I was only six, and not that good a rider. He had to wait for me. Mom was still breathing when we got to the cabin, but then she stopped. I can still remember him calling her name. Over and over as we raced down the road."

She swallowed and opened her eyes. "When we got to the hospital, I was sitting on a chair not far from where they were working on her. They took the baby out and gave him CPR. I was sure he was going to live, but then the doctor shook his head and closed the curtain so I couldn't see any more. A few minutes later, he told Red that they might have had a chance to save the child if we'd gotten there even ten minutes sooner." She sighed. "Ten minutes. If it hadn't been for me, Red could have made that easy."

Nathan turned on the blinker.

Once they were off the highway, he slowed to a stop

and undid his seat belt so he could reach for her. "Oh, sweetheart, I'm so sorry. How come you've never talked about this?"

She shrugged. "I guess I put it out of my head, but seeing Sarah…little Riley…I don't know. The memories just came flooding back."

"Oh, honey. You were six. You were a little bitty girl on a big horse in the middle of nowhere. What happened was just bad luck."

His words weren't new. She'd told herself the same thing, but hearing them from a third party seemed to make all the difference. "Do you think that deep down I've had a psychological fear of getting pregnant? Maybe the real reason it didn't happen for us was me, not your sperm."

"You're too kind. But I had a long talk with my sperm and they told me they've been working out. Any time you're ready, they'd like to give it another go."

His playful tone was just what she needed to take away the residual horror of the past. She almost told him about her suspicion, but at the last second she didn't. Why get his hopes up until she knew for sure, right?

As NATHAN WANDERED around the small, neatly appointed house he felt a bit like Alice falling through the rabbit hole. The furniture was familiar but everything looked different.

They'd barely walked in the door when Jimmy called to ask Casey if she'd go to his place and pick up their infant car seat. A small but critical oversight. She'd changed clothes and raced out the door leaving Nathan alone.

The house itself was perfect—for Casey. He felt that truth and it made him a little sick. How did they get to the point where they had two homes? What would that kind of separation mean to them as a couple?

He didn't know the answers to his questions, but he didn't like the possibilities they presented. And the only way Nathan knew to deal with frustration was to sweat it out. If he were back in the city, he'd find a gym. Here, he didn't even know where to find a city, but on the floor of Casey's closet, he found his old running shoes, which must have gotten stuffed in one of her boxes by mistake.

He knew where to look for socks—Casey always liked to wear his to sleep in on chilly nights when he wasn't around to warm her toes.

He opened the top right bureau drawer. Sure enough. Two size-ten athletic socks rolled into a neat ball. As he grabbed one, his hand brushed a box. The simple oddity of the shape made him look at the label.

His breath caught in his throat. A pregnancy test. He'd seen more than his share over the past year and a half.

Maybe it was left over from before.

But when he picked it up, he spotted a sticker from a local pharmacy. His hand was shaking as he put it back in its partially hidden spot.

Secrets. Not with Casey. She was upfront, direct, honest. Or was she?

He sat down to put on his shoes and socks. He couldn't do anything about the Dockers, but at least he'd worn a white undershirt that morning. He tossed his coat, tie and dress shirt on the bed Casey's aunt had given them as a wedding gift.

He bolted from the house, making the fluffy puppy behind the gate jump up and start barking. He ignored the animal as he looked around, debating which way to go. His tendency was to take to the road, but a path leading into the orchard promised some shade. The road meant blacktop, traffic and exhaust fumes. He started off.

The infantile howl made him stop. Grinning, he turned around. "Okay, dog, you can go, but if you can't keep up I'm not carrying you. Got it?"

He could have sworn she nodded. Her whole tricolor body shook with delight when he opened the gate.

She shot off toward the trees without pause, making him regret his impetuous decision, but when she looked back and realized he wasn't with her, she skidded to a stop, raising a small cloud of dust.

Chuckling, he jogged to her. "Let's get the rules straight. I lead. You follow." Then he set out at a moderate pace.

The weather was a heck of a lot hotter than what he'd come to expect in the city. The breeze had a glass-blower's forge edge to it but he actually liked the way his blood seemed to quicken and stimulate his senses.

He had to keep a watchful eye on the pup because it didn't seem to have perfect depth perception and crossed into his path every few yards. But he was glad for the company. He didn't think he could get lost—the trees had to end sometime, right?

Right. If the map in his head was correct, he and the pup would eventually run into Red's property line and the utility road, beyond which turkey growers planned to build their megahatcheries. His inner GPS kicked in and he turned, startling his canine shadow into giving a sharp bark. An echoing call came from some distance off.

Red's place. And the wild bunch he'd been introduced to the last time he was down. He could do without a close encounter of the dog kind.

"Hush. We don't want to bring out the great thundering horde."

The yipping stopped. With luck, the other dogs would find something else to distract them.

He ran until he came to a fence. When he stopped, his shoes were pale mocha, his socks and the bottom of his Dockers a similar color. Pausing to catch his breath, he stared at the sprawling vista before him. Flat, but not even. Small hillocks covered in knee-high grasses that waved back and forth in the breeze looked friendly and unprepossessing. The kind of Dr. Seuss-like tuft a child might play on.

His and Casey's child, he wondered?

He couldn't make the picture come into focus. A baby on top of all his other responsibilities just seemed too much to ask of him. "I can't do it," he muttered. "Not now."

"But you don't have any choice," a voice said in his head. "You're the man of the family."

Some days he hated that voice. He remembered when he'd become conscious of it. His baby brother had just been born, and Nathan had been left home to care for Christine while their father went to the hospital to pick up their mother and new sibling.

Before leaving the house, Nathan's father had taken

him aside and said, "You know, Nathan, your mother and I are counting on you to take care of things."

And when his father had passed away, Nathan hadn't hesitated to do whatever was asked of him. He might have resented his mother's neediness, his siblings' demands at times, but he'd filled the role he'd been groomed to handle. Just like in the corporate world. Only now, he felt himself sinking beneath the Titanic weight of his obligations: to the staff in his office, to Gwyneth, Eric, Roz and her daughters, to Casey and Red, to his mother and siblings. Enough already, he wanted to cry.

The puppy, who was sitting patiently at his feet, gave a yip.

He realized he had spoken out loud. And it felt good. He looked around. *Nobody here but a dog.*

He took a breath then shouted, "Enough already."

The puppy cocked her head and looked at him as if he was truly mad. Maybe he was. If his life was spiraling out of control, he had nobody but himself to blame. He'd set this play in action by accepting the position in San Francisco. The scenario had made sense at the time. Coming full circle. Close enough to take care of his mother, his brother and sister. Just like his father had instructed.

The problem was he wasn't a little boy trying to fill too big a pair of shoes anymore. He wasn't his father.

Casey's soliloquy at the meeting that morning had made it clear that her goals, her choices, had changed since returning home to the Valley. Nathan had already suspected as much, but hearing her say the words out loud had rocked him. He'd wanted to talk to her about what that change meant to them as a couple, but she'd rushed off.

Nathan refused to believe that she was giving up on their marriage. Casey wasn't a quitter. Look how she'd stood by Red even after years of masking her hurt by distancing herself from the man, the ranch, this way of life.

Distancing herself to mask her hurt. Is that what she's doing now? With us?

He grabbed the closest fence post for support as his sudden epiphany rushed through him like a chill from a fever. Their inability to get pregnant had been humiliating to him but really devastating to Casey. She'd put on a brave face and made jokes about wasting money on years and years of birth control products. But deep down he'd known how badly she was hurting.

And what had he done to ease her pain? Nothing. He'd immersed himself in his work, accepted a job that took even more of his time, moved them to a new apartment she hated and asked a woman she disliked to work for him.

He looked down at the puppy sitting patiently by his feet. "I didn't even want her to have you."

The dog didn't have a tail to wag, so her whole backside moved with vigor when she looked at him. His heart squeezed in a way that made him think of Eric. "Life is precarious," he'd told Nathan when they brought the girls to visit their father. "You just never know, man. You're going along doing what's expected of you, then…blink. It's over. And you realize all those things you put off till you had more time just aren't gonna happen."

Like making your wife happy. Watching her wake up beside you every morning. Seeing her give birth.

Something had to change if he and Casey were going to pull out of this nosedive. He had to change.

He reached into the pocket of his slacks where he'd stashed his phone. He didn't expect to have service, but to his surprise, he had a clear signal. Four bars.

Sitting under the wispy shade of a full-grown pistachio tree, he said, "Kirby's cell."

"Kirby's cell," the mechanical voice answered. "Calling."

Two rings, then, "Hey, Nathan, Mom and I were just talking about you. We got the laundry issue ironed out," he added in a low whisper, then chuckled at his obviously unintentional pun. "Anyway. Today was Casey's big hearing, right? How'd it go?"

"She…we…got a reprieve. And I need a favor."

Nathan kept it short and simple. His brother was a grad student, he didn't need things spelled out.

"No problem. I've got your back, man."

Nathan mumbled a gruff goodbye, finding his throat suspiciously tight. He tried to attribute the prickly sensation across the top of his nose to dust, but when the pup launched herself into his arms and started licking his face, he had to admit that he was choked up by his brother's unequivocal support.

Maybe his family would have been there for him all along if he hadn't been so set on filling his father's shoes. He could picture Christine at age five, furious over some power struggle they'd been involved in at the time, yelling, "You're not the boss of me."

She was right. It had just taken a while for that truth to sink in. He was sick and tired of being the boss, but it wasn't too late to change. At least, he hoped it wasn't.

CHAPTER NINETEEN

NATHAN HAD just started back to the house when a mechanical roar filled the air. He picked up the puppy, just in case, and looked around. Seconds later, a green farm vehicle that looked like it should be carting luggage to and from planes roared to a stop at the end of his row.

Red, in a dusty white cowboy hat, was at the helm. Perched behind him on the open bed sat six dogs. The motley crew of unarmed banditos sent up a noisy, fearsome chorus of barks. The puppy in his arms tried clawing her way under his arm.

"Shut the heck up, you dumb an-i-mules," Red roared.

The dogs obeyed. All except Betsy. The grand dame had the last say with one mighty "Woof."

Nathan couldn't help but grin.

He walked toward the odd vehicle.

"Hop aboard my Gator," Red said. "You look a little winded. I got just the thing."

Thirty minutes later, the pair was sitting under Red's shady veranda staring at the hazy outline of the Sierra foothills in the distance. Nathan and Casey had shared a similar view the afternoon they'd spent at the old homestead. The afternoon they'd made love....

"So, things look pretty crappy for our side, huh?" Red asked, handing him a highball glass filled to the brim with a frothy white liquid that resembled something Nathan might order at Jamba Juice.

"Hard to tell," Nathan equivocated out of habit. He took a sip. The sweet, crisp taste was accompanied by a scent of pine. *Juniper berries.* Gin—not your typical smoothie, he thought with a grin.

Red made a snorting sound that caused Casey's pup to scoot under Nathan's chair, which prompted one of the other dogs that had staked out a certain spot of ground to growl.

Nathan leaned down and picked up the pup one-handed. She settled on his lap with a grateful sigh. It felt surprisingly natural to pet her fine, soft fur while Red ranted. "Lawyer types never can give a straight answer. Not a one of you. I never thought Casey would be that way, but lately she won't even look me in the eye."

Me, either, Nathan thought, picturing the pregnancy kit in her drawer. He still wasn't sure how he felt about that. Hell, he didn't even know if she'd bought it to have on hand for some future go at getting pregnant or…he pushed the thought aside and took another drink.

Better to talk business than think about things that might not be. "Do you know what fairy shrimp are?"

"I could say something but since you're from San Francisco, I won't," Red quipped.

"Thank you. To be honest, I don't know what they are, either, but if there's any chance they exist in the vernal ponds on the property under development, you might be able to get the environmentalists on your side."

Red gave him a skeptical look.

"My brother studies this kind of stuff. One of his teachers is an expert in the field. Even if the planning commission votes in favor of GroWell next week, Casey might be able to get a judge to issue an injunction if we can produce evidence that the habitat of certain endangered species would be threatened."

Red's bushy brows came together in a furrow. "We?"

Nathan felt himself flush under his father-in-law's scrutiny. "This might turn out to be nothing. Casey is an experienced litigator. I'm sure she considered this possibility, but she wasn't around to ask, so I thought, why not get Kirby's take on it?"

"And if it turns out to be something, where's that leave you? Something tells me your bosses ain't gonna appreciate you helpin' out the enemy."

Nathan took a long draw on his drink and closed his eyes to savor the coolness sliding down his parched throat. "I'm not sure I'll be working for them too much longer, anyway. Casey's made it pretty clear that she'd like to live around here, and I want to live with her."

There, he'd said it.

They drank in silence a few minutes with just the sound of swallows zipping past to their messy homes in the eaves of Red's outbuilding, the steady breeze that rustled the leaves of the yucca plant growing a few feet away and the on-and-off scuffle of the dogs as they jockeyed for a place closer to their master.

Nathan expected questions…or triumph. He got neither. When his glass was empty, he looked at his father-in-law and said, "You know, I never got to look at those house plans you put in our picnic basket that day. If we manage to fight off the great turkey menace, I have a feeling Casey and I might be looking for a new place to live. Her little house is nice, but it's kinda small." Especially if there's a baby on the way.

Red leaped to his feet, making the dogs scatter in every direction. "Wait here. I'll be right back."

Nathan eased back in his chair and pulled his phone from his pocket. He tried Casey first, but there still was no answer. He left a message telling her where he was, then he dialed Gwyneth's number.

She picked up on the first ring. "Gwyneth here."

"Hi. Are you in the office?"

"Of course. Made it in record time, but I think our junior associate had to go home to change his skivvies. The wimp."

Her chuckle sounded pure Gwyneth. In her element, triumphant after a positive performance at the hearing and cheating death on the highways. He actually felt sorry for Philip Kim. If Nathan were staying on at Silver, Reisbecht and Lane, he'd have made sure the bright young man saw some immediate advancement.

But he wasn't. Staying on. And he owed Gwyneth the courtesy of hearing his decision from his own lips.

"Gwyn, you handled things very well today. Erudite. Professional. No matter what the final outcome, nobody can say that you didn't give it your all."

"No matter what…? What the hell does that mean? You don't think we'll win? How is that possible? You were there today, Nathan. Those commissioners—the male ones, at least—were putty in my hands. There's no way they can't vote in our favor."

"Your client's favor," he reminded her. "We represent them. We *work* for the home office in Boston, which is three thousand miles away and has no real understanding of what California is facing in terms of land use issues and growth."

"So what? My job is to make sure my client wins."

"But what if they shouldn't?"

She was silent for so long Nathan thought they'd become disconnected. Until she asked, "What's going on, Nathan? Don't tell me your wife came crying to you after the meeting and you let your sympathy for her influence you."

Her tone made it easy to say, "Actually, Casey and I haven't talked about the case. She's the most ethical person I know. But listening to Red's neighbors today made me realize that change isn't always for the better."

"What's that mean?"

"I'm quitting SRL."

"No," she cried. "You can't. I'm not ready to take over. I need more time."

And since everything is about you... He let out a sigh. "Sorry, Gwyn, but life is too short to spend it all at work. I'd appreciate it if you'd keep this to yourself until I can submit my formal resignation. I want to call Nolan Reisbecht myself, but it's a little late today. I'll be in the office tomorrow to get the ball rolling."

"Nathan. This is insane. What will you do?"

He had no idea. Well, one idea. And it involved his wife. Red opened the door and walked out, a rolled-up sheaf of papers in his hands and a wide smile on his face. Nathan couldn't make everybody happy, but he'd obviously given his father-in-law a pleasant surprise—and possibly even a new lease on life.

"I've got to go, Gwyn. We'll talk tomorrow."

CASEY HAD RETURNED home to find Nathan missing. The puppy was gone, too. If they'd been in the city, she wouldn't have worried, but this was the country. And he was on foot. His jacket and tie were on the bed, his shoes neatly to one side of the dresser. *Barefoot?*

Hurrying to the portable phone on the bedside table, she punched in her father's number then walked to her dresser.

"Your husband is over here," Red said without preamble. He had caller ID so he always knew when she was on the other end of the line.

"Is he coming back or are you holding him hostage?"

Red's hoot almost made her smile. "Here. Ask him yourself."

As she waited for Nathan to come on the line, she opened her top drawer. She'd put this off long enough. But as she reached for the home testing kit, her hand started to shake.

Same place, but upside down—label out. She'd left it label down, so it wouldn't taunt her when she reached for her socks.

Nathan had been in her drawer.

"Hi, Case, your dad's teaching me how to make carnitas. We gotta feed a bunch a people. Mom and Kirby are coming."

Casey nearly dropped the phone. "Your mother is coming here? Today?"

"Uh-huh." To someone in the distance, he shouted, "How many limes do you want me to slice?"

The slight slur in his voice made Casey drop the pregnancy kit. "Nathan, are you drunk?"

"I don't think so, but your dad does make a mean fuzzy. I mean fizzy."

In the background, her father's laugh held a tone she hadn't heard for years. He sounded happy. Nathan sounded happy. Tipsy, but relaxed and having fun. "Come on over, Case. This is good stuff. How come we never make carnitas?"

"Um…because you don't like spicy food."

He blew out a raspberry of disapproval. "Well, that's gonna change. Lots of things are gonna change once we find the fairy shrimp."

Fairy shrimp? She knew what they were. She and Sarah had called a dozen leads hoping to find an expert who would testify that the endangered species existed on GroWell land, but none had been willing to stake their reputations on speculation alone. "Yes, the vernal ponds in your area do support a wide variety of fragile ecosystems that would be threatened if the kind of pollution you've described is introduced," one authority in the field had told her. "But without physical samples from ponds on the property, we couldn't say for sure."

"What are you talking about, Nathan?"

"Kirby. I called him. He and his professor…um, thesis advisor or whatever he's called, are going to find you a smoking gun."

Tears filled her eyes and her nose started to run. "Nathan, no. Your bosses might be able to overlook my involvement because this is my dad's property, but bringing in other members of your family? I don't think so. That's reckless, and that's not you."

He laughed and said to her father, who must have been standing nearby, "Red, your daughter doesn't think I'm reckless enough for her."

"That's not what I said."

Her father came on the line. "Maybe you don't know this guy as well as you thought. I'd get my butt over here in a hurry if I were you, Casey T. Things are changing. You gotta keep up."

Suddenly her knees couldn't support her any longer. She slowly sank to the carpet. *You gotta keep up, little girl.* She'd been trying. All her life.

Tears, hot and bitter, were in her eyes. She let go of the phone and curled in a ball, willing her mind to go blank. She closed her eyes. Maybe she slept, because the sound of a door slamming on the first floor made her heart jump. She sat up, dizzy and disoriented.

"Casey?" a voice called out.

Nathan?

She heard him taking the stairs two at a time, and then he was in her room, on one knee beside her. "What happened? Did you faint? Are you okay? Red said he was talking to you one minute then the line went dead."

He helped her get to her feet and sit on the bed. He left her long enough to get her a drink of water then returned. "You look wobbly. Maybe you should crawl into bed and call it a day."

"No. I can't. There's still so much to do."

He sat down beside her and put his arm around her shoulder. "Sure you can. I'm here. I'll handle things."

She closed her eyes and took a deep breath. His warmth and strength were intoxicating, seductive, but this was her cause, not his, and she couldn't let her father down. "I don't know what you meant about Kirby, but—"

He cut her off by pulling her backward until they were lying on their backs looking at the ceiling. "I'll tell you all about it later. The only thing that matters now is you and me."

He was right. She'd left him here alone this afternoon with the excuse that she had to pick up Riley's car seat. But after she'd dropped it off, she'd kept on driving, thinking. And she'd come to a decision. Baby or no baby, she loved her husband. Turkeys or no turkeys, she loved the country. Somehow, she would find a way to stay connected to the land, even if Nathan couldn't bring himself to give up the city. If Red was forced to sell out, maybe they could invest in a small farm in Marin or Napa. Somewhere close enough that she and Nathan—and, she hoped, their children—could join him on weekends.

"I think I might be pregnant," she said, her voice small and strained.

"I saw the test kit in your drawer. How sure are you?"

Ninety-nine-point-nine? Even though she'd never been pregnant before, she knew her body. The changes she'd been experiencing could be due to stress, but she didn't think so.

She sat up. Once the spinning stopped, she scrambled off the bed, picked up the kit and walked into the adjoining bathroom. She knew the drill. It only took a minute, but the wait took a little longer. She left the indicator on the tile counter and returned to her bedroom.

Nathan was sitting on the edge of the mattress, his elbows on his knees. "Your face is red," she told him. "Sunburn?"

"Probably. I went for a jog. Your dad rescued me."

"And got you drunk."

He looked up with a sheepish grin. "I don't think so. Just relaxed."

"Did you take my dog with you?"

"Uh-huh. She begged."

"Her name is Belle, by the way. It came to me while I was driving around...er, driving home today."

Casey changed into shorts and a T-shirt, then walked to where he was sitting. "Tell me what you're thinking? Do you want it to be positive or negative?"

He turned to look at her. His eyes were clear and the look in them intense. "What do you think I went through all those tests for in Boston? That I was humoring you? Just being a good sport?" He gripped her shoulders and squeezed gently. "I love you, Casey. I want a baby. Nine months from now would be great."

"Really?"

He kissed her. "Really. The house won't be finished, but that's okay. This place will do till then."

"W...what house?"

He grinned with a wicked, teasing wink. "You'll see. Has it been long enough?" He stood up and pulled her to her feet. They walked to the bathroom together, which was a good thing because Casey's nerves were making her light-headed again.

Nathan picked up the indicator and held it between them so they both could read the very bold plus sign. Casey started to cry. Nathan swept her into his arms, lifting her off her feet.

"We're pregnant, Casey T. We did it. We're going to have a baby."

He crushed her to his chest and tenderly kissed her lips, her nose, her tears. "I love you, my wife. And I promise I'll do whatever it takes to make our life—our child's life—a happy one."

"Oh, Nathan," Casey cried. "I want that, too, but we—"

He kissed her again. "No buts. I mean it. We have a few logistics to work out, but we will. We have our families in our corner and our love to make sure we do the right thing."

She wanted so desperately to believe him that she didn't mention the obstacles—the turkeys, his job and Gwyneth, for starters. She let him hold her and kiss her and weave a wondrous spell of possibilities around her…until the phone rang.

It was Red.

"People are arriving. Get your butts over here," he commanded loud enough for Casey to hear, even though Nathan had answered the call.

By the time they reached the ranch, there were four extra vehicles scattered about, including Jimmy's truck, which she'd last seen at the hospital five hours earlier. Parked beside it was Doc's mobile vet clinic, followed by a compact sedan she couldn't place, and a bright-red Mustang a few feet away.

"My 'stang," Nathan exclaimed. "Look at it shine."

"You let Kirby drive your car?" she exclaimed.

"Why not?" Nathan answered with a shrug before taking her hand to lead her inside.

The festive atmosphere struck her the instant she stepped through the door. Her father was pouring frosty slush into two salt-rimmed margarita glasses for Doc and Joan, who shared the bench seat at the counter. Kirby and a man Casey had never seen before were attacking a roasted hunk of meat, each armed with long forks and carving knives.

In the corner, sitting in a rocking chair that had been pulled into the room, was Sarah, with Jimmy behind her, hovering like the proud, protective daddy he was.

Although she felt guilty about not greeting her mother-in-law first, Casey hurried to where Sarah was sitting. "What are you doing here? I knew you said the hospital was releasing you today, but I thought you'd go home."

Sarah smiled. "We only stopped by for a minute. Jimmy is making me go home to bed, even though I feel great. But Red said he had a present for Riley, and you know your dad."

She did. Turning to locate her father, she called, "Dad? What were you thinking making Sarah and Jimmy stop here? She just gave birth. She needs to rest."

Red set down the margarita pitcher and walked toward her. "But Sarah's as much a part of this as you are, Casey T. She deserved to be here when the big guns arrived to save the day."

"What big guns?"

The sound of a throat clearing made her turn. "Hmm, that would be me," Kirby said, a blush claiming his youthful cheeks. "And Dr. Henderson." He made a bowing gesture toward the balding man at his side. "Dr. H. rode down with Mom. They were afraid to ride with me in the Mustang. Can you believe that?"

"Survival instinct," Casey's mother-in-law said crisply. "You should know all about that, being an environmentalist. Hello, Casey, it's good to see you."

Casey gave Joan Kent a hug. "I'm so sorry I haven't—"

Joan waved aside Casey's apology, margarita in hand. "You've been busy. Doc has been filling me in on what's been going on around here."

"Um…what exactly *is* going on?"

Kirby grinned. "Your husband has come over from the dark side," he said with a playful wink.

"Chow time," Red's booming voice called.

Riley, startled by the sound, let out a loud wail. Sarah comforted the baby then looked at Jimmy and said, "Bring me food. Now. I'm not going anywhere until you feed me."

Nathan and Jimmy both bolted, leaving Casey and Sarah alone. Casey was tempted to share her good news, but it was too soon. Today was Sarah's day. And Riley's. Casey's fingers itched to hold him.

"Are you sure it's okay for you to be here?"

Sarah let her head fall back against the padded chair. "Never felt better in my life. A little tired and sore, but mostly I'm just starved."

Jimmy returned with a plate piled high with steaming, shredded pork and toppings. He set the plate on Sarah's lap then took Riley from her and transferred the tiny baby to Casey. "The hospital wanted to keep them overnight," he said in a low voice. "But Sarah convinced her doctor she'd get more rest at home. And, believe me, I intend to see she gets it as soon as we leave here."

Casey tightened her grip on the warm little body in her arms. The blue cotton blanket was wrapped snuggly about his body leaving no room for flailing arms. Sarah had explained that current wisdom held that babies liked to be confined since it reminded them of the womb. She wasn't sure she believed that, but until she had her own…

Tear filled her eyes.

"Case, are you okay?"

She looked at her friends, who actually seemed comfortable with each other again. Maybe Riley's birth had been the turning point for them. Casey hoped so. They were so right for each other. Just like her and Nathan. "Uh-huh. Just emotional. He smells so sweet and perfect."

"Our turn next," Nathan said, putting his arm around her. Their gazes met and his smile grew to a heartbreakingly joyous grin that surely would have broadcast their news if anyone had been looking. Fortunately, everyone was intently digging into their meal.

Half an hour later, after Red had bestowed a plethora of gifts that included a stuffed bear twenty times bigger than Riley and a gift certificate from the same breeder who had raised Belle and Betsy—"Every boy needs a dog"—the new family left.

That's when their guests of honor—the big guns—took the floor. Dr. H, as he asked to be called, was in his late fifties. He wore camouflage cargo pants, hiking boots and a loose-fitting vest worn over a Save-The-Wetlands T-shirt.

"When Kirby called this afternoon, I did a quick scan of your area from field maps we have on our database. Although this area is rife with vernal ponds that most likely provide habitat for the fairy shrimp, we've seen big business get around that argument by promising to set aside environmentally protected areas. What I'm hoping to discover is habitat of the bull-nosed spotted salamander. This, my friends, could indeed be your ultimate silver bullet."

Casey shook her head. "Sarah and I tried to get permission to take soil and water samples from the GroWell land and they turned us down."

"Which is why we're going to explore the parts of your father's land that haven't been converted to orchards and other adjoining properties. If endangered species exist in parcels A, C and D, then we can surmise that they'd likely exist in parcel B."

Casey took a bite of the burrito Nathan had made her. "I'm familiar with the argument," she said after chewing and swallowing. The spicy flavor went down easily, despite the frequent bouts of nausea she'd been experiencing. "We talked about how to force the county into demanding a full EIR and decided we lacked the manpower and expertise to do the legwork. If the collection isn't done correctly, we run the risk of having the evidence thrown out."

"That was before your husband jumped ship and called in reinforcements," Red said.

"'*Jumped ship*'?"

"Bring your wife up to speed, son," Red chided Nathan. "The rest of the troops are gatherin' at Maude's place. We gotta git over there before we lose our light."

Casey's heart was racing, but she wasn't sure if her primary emotion was hurt, anger or fear. Red had done it again—usurped her control, sent her packing. Not literally, like last time, but he obviously was running things, now. But what worried her most was that Red had somehow dragged Nathan into the mix.

She waited until the room was empty before she turned to her husband and said, "Nathan, I don't know what all of this means, but I do know that if you don't distance yourself from this mess right away, your career will be down the toilet. If word gets out that you helped us…"

He shrugged. "Word already is out, Casey. I called Gwyneth. She claims she isn't a spy, but I can almost guarantee that Boston knows by now. I'm giving my formal resignation tomorrow."

"Your resignation?"

"Having two residences—one in the city, one in the country—isn't working for me. And since I married a country girl, I'm going to give this place a try. It's the least I can do since you did the same for me."

"I did?"

"You made a good life for us in Boston. You threw yourself into that lifestyle with such enthusiasm you made me think you were happy. But you weren't. Not deep down."

"Nathan, no…I loved Boston. Meg and—"

He stopped her. "I'm not denying that you loved your aunt. And me. But you've blossomed since you moved back to this valley. It's almost as though a part of you was still here—on the land. I can't say I feel the same way, but I do feel something. I don't want to see Red lose this place. I want our children to know what running barefoot with a pack of wild mutts is like."

"But the city. You'll miss it."

He smiled. "That's what four-star hotels are for, my dear. Any time I need to see a museum or I crave an honest-to-goodness espresso, I know where to find it."

"What about your career?"

"Your father was telling me about a friend of his who is thinking about retirement. He's a judge now, but still has his fingers in a little practice that might be right up my alley." He leaned down and kissed her. "Right up *our* alley. I could use someone who's good with people and knows the lay of the land, so to speak."

She blinked back tears. "I appreciate what you're trying to do. I mean that. You made a noble sacrifice, but don't you think I thought of this EIR option? This is my job, Nathan. I called half a dozen experts and was told that even if we found an active colony of extinct dodo birds nesting on the ranch, all GroWell has to do is promise to set aside a tract of land to appease the environmentalists."

She paced to the sliding glass door and looked out. "The only truly effective deal-breaker is public outcry. You get that by effective use of the press. I tried. The papers aren't that interested. Turkeys. Big deal."

"What if there was a scandal? Say GroWell never

intended to build a hatchery on that land but wanted to make it look that way so another county would give them tax breaks and other perks."

She spun around. "You know about the Mono County plan?"

His stunned look told her he hadn't expected her question. "Of course, but how the hell did you hear about it?"

She looked down. "I'd rather not say."

"Eric."

"It wasn't Eric."

Roz. Of course. Unlike he and Casey, the couple talked business all the time. "Jeez, Casey, if you knew about GroWell's Plan B, why haven't you done something with it? This planning board would be outraged to find out they were being played. There would be talk of tar and turkey feathers."

"Because GroWell is buying that other parcel through a holding company. I tried to find a concrete link through the usual channels, but there wasn't one. Or if there was, I couldn't find it in the time I had to work with. There was no way I could wave that flag without everyone assuming I got inside information from you. Your reputation would have been ruined. I couldn't do that to you, Nathan. I love you."

She chose him over the land. Over her father. Over the expectations of everyone around her. She had been prepared to disappoint Red to save him.

He took her in his arms. "You're my hero, Casey T., but if it's okay with you, I think we should call a press conference."

"We?"

"As your father so aptly put it, I jumped ship."

"But being made partner of Silver, Reisbecht and Lane has been your goal for as long as I've known you."

"Being a partner in a prestigious law firm is one thing. Being a partner with you is another. I love you, Casey Tibbs Buchanan-Kent. I love being married to you and spending time with you. And I would do anything to keep us together and happy. We can be happy again, can't we?"

She looked at him as if he'd lost his mind. "Again? I've never *not* been happy being married to you, Nathan. Things got a little crazy for a while, but I never stopped loving you."

He hugged her tight. "That's my Casey T. Is it time to start thinking up baby names?"

She kissed him—an open-ended invitation that robbed him of the ability to worry, then she added, "We have time. After all, some names only fit after you meet the baby. We'll know for sure who this little person is eight months from now."

"I can't wait, but we have a lot to do to get ready for him or her. A house to build. A business to set up. If Eric resigns from SRL, as I think he will, I might ask him to join us. He and Roz definitely want to get out of the city and…"

Casey linked their arms together and started leading the way to the car. They already had a temporary house—and a bed that needed christening. She'd be at his side every step of this new adventure. And Abigail Margaret Kent—plus any future siblings her parents might provide—would be there, too.

She'd lied, of course. The moment she'd realized for certain she was pregnant—maybe even before that instant—she'd known the name of the baby growing within her. Abigail Margaret. As her father once told her, some names just fit.

EPILOGUE

One year later

NATHAN LOOKED AROUND and couldn't help but feel proud. Together, he and Casey had pulled it off. Today was the grand opening of Kent and Mathers Law Offices in a refurbished brick building just off Robertson Boulevard in Chowchilla.

His whole family was here. Joan was holding three-month-old Abby, dressed in lavender frills that she seemed to tolerate for her grandmother's sake alone. Instead of moving into an adult-living center, Joan had taken up Casey's job offer: part-time nanny to Abby. His mother had moved into the little house Red had built for Casey just weeks after Nathan and Casey moved out. Their newly completed home, which sported wraparound verandas and had a great view of the foothills, was nestled beneath the stately palms of the original homestead.

"Looking good, isn't it?" Eric asked, beaming.

Thirty pounds lighter and strikingly fit, Eric had come through his near miss with flying colors. He'd embraced every healthful dietary habit his wife suggested, including downsizing. When Nathan suggested a partnership in a small town in the Central Valley, they'd jumped at the offer.

"Come on, you two," Roz called. "Photo op." With the help of Eric's daughters, the men playfully snipped the ribbon at the door of the offices. Then both families posed for the reporter from the local paper.

After Casey hustled their guests inside for coffee and cake, she grabbed Nathan's hand. "Jimmy and Sarah are anxious to leave. You're sure you're okay with us babysitting Riley overnight?"

"Jim's anxious to leave," he corrected. "I don't think Sarah is all that thrilled about leaving her baby boy behind."

Casey tossed her head and laughed. "Wrong. As a breastfeeding mom, I can assure you that the first chance I get to run away for a romantic tryst after Abby is weaned, I will be the one pulling you out the door."

After the exchange of diaper bags and contact information, Sarah handed Riley to Nathan. Holding the twenty-three pound toddler, who was dressed in cowboy boots and snap-crotch jeans, made Nathan realize how fast babies grow and change.

As if picking up on his emotional state, Sarah stood on her toes to plant a peck on Riley's cheek. "Isn't it amazing how things worked out? A year ago, I never could have predicted that we'd all be together—good friends with two babies. I'm so happy I could cry."

"Does that mean you don't want to go on our trip?" Jimmy asked.

Casey kicked him playfully. "Don't be a boob. Of course she wants to go. That's just hormones talking.

And unless you want Riley to have a sibling sooner than you'd planned, you'd better be careful. These maternal juices are potent things—and contagious. Nathan is already planning for child number two."

"I'm not surprised," Sarah said, wiping away a tear. "The only father who dotes on his kid more than Nathan dotes on Abby is Jimmy."

Casey agreed. Their husbands were turning into amazing fathers. And Red, who'd bounced back after his cancer treatments with his usual orneriness, was "Grandpa" to all the children in their newfound community—Riley, Abby and the Mathers girls. He and Joan shared babysitting duties on the three mornings a week that Casey worked in the law office.

Casey had worried that Joan would be homesick for Sacramento, especially since she was used to being so close to Christine and Kirby. But everyone had adapted to the change. Chris and her family visited the ranch at least one weekend a month, and Kirby, who'd graduated a few months earlier, had just accepted a teaching position at the new university in Merced.

Although GroWell was history, there were plenty of other land issues to keep Casey busy once she'd attained permission to practice law in California. She'd begged Nathan not to burn any bridges when he quit Silver, Reisbecht and Lane, but he'd explained his position to Gwyneth quite succinctly. If GroWell persisted in the application, he'd alert the media to their unethical practices. The company dropped their plans to build and promptly sold the property—for a substantial profit— to a farmer who planned to grow organic wine grapes.

Gwyneth had taken over the San Francisco office after Eric and Nathan left, but according to Roz, who remained in touch with several of her husband's ex-colleagues at SRL, she hadn't even lasted the month. The barracuda was back in Boston.

Casey had expected to feel relief when her beautiful nemesis left the west coast, but, in truth, she'd been too happy—and busy—to notice. Her life was chaotic at times, Abby and Red made sure of that, but, at least now, she didn't have to worry about keeping up. Not with Nathan at her side.

* * * * *

Look for Debra Salonen's
next Superromance story,
"THE MAX FACTOR,"
in the anthology, WHO NEEDS CUPID?
available in January 2007,
wherever Harlequin Superromance books are sold.

Design Tip of the Day

Ambience is everything. Imagine eating a foie gras at a luncheonette counter or a side of coleslaw at Le Cirque. It's not a matter of food but one of atmosphere. Remember that when planning your dining room design.
—Tips from *Teddi.com*

"Now that's the kind of man you should be looking for," my mother, the self-appointed keeper of my shelf-life stamp, says. She points with her fork at a man in the corner of the Steak-Out Restaurant, a dive I've just been hired to redecorate. Making this restaurant look four-star will be hard, but not half as hard as getting through lunch without strangling the woman across the table from me. "*He* would make a good husband."

"Oh, you can tell that from across the room?" I ask, wondering how it is she can forget that when we had trouble getting rid of my last husband, she shot him. "Besides being ten minutes away from death if he actually eats all that steak, he's twenty years too old for me and—shallow woman that I am—twenty pounds too heavy. Besides, I am *so* not looking for another husband here. I'm looking to design a new image for this place, looking for some sense of ambience, some feeling, something I can build a proposal on for them."

My mother studies the man in the corner, tilting her head, the better to gauge his age, I suppose. I think she's grimacing, but with all the Botox and Restylane injected into that face, it's hard to tell. She takes another bite of her steak salad, chews slowly so that I don't miss the fact that the steak is a poor cut and tougher than it should be. "You're concentrating on the wrong kind of proposal," she says finally. "Just look at this place, Teddi. It's a dive. There are hardly any other diners. What does *that* tell you about the food?"

"That they cater to a dinner crowd and it's lunchtime," I tell her.

I don't know what I was thinking bringing her here with me. I suppose I thought it would be better than eating alone. There really are days when my common sense goes on vacation. Clearly, this is one of them. I mean, really, did I not resolve less than three weeks ago that I would not let my mother get to me anymore?

What good are New Year's resolutions, anyway?

Mario approaches the man's table and my mother studies him while they converse. Eventually Mario leaves the table with a huff, after which the diner glances up and meets my mother's gaze. I think she's smiling at him. That or she's got indigestion. They size each other up.

I concentrate on making sketches in my notebook and try to ignore the fact that my mother is flirting. At nearly seventy, she's developed an unhealthy interest in members of the opposite sex to whom she isn't married.

According to my father, who has broken the TMI rule and given me Too Much Information, she has no interest in sex with him. Better, I suppose, to be clued in on what they aren't doing in the bedroom than have to hear what they might be doing.

"He's not so old," my mother says, noticing that I have barely touched the Chinese chicken salad she warned me not to get. "He's got about as many years on you as you have on your little cop friend."

She does this to make me crazy. I know it, but it works all the same. "Drew Scoones is not my little 'friend.' He's a detective with whom I—"

"Screwed around," my mother says. I must look shocked, because my mother laughs at me and asks if I think she doesn't know the "lingo."

What I thought she didn't know was that Drew and I actually tangled in the sheets. And, since it's possible she's just fishing, I sidestep the issue and tell her that Drew is just a couple of years younger than me and that I don't need reminding. I dig into my salad with renewed vigor, determined to show my mother that Chinese chicken salad in a steak place was not the stupid choice it's proving to be.

After a few more minutes of my picking at the wilted leaves on my plate, the man my mother has me nearly engaged to pays his bill and heads past us toward the back of the restaurant. I watch my mother take in his shoes, his suit and the diamond pinkie ring that seems to be cutting off the circulation in his little finger.

"Such nice hands," she says after the man is out of sight. "Manicured." She and I both stare at my hands. I have two popped acrylics that are being held on at weird angles by bandages. My cuticles are ragged and there's marker decorating my right hand from measuring carelessly when I did a drawing for a customer.

Twenty minutes later she's disappointed that he managed to leave the restaurant without our noticing. He will join the list of the ones I let get away. I will hear about him twenty years from now when—according to my mother—my children will be grown and I will still be single, living pathetically alone with several dogs and cats.

After my ex, that sounds good to me.

The waitress tells us that our meal has been taken care of by the management and, after thanking Mario, the owner, complimenting him on the wonderful meal and assuring him that once I have redecorated his place people will be flocking here in droves (I actually use those words and ignore my mother when she rolls her eyes), my mother and I head for the restroom.

My father—unfortunately not with us today—has the patience of a saint. He got it over the years of living with my mother. She, perhaps as a result, figures he has the patience for both of them, and feels justified having none. For her, no rules apply, and a little thing like a picture of a man on the door to a public restroom is certainly no barrier to using the john. In all fairness, it does seem silly to stand and wait for the ladies' room if no one is using the men's room.

Still, it's the idea that rules don't apply to her, signs don't apply to her, conventions don't apply to her. She knocks on the door to the men's room. When no one answers she gestures to me to go in ahead. I tell her that I can certainly wait for the ladies' room to be free and she shrugs and goes in herself.

Not a minute later there is a bloodcurdling scream from behind the men's room door.

"Mom!" I yell. "Are you all right?"

Mario comes running over, the waitress on his heels. Two customers head our way while my mother continues to scream.

I try the door, but it is locked. I yell for her to open it and she fumbles with the knob. When she finally manages to unlock and open it, she is white behind her two streaks of blush, but she is on her feet and appears shaken but not stirred.

"What happened?" I ask her. So do Mario and the waitress and the few customers who have migrated to the back of the place.

She points toward the bathroom and I go in, thinking it serves her right for using the men's room. But I see nothing amiss.

She gestures toward the stall, and, like any self-respecting and suspicious woman, I poke the door open with one finger, expecting the worst.

What I find is worse than the worst.

The husband my mother picked out for me is sitting on the toilet. His pants are puddled around his ankles, his hands are hanging at his sides. Pinned to his chest is some sort of Health Department certificate.

Oh, and there is a large, round, bloodless bullet hole between his eyes.

Four Nassau County police officers are securing the area, waiting for the detectives and crime scene personnel to show up. They are trying, though not very hard, to comfort my mother, who in another era would be considered to be suffering from the vapors. Less tactful in the twenty-first century, I'd say she was losing it. That is, if I didn't know her better, know she was milking it for everything it was worth.

My mother loves attention. As it begins to flag, she swoons and claims to feel faint. Despite four No Smoking signs, my mother insists it's all right for her to light up because, after all, she's in shock. Not to mention that signs, as we know, don't apply to her.

When asked not to smoke, she collapses mournfully in a chair and lets her head loll to the side, all without mussing her hair.

Eventually, the detectives show up to find the four patrolmen all circled around her, debating whether to administer CPR, smelling salts or simply call the paramedics. I, however, know just what will snap her to attention.

"Detective Scoones," I say loudly. My mother parts the sea of cops.

"We have to stop meeting like this," he says lightly to me, but I can feel him checking me over with his eyes, making sure I'm all right while pretending not to care.

"What have you got in those pants?" my mother asks

him, coming to her feet and staring at his crotch accusingly. "*Baydar*? Everywhere we Bayers are, you turn up. You don't expect me to buy that this is a coincidence, I hope."

Drew tells my mother that it's nice to see her, too, and asks if it's his fault that her daughter seems to attract disasters.

Charming to be made to feel like the bearer of a plague. He asks how I am.

"Just peachy," I tell him. "I seem to be making a habit of finding dead bodies, my mother is driving me crazy and the catering hall I booked two freakin' years ago for Dana's bat mitzvah has just been shut down by the Board of Health!"

"Glad to see your luck's finally changing," he says, giving me a quick squeeze around the shoulders before turning his attention to the patrolmen, asking what they've got, whether they've taken any statements, moved anything, all the sort of stuff you see on TV, without any of the drama. That is, if you don't count my mother's threats to faint every few minutes when she senses no one's paying attention to her.

Mario tells his waitstaff to bring everyone espresso, which I decline because I'm wired enough. Drew pulls him aside and a minute later I'm handed a cup of coffee that smells divinely of Kahlúa.

The man knows me well. Too well.

His partner, whom I've met once or twice, says he'll interview the kitchen staff. Drew asks Mario if he minds if he takes statements from the patrons first and gets to him and the waitstaff afterward.

"No, no," Mario tells him. "Do the patrons first." Drew raises his eyebrow at me like he wants to know if I get the double entendre. I try to look bored.

"What is it with you and murder victims?" he asks me when we sit down at a table in the corner.

I search them out so that I can see you again, I almost say, but I'm afraid it will sound desperate instead of sarcastic.

My mother, lighting up and daring him with a look to tell her not to, reminds him that *she* was the one to find the body.

Drew asks what happened *this time*. My mother tells him how the man in the john was "taken" with me, couldn't take his eyes off me and blatantly flirted with both of us. To his credit, Drew doesn't laugh, but his smirk is undeniable to the trained eye. And I've had my eye trained on him for nearly a year now.

"While he was noticing you," he asks me, "did *you* notice anything about him? Was he waiting for anyone? Watching for anything?"

I tell him that he didn't appear to be waiting or watching. That he made no phone calls, was fairly intent on eating and did, indeed, flirt with my mother. This last bit Drew takes with a grain of salt, which was the way it was intended.

"And he had a short conversation with Mario," I tell him. "I think he might have been unhappy with the food, though he didn't send it back."

Drew asks what makes me think he was dissatisfied, and I tell him that the discussion seemed acrimonious and that Mario looked distressed when he left the table.

Drew makes a note and says he'll look into it and asks about anyone else in the restaurant. Did I see anyone who didn't seem to belong, anyone who was watching the victim, anyone looking suspicious?

"Besides my mother?" I ask him, and Mom huffs and blows her cigarette smoke in my direction.

I tell him that there were several deliveries, the kitchen staff going in and out the back door to grab a smoke. He stops me and asks what I was doing checking out the back door of the restaurant.

Proudly—because, while he was off forgetting me, dropping by only once in a while to say hi to Jesse, my son, or drop something by for one of my daughters that he thought they might like, I was getting on with my life—I tell him that I'm decorating the place.

He looks genuinely impressed. "Commercial customers? That's great," he says. Okay, that's what he *ought* to say. What he actually says is, "Whatever pays the bills."

"Howard Rosen, the famous restaurant critic, got her the job," my mother says. "You met him—the good-looking, distinguished gentleman with the *real* job, something to be proud of. I guess you've never read his reviews in *Newsday*."

Drew, without missing a beat, tells her that Howard's reviews are on the top of his list, as soon as he learns how to read.

"I only meant—" my mother starts, but both of us assure her that we know just what she meant.

"So," Drew says. "Deliveries?"

I tell him that Mario would know better than I, but that I saw vegetables come in, maybe fish and linens.

"This is the second restaurant job Howard's got her," my mother tells Drew.

"At least she's getting *something* out of the relationship," he says.

"If he were here," my mother says, ignoring the insinuation, "he'd be comforting her instead of interrogating her. He'd be making sure we're both all right after such an ordeal."

"I'm sure he would," Drew agrees, then looks me in the eyes as if he's measuring my tolerance for shock. Quietly he adds, "But then maybe he doesn't know just what strong stuff your daughter's made of."

It's the closest thing to a tender moment I can expect from Drew Scoones. My mother breaks the spell. "She gets that from me," she says.

Both Drew and I take a minute, probably to pray that's all I inherited from her.

"I'm just trying to save you some time and effort," my mother tells him. "My money's on Howard."

Drew withers her with a look and mutters something that sounds suspiciously like "fool's gold." Then he excuses himself to go back to work.

I catch his sleeve and ask if it's all right for us to leave. He says sure, he knows where we live. I say goodbye to Mario. I assure him that I will have some sketches for him in a few days, all the while hoping that this murder doesn't cancel his redecorating plans. I need the money desperately, the alternative being borrowing from my parents and being strangled by the strings.

My mother is strangely quiet all the way to her house.

She doesn't tell me what a loser Drew Scoones is—despite his good looks—and how I was obviously drooling over him. She doesn't ask me where Howard is taking me tonight or warn me not to tell my father about what happened because he will worry about us both and no doubt insist we see our respective psychiatrists.

She fidgets nervously, opening and closing her purse over and over again.

"You okay?" I ask her. After all, she's just found a dead man on the toilet, and tough as she is that's got to be upsetting.

When she doesn't answer me I pull over to the side of the road.

"Mom?" She refuses to meet my eyes. "You want me to take you to see Dr. Cohen?"

She looks out the window as if she's just realized we're on Broadway in Woodmere. "Aren't we near Marvin's Jewelers?" she asks, pulling something out of her purse.

"What have you got, Mother?" I ask, prying open her fingers to find the murdered man's ring.

"It was on the sink," she says in answer to my dropped jaw. "I was going to get his name and address and have you return it to him so that he could ask you out. I thought it was a sign that the two of you were meant to be together."

"He's dead, Mom. You understand that, right?" I ask. You never can tell when my mother is fine and when she's in la-la land.

"Well, I didn't know that," she shouts at me. "Not at the time."

I ask why she didn't give it to Drew, realize that she

wouldn't give Drew the time in a clock shop and add, "...or one of the other policemen?"

"For heaven's sake," she tells me. "The man is dead, Teddi, and I took his ring. How would that look?"

Before I can tell her it looks just the way it is, she pulls out a cigarette and threatens to light it.

"I mean, really," she says, shaking her head like it's my brains that are loose. "What does he need with it now?"

In February, expect **MORE**
from

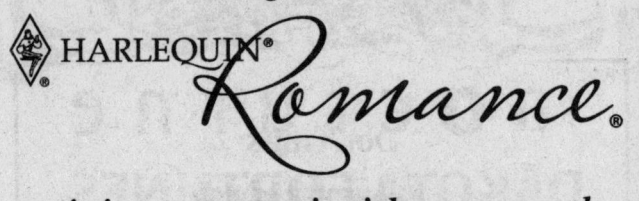

HARLEQUIN® *Romance*®

as it increases to six titles per month.

What's to come...

Rancher and Protector

Part of the

Western Weddings

miniseries

BY JUDY CHRISTENBERRY

The Boss's Pregnancy Proposal

BY RAYE MORGAN

Don't miss February's
incredible line up of authors!

Don't miss
DAKOTA FORTUNES,
**a six-book continuing series following
the Fortune family of South Dakota—
oil is in their blood and privilege
is their birthright.**

This series kicks off with
USA TODAY bestselling author

PEGGY MORELAND'S
Merger of Fortunes
(SD #1771)
this January.

USA TODAY bestselling author

ANN MAJOR

He always got what he wanted.

Pierce Carver was one of Austin's most successful surgeons. He was going to marry trauma nurse Rose Marie Castle and put her aching feet into glass slippers. But he couldn't give up his womanizing ways, so he jilted Rose Marie....

Then someone wanted him dead.

Things were looking bad for Rose Marie. After her ex was murdered she became the prime suspect. Worse, her high school sweetheart was the investigating detective. But if Rose Marie didn't kill the not-so-good doctor, who did?

THE SECRET LIVES
OF DOCTORS' WIVES

"Ann Major's name on the cover instantly
identifies the book as a good read."
—*New York Times* bestselling author Sandra Brown

*Available the first week of December 2006,
wherever paperbacks are sold!*

MIRA®   www.MIRABooks.com   MAM2346

REQUEST YOUR FREE BOOKS!

2 FREE NOVELS PLUS 2 FREE GIFTS!

HARLEQUIN®

Super Romance®

Exciting, emotional, unexpected!

YES! Please send me 2 FREE Harlequin Superromance® novels and my 2 FREE gifts. After receiving them, if I don't wish to receive any more books, I can return the shipping statement marked "cancel." If I don't cancel, I will receive 6 brand-new novels every month and be billed just $4.69 per book in the U.S., or $5.24 per book in Canada, plus 25¢ shipping and handling per book and applicable taxes, if any*. That's a savings of close to 15% off the cover price! I understand that accepting the 2 free books and gifts places me under no obligation to buy anything. I can always return a shipment and cancel at any time. Even if I never buy another book from Harlequin, the two free books and gifts are mine to keep forever.

135 HDN EEX7   336 HDN EEYK

Name	(PLEASE PRINT)
Address	Apt.
City	State/Prov.	Zip/Postal Code

Signature (if under 18, a parent or guardian must sign)

Mail to Harlequin Reader Service®:

IN U.S.A.
P.O. Box 1867
Buffalo, NY
14240-1867

IN CANADA
P.O. Box 609
Fort Erie, Ontario
L2A 5X3

Not valid to current Harlequin Superromance subscribers.

Want to try two free books from another line?
Call 1-800-873-8635 or visit www.morefreebooks.com.

* Terms and prices subject to change without notice. NY residents add applicable sales tax. Canadian residents will be charged applicable provincial taxes and GST. This offer is limited to one order per household. All orders subject to approval. Credit or debit balances in a customer's account(s) may be offset by any other outstanding balance owed by or to the customer. Please allow 4 to 6 weeks for delivery.

HSR06

Silhouette®

SPECIAL EDITION™

Logan's Legacy Revisited

**THE LOGAN FAMILY IS BACK
WITH SIX NEW STORIES.**

Beginning in January 2007 with

THE COUPLE
MOST LIKELY TO

by

LILIAN DARCY

Tragedy drove them apart. Reunited eighteen years later, their attraction was once again undeniable. But had time away changed Jake Logan enough to let him face his fears and commit to the woman he once loved?